AF610483

WALKERS

JACK CRAFT

Order this book online at www.trafford.com/08-0268
or email orders@trafford.com

Most Trafford titles are also available at major online book retailers.

Edited by Paul Singh
Cover Design/Artwork by Paul Singh
Designed by Paul Singh

Note for Librarians: A cataloguing record for this book is available from Library and Archives Canada at www.collectionscanada.ca/amicus/index-e.html

ISBN: 978-1-4251-7240-4

We at Trafford believe that it is the responsibility of us all, as both individuals and corporations, to make choices that are environmentally and socially sound. You, in turn, are supporting this responsible conduct each time you purchase a Trafford book, or make use of our publishing services. To find out how you are helping, please visit www.trafford.com/responsiblepublishing.html

Our mission is to efficiently provide the world's finest, most comprehensive book publishing service, enabling every author to experience success. To find out how to publish your book, your way, and have it available worldwide, visit us online at www.trafford.com/10510

www.trafford.com

North America & international
toll-free: 1 888 232 4444 (USA & Canada)
phone: 250 383 6864 • fax: 250 383 6804
email: info@trafford.com

The United Kingdom & Europe
phone: +44 (0)1865 487 395 • local rate: 0845 230 9601
facsimile: +44 (0)1865 481 507 • email: info.uk@trafford.com

10 9 8 7 6 5 4 3

For Lynda,
And you, the reader:

INTRODUCTION

What exactly are the characteristics that define a monster? Is it by the way that he, she, or it looks? On the other hand, perhaps, by its actions. If something is so hideous, that it repulses one to look at, could that possibly constitute a monster? The dictionary defines a monster as an animal that has features combined with that of a human, or any creature so ugly or grossly deformed as to frighten people. Then what is beauty? Is it not in the eye of the beholder? The dictionary also describes a monster as any person who excites horror through wickedness, or cruelty. If this is the case, with all the crime, hatred and atrocities flowing across the planet, are we not already living amongst the monsters?

PATIENT ZERO

I would like you to meet patient zero—me—I am patient zero. I alone would set into play a series of events that would bring about the near extermination of every living soul on the planet. What began as something so harmless, much like the common cold, turned into a battle for the very existence of the human race.

You see, I was born with a very rare blood disorder. A disorder so severe and so unforgiving, that it can make one drop of a stranger's blood deadly. As a child, I grew up having regular bouts of illnesses. Mostly, they were chronic tonsillitis, unexplained nosebleeds that, with each visit to the hospital became harder and harder to stop and reoccurring intestinal infections, that at times became crippling. But first let me go back a bit.

"Beware the demons of the flesh."

My grandmother would always say that to me when I was a little boy.

"Beware the demons of the flesh."

The monsters of the flesh would creep into her bedroom at night and slowly feed on her while she slept. The biting little ghouls fed upon her eyes and skin causing her to go blind and get little brown spots on her skin. Those were the scars. It wasn't from getting older. It was them—the monsters of the flesh. Or at least that is what grandma believed.

Grandma suffered from dementia. Every day she would wander aimlessly around the house babbling about the monsters of the flesh attacking her. At night, she would sneak around stuffing towels at the bottoms of doors and into the heating ducts. Everyday grandma would seek out any cracks in the walls and after making sure no one was watching, fill them with her denture cream. All this was in a bid to keep out the demons of the flesh.

My parents eventually got tired of grandma constantly uttering nonsense and wrecking the house so they put her in a home. I did not see or hear much of her ever again. No one in our house took grandma seriously—except for me. The demons of the flesh tormented me every night.

They make those tiny cracks that appear in the walls. Those little knocks and bangs that you hear in the middle of the night, they are the demons of the flesh. They are the itches and the scratches that tickle you while you sleep. You may think that is your clock ticking away. It's not. It is the demons of the flesh. They are the glowing lights in your stereo. When you turn off your television and that little dot that remains behind—it is their eyes—watching you. Hiding and waiting, they lurk in the shadows for a chance to attack, for a chance at the feast of flesh.

Sliding under the door cracks and climbing out from inside the heat registers—they enter. From within the walls of the room—they come. Making their way out of the narrow slits of the wall sockets—they pour in. They come from every crack and fissure that the darkness has hid from the light.

The monsters would attack in the middle of the night, usually seeking out sleeping children or the elderly. They would sneak in as their victims lay helplessly in bed. Fast asleep, they were oblivious to the kinds of things that went on after the darkness of night crept across their pillows.

The demons of the flesh were already dead and they wanted you with them. As the flesh slowly decayed from their tiny little rotting corpses, they searched for a feast of new flesh. The monsters of the flesh would come and crawl inside you as you slept and slowly feed on your body.

They creep in through your nose, your mouth, or your ears. From there they could disperse throughout your body. Their tiny teeth stab into your tissue as they feast, leaving little pockmarks. As they try desperately to satisfy their appetites the ghouls leave behind their toxic bacteria ridden saliva.

That is where the tummy aches, chest congestion, and sore throats come from—the demons of the flesh. The bacteria filled saliva that they left behind slowly wreaking its havoc on your insides.

Each day before bed, I would go about my nightly ritual of trying to seal the demons out. Like grandma, I stuffed towels at the bottom of my doors, hoping that would help keep them out. I went around the room and filled every crack I could find with gum. In the winter, my windows would frost up from having the heat registers closed tight. I did everything I could apart from sleeping with the light on, which I sometimes did, but to no avail. The monsters of the night came almost every time.

During the middle of the night, while I lay fast asleep in bed, the evil little demons would creep into my bedroom and pay me a visit. Once the darkness of night cast it shadow over my pillow, they came to haunt me—to torture me. To feed on me as I lay there not knowing what type of cellular destruction they had in store for me each night.

Their rotting little corpses made their way into my room and towards me, being careful to stay out of the dim glow of the nightlight. They did not fear the light. They did not fear anything. Occasionally, they attacked during the day but it was more fun at night when their prey was more vulnerable.

Skulking across the carpeted floor, the wave of dark deformed demons crept over to my bed. At the foot of my bed, they planned their attack. The miniature monsters climbed slowly up my bedpost. Their tiny little claws carving deep into the oak wood as they rose. On top, one by one they crawled under the sheets and into my bed.

Armed with their tiny teeth, they would sneak up onto my face and crawl inside of my nostrils. That's why you sneeze and why you cough. It is the demons of the flesh trying to make their way inside. They made their way through my body as they slid down my throat and into my intestines. Once free from being spied by the outside world and hidden from the light that they hated so much, they searched for their targets.

Seeking out my tonsils, my intestinal track, and the small veins located within the thin lining of the nose, they prepared for their attack. The demons fed off the insides of my body and my nostrils while dancing around in the darkness that they so loved. Biting and chewing at the soft tender flesh, they gorged themselves. Feeding until the blood and infection began to flow freely.

I would wake up in the morning, the side of my head being sticky and wet from the blood that had flowed from my nose all night. My pillow now stained brownish-red and saturated with my lifeblood, I knew the monsters had come.

The nosebleeds I repeatedly suffered from always bled from one nostril, which was abnormal, since normally a nose bleeds from both nostrils at the same time.

The nosebleeds were so bad that sometimes the demons of the night would be brave and show themselves during the day. I would just be standing there as the tap of blood opened up. Somehow, they managed to get passed me and have their feast of flesh.

The red liquid would come pouring from my nose, feeling like a warm thick waterfall rushing over my lips. The salty taste of the gelling blood choking me as it ran down the back of my throat. I was having between two to three nosebleeds a day that would last for about forty-five minutes.

The doctor told my parents that if the flow of blood could not be stopped before fifteen minutes then they were to rush me to the Emergency. So after fifteen minutes of bleeding, my parents would rush me to the hospital every time. I spent more time in the Emergency waiting room than I did outside playing as a kid. They had some weird idea that I would bleed to death. I had never heard of anyone dying from a bloody nose before.

Eventually, in my teens I stopped believing in the little monsters of the night. I also began refusing to make the trip to the hospital. They did not have any more luck than I had in stopping the bleeding. I would just stand over the sink, letting the liquid of life pour down the drain until it finally stopped on its own.

As the blood coagulated in my nose and throat, I could always feel the long clot gagging me until, after letting out a series of throaty belches; I either hacked or puked it into the sink. The clots were usually the size of a small hamburger patty. They would cling to the bottom of the sink, jiggling like Jell-O and looking like a hunk of raw liver. I was about the age of sixteen when I did finally receive a normal bleeding nose.

While playing hardball over at the local schoolyard, I was out at shortstop getting ready for the next hit. I heard the crack of the bat as a ground ball came racing across the infield towards me. I bent down on one knee, placing my glove onto the dusty field to stop it. About a foot in front of my glove, the baseball skipped off a rut in the dirt. Leaping up into the air, the hardball smacked me right in the middle of my face and right off my nose.

My nose became numb and tingly as I began to feel the warm sensation of blood trickling down over my mouth one more time. The salty taste of the thick dark liquid flavored my pallet as I licked my lips. The deep red stream flooded down my chin and onto my t-shirt.

I raised my arms in the air and jumped up making an attempt at some crazy man's jig. Dancing around on the baseball diamond, I became overjoyed at the fact that I had, for the first time in my life, a normal bloody nose. I will never forget the look of surprise and then horror on the faces of my fellow teammates as they ran to my aid. Panicked by the geyser of dark red liquid spilling from my face and shocked at the fact that I was elated.

Many times my illness was very bad. If I became sick, it was usually severe and dragged on for months. Growing up, I would make every possible effort to stay away from other sick people. However, you always had those kids that went to school or the adults who went to work that would cough, sneeze, and hack all over everything. To many people it was funny. Some would purposely go out of their way to try and cough on me.

Some people took me as rude since I would always try to stay farther away than most people did. My personal bubble was a little larger than most others were. If you coughed, I would turn my head and cover my face with my shirt. When offered cookies from a plate or pizza from an already opened box, I would always decline. I was just trying to be safe and stay healthy but being an adult now, I can understand how some could think me as rude and abrasive.

The doctors just took all my symptoms as normal childhood ailments. As I became older, I began to think that maybe they were right. The nosebleeds eventually stopped, except for on the rare occasion. The tonsils settled down and the infections became less frequent.

It was not until I was in my late 30's that I had problems again. It began with the occasional case of the runs. Not thinking it was anything serious, I ignored and dealt with it. I figured I just drank too many beers the night before, ate too much fibre or maybe had some bad wings. After some time, my symptoms became more frequent and more intense. My dysentery eventually becoming so often, that mid-meal I was in the bathroom.

My appetite was undying, never being satisfied. I could eat and eat, yet still, I was constantly feeling hungry. My meals grew in size and frequency, up to the point where I was having five or six large feedings in a day while still snacking in between.

My waist, which should have been expanding, was instead, shrinking. I began to shed weight drastically. In one month, I lost thirty-five pounds, leaving my small frame looking like I just crawled out of a Nazi concentration camp. All the medical specialists, to which my doctor referred me to see, had absolutely no idea why my weight was dropping so fast. But I knew. The demons of the flesh were back and they were out to make up for lost time. This time they were very hungry.

I sat in the waiting room eavesdropping on the doctors as they discussed my symptoms. I could barely make out what it was that they were saying but I could sense the stress in their voices. I overheard one word repeated several times.

"Cancer."

Every test I had done up until that point had come back negative for any other illnesses so what else could it possibly be. Then, I received an Ultrasound.

I lie back on the table as the technician moved the ultrasound probe up and down my abdomen. The gel used to glide it around felt cold and sticky against my skin. Curious, the technician looked at me,

"Are you in any pain?"

Wild thoughts raced through my mind as I tried to picture what the technician was seeing on the monitor before him. I replied, half-panicked,

"No, am I supposed to be?"

The technician never answered back. I went home that day wondering it was that he had seen. It had to be bad. No one asks you if you are in pain unless it is bad. That day, I looked through every medical resource available to see if I could find out what it was that I could possibly have. Of course, the only things I managed to convince myself that I had were exotic and rare diseases like the Ebola virus or some other kind of hemorrhagic fever.

For two weeks I sat by the phone at home waiting for the doctors call that would confirm my horrors. The call never came. On the third week, I decided to call them. Asking the nurse,

"Have you had any word on the results of my Ultrasound?"

The nurse replied,

"We have not received them yet."

Shocked, I yelled into the phone at her,

"It has been three weeks!"

The nurse quickly answered,

"I'll call the lab and call you right back."

Sheepishly, she asked in a quiet voice,

"Do you know which one you went to?"

Unfazed by her ignorance, I said,

"Aren't you supposed to?"

I slammed the phone down and waited.

After an hour, the nurse called back. She told me the lab forgot to send them in and they would be couriered over immediately.

The ultrasound I had received showed inflammation running the length of my intestines. The Internal Specialist thought it best to scope me from both ends so that he could actually look inside and see what was happening in there.

I lay back on the table once more but as the doctor readied his long camera cables. I asked what I thought at the time to be a valid question,

"You're going to put that in my mouth first, right?"

The doctor laughed,

"Yes, there is a scope for each one."

When I think about it now, it was kind of ridiculous to think that they used the same camera for each exam. Even after sanitizing the hell out of it, I could not see me or anyone else for that matter, allowing them to stuff it down my throat after it had just been up someone else's ass.

Moving the camera around the specialist took a variety of photos. The pictures revealed that tiny polyps lined the sides of my entire intestinal track.

A week later, my wife and I went to the doctor's office to talk with him about what he found. The Specialist sat back in his large leather chair staring at the photos he had snapped of the length of my innards. He looked up at my wife and me,

"It looks like cancer but just to be sure, I'm going to send it out to my friend at the CDC for a second opinion."

The Center for Disease Control? What in the hell did I have? The whole process took six months.

When the second opinion did finally came back, the diagnosis was a common infection that had progressed farther than any they had ever seen before and in the end would have been fatal. The infection thrived as it fed off everything I ate. For the past six months, I had been starving to death!

The demons of the flesh were back. And this time, they did not want to leave. The tiny monsters had made a home of my insides. Burrowing into every tissue, every muscle, they nested in the minute fissures of my body. Everything I ate, they stole. Every scrap of food and every ounce of liquid they took for their own. They would not rest until I had joined them and was dead.

The Internal Specialist prescribed some pills that would rid my body of the sickness. The pills worked like a charm. Only problem was, he said that the disease would always remain, lying dormant, ready to spring back at anytime and without warning. It was no shock when I heard that. I already knew that. The monsters never left. They just went into hiding.

Because of the pills, I could not drink any alcohol for two months. Boy was that tough. It felt like I was doing the twelve-step program in Alcoholics Anonymous. One time, I made the mistake of taking some cough syrup that contained a small alcohol content. That night, I hung my head over the toilet bowl getting violently ill for hours. I would be sure not to make that mistake again.

The infection that had been slowly killing me was a common

ailment that my body should have been able to fight off in a few weeks at most. Why did it not? The doctors were puzzled. Sending me for a more in-depth blood test to a Hematologist, they found my disorder.

My body was producing blood of one type and anti-bodies from another type. In the middle of all that, it was missing a bunch of other stuff that, unless you are a Hematologist, is far too complicated to explain. Basically, I was born with a non-existent immune system. But I was also naturally immune to certain illnesses and would become a carrier of these diseases.

The Hematologist I was seeing set up an appointment for a shot to help boost my immune system. I was to go every month for it. It was supposed to be a routine injection that was to help my body fight off common illnesses that, up until that time, I did not know could kill me.

I sat back in the chair for the first time, waiting for my elixir of health. I was accustomed to being poked and prodded by doctors and specialists, doing test after test, so a little needle was not a big deal. So I thought.

As soon as the nurse began the injection, my heart began to thump. Harder and harder it pumped. I could feel it crashing into my chest wall as if it were about to pop out. Beads of moisture formed on my brow. With sweat trickling down my forehead, I said,

"I don't feel right."

My lungs tightened, making it difficult to breathe. Drops of salty water ran down into my eyes, stinging them. My brain, throbbed against the inside of my skull, feeling as if it would burst and leak out of my ears. I continued, as a panic began to settle in,

"Something's wrong."

The nurse stared at me muddle-headed and replied,

"You're just nervous."

My jaw clamped shut, clenching my teeth solidly together. I thought that they might shatter in a puff of chalky white dust as my eyes squinted with the pain of my ordeal.

My fingers gripped the arms of the chair tightly, my knuckles turning white as if trying to rip the seat apart. I was going into anaphylactic shock and this bitch did nothing! Unable to breathe, I could feel myself dying as the nurse stood idly by. Was she just a simpleton or did she have some kind of sick twisted fetish on watching people slowly die? Was it not obvious that I was in respiratory distress?

If it had not been for an alert expeditious doctor who happened to be passing by, I would not be telling this tale. The sharp-witted doctor took notice of my ailing condition and hastily ran to retrieve an adrenaline needle. Stabbing me in the chest with the huge injection of mortality, he delivered me from what was certain extinction.

It turns out, I was allergic to all blood products and blood, accept for my own. The doctors dubbed it "clean blood" saying everyone was born with "dirt" in their blood—except me. It meant that I was an ideal candidate to donate to other people. The "dirt" in the blood is the part that people rejected. There was no way they could reject mine. The Hematologist suggested banking my own blood in the event that I was ever in need of a transfusion.

So, away I went to the Blood Bank. They were to store my blood for me by freezing it. That was until the Blood Bank said that they could use it for someone else if need be.

"Well, isn't that just great."

I stared dumbfounded at the nurse.

I used to donate blood habitually and still had them calling me once a week not knowing I had just been there. I was not even eligible to give again.

Constantly, the Blood Bank badgered me to bestow more of the juice of life upon them, saying that they were out and in need of my blood type. If this was the case, I knew there was no way in hell, if I stored blood, it would be there when I needed it. Hanging my head low, I turned and walked out, never to return.

My illness was not all bad though. The benefit was, when I was healthy, it looked like I was on steroids. My body would bounce back from an illness at an alarming rate. The muscles in my arms and chest stayed ripped due to my lack of body fat.

When people commented on the weight I had gained, I would suggest that it must be my tan or that I just had my haircut. This seemed to work most of the time. Sometimes I did get a small chuckle out of them with the response of,

"Yeah, right."

My family doctor always said to me that if I could bottle what I had, I would be rich. There was no need for money now. Food, shelter, and ammo are all the basic necessities you need.

It all started when the demons showed themselves once again. I had paid a visit to the doctor's to see about a sore throat that the monsters had been feeding on for over a month. I was the type of person that, even with the severity of my ailment, I still hated to go to the doctor's office. I did not want to sit in the waiting room surrounded by ill people that were usually there because they had the common cold. I would wait until the last possible moment, when I could not stand the pain anymore, before I would seek treatment.

The doctor was on holidays for two weeks. Great, just my luck. My doctor always seems to be on holidays or involved in some clinic whenever I needed an appointment. So, they sent to me to another doctor, a Doctor Janik.

Parking the car across the street from Dr. Janik's office, I stepped out into the cold morning air. The sharpness of the breeze made my throat feel raw and yet somehow at the same time, soothed the pain.

With the warmth of the sun beating down on my face, I walked, tilting my head back, and closing my eyes as I basked in its golden glow. I crossed the quiet morning street with the only perceivable noise in my ears being the chirps of the many tiny birds flitting about as they scouted for food to feed their young.

The beautiful day outside had given me some newfound energy in life as I walked, enjoying the morning air. Taking a deep breath, I smiled, thinking how good it was to be alive.

The screeching of a car's tires sent my diving for cover onto the sidewalk. I went tumbling into a trashcan, knocking it over, its contents spilling to the ground. My heart raced and my eyes bulged out of my head. Looking down, I realized I was lying in a pile of discarded newspapers, coffee cups, and left over lunches.

Rolling over in the heap of stinking garbage to face my narrow escape, I gazed out into the street. A car full of teens sat at the corner, an empty cardboard box blocking their path. They hung out the car's windows pointing to me, laughing hysterically, hurling insults,

"Loser!"
"Garbage picker!"
"I smell shit!"

"I bet it's in his pants!"

As the teens slowly pulled away still laughing, I stood up peeling off a piece of two day old lettuce from my jacket, the mayonnaise that soaked it, leaving a white slimy smear. Looking down at the filth that covered the front of my jacket and hands, I muttered in disgust,

"Nice."

I entered Dr. Janik's office still staring down as I continued to attempt to brush off the grime from the front of my jacket. I paused, glancing up. This place looked like something out of a third world country.

As my eyes scanned the waiting room, the 60's era orange carpet caught my eye. The mismatched ceramic tiles on the wall, some of them missing, showed the cheap glue that used to hold them in place. It made me wonder if this guy was even a legitimate doctor.

Bookshelves, made from rough unstained wood teetered against the walls. Old children's books, many with the covers torn off, sat scattered on the shelves.

As I stood taking in the filth of the ragged room before me, a craggy voice behind me, queried,

"Can I help you?"

Turning around, the sight that filled my eyes yet again shocked me.

The voice had cackled out of an elderly woman, the phlegm distorting her words causing me instinctively to clear my own throat. Her hunched back made me wonder if when she answered questions, the reply would be,

"Yes, master."

At her age, I would have thought she should be retired by now. It was not the age or look of the haggard old woman that shocked me. It was the desk she stood behind—yes—stood behind. There was no chair.

The aging decrepit receptionist stood behind what looked like a police line-up window, complete with bulletproof glass. She spoke through a small hole in the thick glass.

I leaned towards the glass,

"My doctor is away on holidays and
she referred me to Dr. Janik for an
appointment."

The elderly woman slowly shuffled to the heavy door closing her in her little booth.

As she tugged on the big door, I began to think the receptionist bunker was more to keep her from straying away instead of for her protection. Waddling out from behind her interrogation room, she led me down the hall and to the lone examination room in the office.

As I walked behind her watching her teeter back and forth, her head became almost invisible as it ducked behind the giant hump that towered on top of her back. I almost let out a giggle as I followed this headless old woman to the examination room.

Reaching the examination room, the old woman stretched up, dumping my chart into the wooden box that hung on the open door. As she turned towards me, her head reappeared once more sending me back in shock from seeing her ugliness so close. As I stepped back, a

"Yeesh!"

flashed out. I am not sure if I had just thought it or if I actually said it aloud. I must have just thought it since the old woman never flinched at my reaction.

Maybe the ugly woman had received the same reaction so often that she had grown accustom to it over the years. With her head still bowed down, the receptionist teetered off, back to her holding cell, her head disappearing once more as I watched her.

The examination room was the only part of the office that appeared rather up to date and clean. The doctor's certificates of training, encased in cheap metal picture frames, hung on the walls, along with a few "smoking is bad for you" posters. The school names, which I did not recognize, looked like they also came from some third world places.

An examination table complete with stirrups stretched across one wall. A vanity ran half the length of the back wall with a sink. A single, metal framed, vinyl chair sat against the wall by the door. A light shade of mint green paint coated the plaster.

Walking over to the sink, I reached for a roll of paper towels that sat on the vanity counter. Tearing off a strip, I wet them under the tap and began to clean off more of the filth from my run in with the trashcan. I heard my chart sliding from its resting place on the open door behind me as the doctor entered the room, chart in hand.

Doctor Janik was an older Polish gentleman, who appeared pleasant when I met him. Asking me to have a seat, he opened up my file.

Giving me the usual,

"Aww"

Dr. Janik flashed his penlight into my mouth and glanced at my throat. Without looking up, he took out his pad and wrote a prescription. He handed it to me saying with a strong Polish accent,

"Deez vill get rrrid of vhat ju haff."

What did I have? He never said.

Arriving at the Pharmacy to acquire my miracle pills, the Pharmacist, his eyeglasses hanging from his nose, continued to stare down at his computer monitor as I handed him the prescription. Still deeply engrossed in his work, he said,

"One hour."

I wandered around the mall for an hour doing the dreaded time killing window-shopping, as I waited for the pills to be counted and bottled. I thought to myself,

"I hope these pills work fast. I can't
take any more of this sore throat."

Living off soups and soft foods for the last month, I could not remember the last time I enjoyed a real meal. As I walked by the food court in the mall I stopped, and stood, staring at all the wonderful fast food joints. I imagined buying from all of them. Picking out my fictitious orders and sitting down to gorge myself on the fatty foods that I did not eat often but had missed so dearly.

Heading back to the Pharmacy, I stepped up to the counter spying my medication already bagged and ready to go. The Pharmacist dropped everything and rushed over as I spoke my name to the girl on the register. Picking up my prescription, the Pharmacist stared at me. His eyes were wide and glistening. He bounced around all happy like a teenage girl in love, saying,

"These are great pills; it's kind of
like getting a two pronged attack".

It is a good thing he was happy because I felt like shit and could not give a flying fuck what he thought about the pills. I just wanted the nagging pain in my throat to be gone.

"Just give me the fucking pills!"

I thought to myself.

With due diligence, I finished the pills as two more weeks went by. The sore throat seemed to get better for a few days but it persisted.

Calling my doctor back to request a repeat visit, the office informed me that a nurse would look at my throat for me. I sat in the waiting room and watched as my doctor went back and forth between examination rooms. What the hell? If the doctor is here, why can't she see me? Looking around the waiting room filled with mothers and their babies, it struck me. She was doing some kind of prenatal crap.

I always hated our health care system. Almost everything was offered free except for the things that were an absolute necessity, such as eye care.

If you bitched about being too overweight enough, they would staple your stomach for you free of charge. But if you needed a pair of eyeglasses to see—forget it. Pay for your own.

Then you had the habitual,

"I have a sniffle so I must go to the doctor's."

And don't forget the,

"Well, it's free so I may as well visit my doctor once a month."

With people like these in today's society continually hogging up all the medical resources, the ones that do really need to see a medical professional, sit there—left in the wings—waiting.

It is no wonder that there are so many outbreaks of illnesses in the world that, had those first patients received a diagnosis or treatment in a timely fashion, the ensuing epidemic probably might have been prevented.

There I sat in the waiting room, hoping that my turn to enter was soon. Patiently waiting, I perused the usual celebrity magazines that were at least six months old. The ones that gossiped on which movie star slept with whom.

After about a half hour, the call finally came to enter an examination room. Sitting in the examination room, the nurse entered and asked me,

"What did Dr. Janik say you had?"

I replied,

"Nothing, he never told me anything."

"He just gave me a prescription."

The nurse gave me an odd look,

"There is definitely an infection."

I was stunned,

"Well, no shit!"

It was evident that the thousands of dollars spent and the years of medical schooling really paid off. A fucking genius she was. Any imbecile could see that there was an infection.

She left the room and came back with yet another prescription for me. Handing me the piece of paper, the nurse said,

"This should work. If not, just call back."

I grabbed the paper and began to walk out trying to read, whatever the hell language, the chicken scratch that covered it was supposed to be. As I stepped out the front door, I stopped,

"Wait a minute! She never said what I had either."

What the hell kind of medical profession is this? I just shook my head and went home.

Eye drops, nose sprays, inhalers, every medication imaginable, they shoved my way. I tried anti-biotics and more anti-biotics, anti-viral medications, anti-bacterial medications, and yet the sore throat nagged on.

Becoming desperate at finding a solution to the constant aggravation of my throat, I eventually went to the hospital to see if they could do something for me.

After sitting in the hospital waiting room for six hours, and watching all the nurses standing around with their thumbs up their asses, I had had enough.

Clearly unimpressed, I walked up to the triage nurse,

"I am going home with no treatment received."

The nurse, looking at me as if this type of wait should be normal, said,

"But you're at the top of the list."

The nurse then asked my name. I told her who I was and stood there watching her search for my file, the nurse's fat ass jiggling as she hurriedly rooted through the stacks of envelopes. Top of the list my ass. She could not even find my chart. Tax dollars hard at work.

I grabbed a pair of small scissors from a nearby desk, cut the administration band off my wrist, and began to walk out. The nurse, acting as if I received treatment and was better said,

"If you have any more problems just
come back."

Stunned, I paused. As everyone sat in the waiting room staring at the commotion I caused, I turned and raised my voice,

"Why, so I can come back and sit
here for another six hours?"

Shaking my head in disbelief, I walked out.

As I went home that day, I couldn't help but think,

"What would happen if the demons
of the flesh escaped to roam the
streets freely instead of the body,
seeking out and searching for their
feast of flesh? I already knew.
Mankind would cease to exist."

Perhaps, if the doctors would have examined me that day at the hospital, they might have prevented the ensuing outbreak—but it is too late to ponder that now.

THE PLAGUE

After a few more months, the demons calmed down and my sore throat did eventually fade or at the least, become tolerable. I could tell that the infection was still there but it was now manageable with a pain pill every so often. I gave up on the art of medicine in finding a cure. It was possible for modern medicine to cure a variety of exotic illnesses but it seemed they could not or did not have the desire to cure the simple ones such as a sore throat or the common cold.

They say that the flu virus mutates every year. Should it not have a base gene in its DNA that does not change? I am not a biologist but everything has a base in which to grow from. Could something in it that is stable and common in every virus be targeted and wiped out? Cold remedies are big business though. Nevertheless, I had given up on modern medicine and their so-called cures.

Then cases of a strange and new sickness started popping up. A virus that lay dormant for months then take three days to incubate and kill its host. The symptoms were minimal. The host might have a slight sore throat and possibly show a low-grade fever. More times than not, the disease put forth no symptoms at all. As the virus slowly took hold, the host was in complete darkness about the death that they carried in their blood. It was not until the last day of the incubation period that the virus really showed itself.

The host's chest cavity exploded internally in a giant wave of puss and liquid, drowning the victim in his or her own bodily fluids in a matter of seconds. The disease pumping out of the mouth in a blackish froth as the host died. The virus had a one hundred percent mortality rate and spread slowly, leaping from person to person. The medical community gave the virus the name of D.R.E.D. They called it the Deadly Respiratory Excretion Disease.

In the end, I would find out that I was the initial carrier of the virus and apparently, immune. Not knowing, my wife was also immune from having intercourse with me. The result being, the tiny lacerations from having unprotected sex passing on my blood and immunity. Kind of like getting an AIDs virus that keeps you alive instead of slowly killing you.

In the beginning, the virus was not deadly. It sat dormant in its host, waiting for its opportune time to mutate. No one knows when exactly it became terminal or what the catalyst for its change was.

They traced the first known case to a young Chinese boy, whose mother had brought him into the hospital on the same day that I was there. I remember thinking that day, how it was a waste of medical resources for her to bring her son into emergency over a lost tooth. The kid's bleeding would stop and another tooth would eventually grow in. If anything, she should have visited a dentist.

The woman and her son were taking a trip back to their homeland. She wanted her son to look healthy when she returned home, showing everyone that their newfound country was indeed great. Travelling the world, their cross-global jaunt passed on the illness as they went.

As the sickness spread, people started to die in groups of tens. They were mostly the old that resided in retirement homes and those that lived in places like shelters or refugee camps, so people did not really care. The old were near death anyways and expected to die soon. The conditions are horrible in shelters and refugee camps so it barely made the news when the people died there. Small pockets of people here and there were dying but it was becoming a global issue. Any place where groups of people were in constant contact with one another the virus would spread.

With the D.R.E.D. virus not showing any signs of infection until the final stage, it was impossible to tell who was a carrier. Behind closed doors, governments started to panic and thought about imposing a worldwide one-week mass quarantine but the majority of the people in the world remained calm and that type of action was sure to cause chaos. Some survivalist types got scared and ran to the hills for their secret hideouts. But without the widespread panic, the government would take no action. How do you prevent a virus from spreading that you cannot find?

The D.R.E.D. disease grabbed hold of the world on New Years Eve. At the stroke of twelve, everyone kissed and hugged their loved ones and total strangers. Little did they know is that they were spreading the virus, only now on a massive scale.

The people's lips pursed together and their hands stuck out, all preparing for their loving embrace. The D.R.E.D. waited, preparing itself to carry on its embrace of death. As the clock struck twelve, lips touched and hands grabbed. And the sickness began its slide from happy victim to happy victim. The disease leapt from hand to hand and mouth to mouth, winding its way from host to host.

Scientists from all nations came together, trying to find a cure. It seemed no one was immune to the Deadly Respiratory Excretion Disease. Working around the clock, the scientists quickly came up with a new anti-viral vaccine that was supposed to cure everyone.

A few months had now gone by and in smaller countries panic was slowly beginning to set in. By now, it was on a worldwide scale and even the armed forces of the world had become decimated with the growing number of fatalities.

The virus, spreading easily and quickly, swept across the earth like a raging wildfire of death. It was no longer groups of tens dying. Now, they were falling by the tens of thousands.

The World Health Organization had in the past, always warned the world of a coming global pandemic but everyone I knew thought it was some kind of conspiracy to get us to pay more taxes.

However, oddly enough, even with a widespread pandemic, the western world kept right on going as if nothing was happening. Because the disease showed no signs of symptoms, everyone that was not sick still went to work, shopped and continued with his or her daily lives, ignorant to the masses dying around them.

A few of the more paranoid people wore those little white dust masks, which in reality would not do a thing for them. If it does not affect you, why worry, right?

Concealed well by the government, maybe they did not have a contingency plan and all of the pandemic hype was just a conspiracy. On the other hand, was it just plain human ignorance? Who knows? I will say the latter.

I guess because most of the mass numbers of deaths were in other countries like China, Africa, the Middle East, and other places that most people in the Western world do not give a crap about. The rest of the people in the world just ignored it. In addition, we had the scientists that had found a cure. Everyone would get his or her anti-viral shot and end of plague, end of story.

They called the antidote DRED-not. The DRED-not was to be the magic potion that was going to keep the people from succumbing to the deadly new strain that had begun to ravage the globe.

Commandeering any facility that could make the shot, the factories produced the DRED-not in mass quantities. They made enough for every person on the planet.

On television, there were no longer any new shows. Everything aired was a re-run consisting of the usual sitcoms, forensic shows and of course, the reality TV.

The only new thing on TV was a DRED-not commercial. It was the only commercial. They aired it about every ten minutes and in every language imaginable. It was to get your DRED-not.

I do not really remember exactly how it went since I hated commercials and always muted them but it went something like this,

"DRED-not. Take care of the
D.R.E.D. virus—before it takes care
of you.
Possible side effects include gas,
bloating and anal leakage."

People lined up for blocks and blocks, in every part of the world. In the rain, snow, bitter cold and searing heat, they stood. Waiting for hours upon hours, they all hoped to be the first to get their reprieve from the viral death know as D.R.E.D. that was sweeping across the planet.

Being impatient and pig headed, I never stood in lines, never paid initiation fees and refused to pay cover charges. I would rather leave. I was sure as hell not going to be one of those people wasting my time by standing in line all day.

I really did not want the DRED-not anyways. The only time I had ever gotten the flu in my entire life was when I went to the doctors for my free flu shot to prevent it. Everyone I had ever known to receive a preventative flu shot always became severely ill with the flu. So I remained highly skeptical that the DRED-not would even work.

One by one, the whole of society, save for the few that thought the same as I, lined up for their needles. One by one, the recipients; his and her names catalogued, stepped up, and were given their antidote.

Of course, the government, military, and law enforcement officials received the first doses. If there was chaos from the outbreak then there had to be people in charge. Little did they know the disease would claim most of them first.

Unfortunately, the scientists were in such a hurry to save the world and become heroes; and since the virus showed no signs of symptoms, they never did do any actual human trials of the vaccine. They only had the corpses of the fallen to work with. There were no live specimens. I believe they just tested the DRED-not on some pigs and then rushed it all over the globe. Pigs were close to us in DNA—right?

Oh, it kept the people alive all right. DRED-not worked perfectly. The problem was; it began to work after the D.R.E.D. had killed them already. One by one, the bodies of the dead began to rise—attacking the living.

I remember hearing someone in my travels refer to them as,

"Walkers."

One bite from the newly departed infected the victim with both the D.R.E.D. virus and the DRED-not. The living host had at most, three days, depending on the severity of the wound, before they died and became one of the undead.

They had injected everyone with DRED-not on such a mass scale that when the dead did finally re-animate, the hordes were so great, and had infiltrated every level of government, military branch, and law enforcement, that they overpowered the living with ease. And they ate or infected everyone in the vicinity. The demons of the flesh were now outside the body, free to roam the lands instead of your insides and there seemed to be no stopping them.

There were few survivors left alive to tell people what was happening back in the early stages. If, by chance, a survivor did make it out to tell, who was going to believe them? The dead—walking? Fruitcake. They would just sedate them and lock them up in the Looney bin. Although, being in the nuthouse was probably safer than being outside. Maybe it was from the few early survivors that the reference to "walkers" came about.

As the walkers rose in homes around the world, domestic disputes, or what were believed to be, became commonplace. Neighbours, hearing the screams and commotions called for the Police to intervene.

Upon receiving the call about the ongoing domestic dispute, it would not be the usual two or three cop cars that would normally cruise up consisting of the usual female officer backed up by a couple of giant male constables. No, this time, due to the short staffing left by the sudden spike of no-shows that had already fallen victim to the rising dead or were, they themselves claimed by the virus, you were lucky to get one car if any at all.

Pulling their vehicles up to the address of the infracting dwelling, the police officers became confused. From the report, there sounded like an all out battle was taking place next door. The 9-1-1 operator could hear the screams of terror travelling over the phone line while they talked with the neighbors. Now all was quiet and appeared normal.

The Police had made the call, so they had better make sure that everything was fine. After knocking in vain on the door, the officers investigated further by gaining entry. Seeing the carnage inside stunned the officers, allowing for the family full of ghouls to take them down easily.

The cops never had a hope in hell to fight off a group of walkers as the officers pepper sprayed and beat the ghouls with their batons in an attempt to subdue them.

Any shots fired by the dispatched officers were to the body and ineffective. They definitely were not prepared for what they ran into. After all, it was only a domestic dispute.

Joining the multiplying mass of the undead, one by one the police radios went silent. When the responding officers did not return the repeated requests from their dispatch, the authorities fueled the undead wildfire, by sending any back up they could.

With Police forces becoming almost non-existent overnight, the cities became lawless.

The carnage that the undead brought spread globally in a matter of days. The dead were consuming entire cities one at a time and the rest of the world had no idea. Most places that the undead attacked never even had a chance to ask for help. Those few that could chose not to, as the leaders feared their country would seem weak and unable to cope to the rest of the world. Local governments would deal with the uprising in their own way, fearing that if they failed, they would not be re-elected. It was politics at its finest.

The entire globe became a massive Bermuda Triangle. I can recall watching the news about a cargo plane leaving for Iraq on a re-supply mission. The plane just vanished, never to be heard from again. The military recorded the disappearance as a mechanical failure. Stating it had crashed in the ocean on route, with the total loss of aircraft and life.

All around the world, places were falling off the map, becoming silent to the rest of the planet. Phones sat, ringing, in empty houses, as the dead and decaying shuffled past, unable and unwilling to answer. The traffic in the airport terminals gradually became less and less as the departing flights did not return and the incoming flights slowed.

Sure, some became curious. For the visitors playing detective on their own that had decided to make the trip, attempting to find out what the fate of their loved ones was, it became a one-way journey into oblivion. As if, the void of a black hole had grabbed them and pulled them into its grasp of eternal darkness. Anything or anybody that went to these places never came back.

I still, to this day have nightmares, watching people, one by one, walking into the darkness, only to return all at once—dead. As the shadowy figures of the dead slowly advance, their lifeless eyes burn a green hue. The black mass of undead creeping towards me, they come. With their arms outstretched, they grasp at the air towards me, the tattered flesh hanging from their rotted fingertips, still dripping with the remnants of their last meal. The only light being the peppering of their bright staring orbs as they come ever so closer.

The odd thing is; they are not trying to eat me. It is more as if they are trying to coax me along, to join them, as if it was better where they are. Who knows, maybe it is better. Maybe they have found some kind of peace in the void that they now belong. When I wake up at night, drenched in a cold sweat, I cannot help but think—anywhere has to be better than here.

Some governments deployed Search and Rescue teams. Outfitted with biohazard equipment, they went to several locations in an attempt to find out why communications had been lost from some of the smaller rural areas. Was the plague really getting that bad and widespread that it was wiping out entire communities? Wild reports came back from some of the Search and Rescue teams that had managed to last long enough to describe the chaos that they witnessed on the ground.

In Russia, one Search and Rescue team reported that the local civilians wandered aimlessly around the snow-covered ground in large groups as if drugged. Their skin appeared pale in colour with a leathery look. The eye sockets seemed hollow and their cheeks sunken. Their clothes and flesh were tattered and smeared with blood. The cold did not appear to affect them either.

On the hands and around the mouths of the civilians, dried blood caked their skin. As the group of people wandered around not caring about the cold, without warning they would turn to attack a curious onlooker, devouring them in a frenzied horde.

Not knowing that the dead were roaming the earth, the team's reports detailed the slaughter on the ground. Calling it a widespread panic of some sort, the small team moved in to investigate. Armed with only pistols, the Search and Rescue team parked their vehicles. It would be easier for them to get closer on foot. They were not there to fight. The team had come to lend a hand in assisting as to why these places were not responding to the repeated attempts at communications. They were merely observers.

From behind the cover of a snowy embankment, the team watched in horror as the packs of mindless humans stalked their victims. The people ran from the mass of cannibals. Just then, a Russian Hind military helicopter swooped down into the center of the village, its blades kicking up a small snowstorm as it hovered above.

Four ropes dropped down from the hovering helicopter. A squad of fifteen heavily armed troops rappelled down, right into the middle of the carnage. The clatter of machine gun fire filled the air as the door gunner laid down suppressing fire for the descending soldiers. They were going to end this here and now.

The Search and Rescue team watched as the Spetsnaz began to set up a defensive perimeter. Having unloaded its cargo, the helicopter floated off into the horizon, leaving the soldiers to fend for themselves.

The Spetsnaz were Russia's elite of the elite. Highly trained and well disciplined to do one thing—not to negotiate or reason with the crowd—but to kill.

The Russian super troopers open fired with their AN-94 assault rifles and RPK light machine guns as the crowd of cannibals tried to engage them. The rounds smashed into their flesh, forming fresh cherry blossoms. Their blood ran free, speckling the white glistening snow with dark red splotches. The constant barrage of bullets smashed into the advancing horde, thumping harmlessly into their torsos. They seemed unstoppable. The flesh-eaters crept closer, slowly encircling the Spetsnaz.

As the unruly mob of cannibals closed in, the circular defence of the Spetsnaz shrank. One by one, their weapons ran dry as the machine gun fire slowly began to fade. They pulled their knives from their sheaths as the last rifle fell silent. Back to back now, the super troopers looked at each other one last time before charging off into the crowd of flesh-eaters. Slitting throats, and breaking bones to no avail, the crowd of death quickly enveloped them, tearing at their limbs, leaving rivers of deep red trickling across the snow covered ground.

Seeing the fate of the Spetsnaz, the Search and Rescue team turned to flee back to their vehicles. As they struggled to run across a snowy field, a small pack of staggering villagers closed in on them. Pushing on through the deep snow, the team began to tire and one after another suffered the same fate as the Spetsnaz.

One Rescue member did manage to make it back to the vehicles. He fell onto the front seat, the blood from fresh bite marks staining his winter camouflage, the pain coursing through his body. He sent a broken radio message,

"God help us—god help us."

The world as humans had known it was slowly spiraling out of control. What could be causing masses of people to commit to cannibalism? The small Search and Rescue teams did not have the manpower or the resources to cope with such a large-scale riot. The swarms of walkers engulfed them, forcing them to join the ever-growing masses of the undead.

Sending larger riot control forces in on the ground was definitely out of the question. The legions of unruly had grown to the thousands and it was going to take a large military mobilization to deal with this sort of crowd.

On hearing of the spread of D.R.E.D. in India, Pakistan attacked, pushing through the Kashmir valley with all the soldiers it could muster. Forcing all of its civilians, able bodied or not, to join the fight. India repelled the attack by sacrificing its own troops and launching a tactical nuclear warhead into the valley on top of the oncoming Pakistanis, wiping them out.

With the civil unrest out of control in China, they launched several small nukes within their own borders in an attempt to stop the spread of disease and chaos. They killed millions of their own people in a blink an eye. Asia was now a mass of a billion irradiated undead roaming over the lands, in the hills and through its lifeless cities.

Iran sent its forces into Iraq to squash the few healthy remaining American Infidels that still occupied it. They vanished. In a matter of days, the Iranian soldiers returned over the border and back into Iran. Now they fought side by side with American soldiers—as members of the army of the undead. Some suicide bombers detonated themselves as the masses of undead swarmed over them. Some drove car bombs at them to try to drive them back. Some still wore their deadly vests of explosives as they crossed the countryside now in search of the feast of flesh.

Hordes of Palestinian refugees swept over the West Bank into Israel bringing with them the thousands upon thousands of walking dead that followed closely behind. The Middle East now belonged to the undead, the sandstorms blasting at their flesh as they roamed freely and without opposition.

In Africa, the outbreak of undead did what so many others had failed to do—stop the fighting that existed between the various tribes. Now, they all fought on the side of the undead. It could be said that the Africans may have put up the best fight in the beginning against the growing masses of undead. Almost everyone there owned a machete and they hacked and slashed at the undead as best they could. In the end, it left the most gruesome horde of all, one missing limbs and multiple hunks of flesh from their bloody, battered bodies. With their arms, legs, and faces hacked off, the monsters roamed the deserted landscape, their dried up flesh cracking like the mud beneath their feet in the constant hot sun.

The numbers of undead arose from the several ghettos and shantytowns spread out across South America. Sweeping into the larger cities, they brought with them their wave of death and destruction. From there, the demons crossed into Central America, joining forces with the growing multitude of undead that had already begun their rampage.

No one knows what exactly happened to the United Kingdom. Their communications slowly trickled off, only to one day, suddenly fall silent. The plague of the walking dead consumed them as it had claimed so many others in so many countries.

Some small islands might still be safe. Being isolated, there was no access to the DRED-not vaccine and were spared from the initial outbreak of the undead. Now, who knows? Who knows how far the carnage has spread?

Perhaps the roaming masses of dead had not made it up north to the coldest regions. Would they freeze if they tried? Either way it was a hostile place for both man and monster. How long could you survive up there in the cold? And with up to six months of total darkness, it would surely be a terrifying hell if the undead did make it. With limited supplies and lack of available shelter, you had better hope that you did not have to relocate in a hurry.

What do you do when everyone and everything you send somewhere just vanishes, being swallowed up by the unknown? You eventually stop sending until you can figure out what in the hell is happening.

As the numbers of the living decreased, the numbers of the dead soared, the victims having enlisted unwillingly into the growing army of the undead walkers that had begun to stalk the earth.

Looking back, is it really my fault or the scientists? As much as I try not to, I still take the blame. If only I had stayed at the hospital—maybe—just maybe...

THE HORDES

It was unknown to everyone in the beginning what the catalyst was to make the dead rise. It did not take long for people to figure it out. It had to be the DRED-not. In a matter of hours, the entire planet was battling a new foe. A foe unlike any other they had ever seen. They looked like humans and walked upright like humans but they did not die like humans. This new undead adversary was definitely not human. They were the demons of the flesh. They were the monsters that craved one thing—the feast of the flesh.

No one knew if you had the DRED-not vaccine in you to bring you back if you became sick. If you did have it, you were not going to admit it. Those foolish enough to admit to taking the DRED-not; were hastily shot or dragged out into the street and beaten to death by the mobs of terrified civilians.

Everyone became a potential walker. Everyone became an enemy. The demons of the flesh were inside us all—and they were waiting to get out. Entire cities, even nations, exiled themselves away from everyone else to try to keep safe. Locking their doors and boarding their windows, hoping desperately that that was somehow going to save them from the escalating horrors and atrocities now taking place outside.

To go next door to borrow a hammer or some nails usually

resulted in deadly consequences. The visitor receiving several bullets into his or her body, fired from homemade gun ports built into the makeshift fortifications.

The streets became vacant of life. The only life on the streets—was not alive. They were the walking dead. Shuffling down streets, farmlands and out of buildings, they came from everywhere. That is when the real hordes showed up.

Hundreds of thousands of rotting, roaming undead came searching for the living, trying desperately to satisfy their voracious appetite for the flesh. They had come from the areas where all communications were lost—from the voids.

The hordes came, travelling street by street, door by door, almost systematically, tearing apart and ravenously eating every living thing in sight. I did see some bitten animals, which did seem to be immune to the virus. I guess it was something that only affected humans.

As the death and decay spread, the darkness of night concealed the walkers' movements. Their image appearing then fading as they walked, passing through stray beams of light. Creeping ever so closer, stalking their prey. Millions of feet, dragging and shuffling, pounding the ground, shaking the earth. It was enough to drive even the most hardened battle veteran mad.

The moans—I guess they are not really moans since technically the dead do not breathe. The gaseous sound of the decaying flesh from previous victims as it sat rotting in their stomach is more like it. The wail of the encroaching entourage of evil emanated for miles. Some have likened it to a kind of freakish rock concert.

The bright greenish glow of the walker's staring dead eyes came piercing through the blackened streets. Like tiny little fireflies—of death. Something in the DRED-not made the deads' eyes appear to glow a sickly fluorescent green. It also accelerated and then suddenly stopped the rate of decay.

The dried out leathery flesh hung from the undead demons, tattered like the clothes they wore. They came streaming steadily out of the smoke, out of the despair that they had left behind. I have never actually heard or seen a true Horde. To be honest, I hope I never do.

Very few people have heard the hordes and lived to tell the tale. Seeing or hearing a horde seemed to drain the life force from every living soul, even before the undead attacked.

Many killed themselves, rather than fall victim to the agonizing death that the walkers would bring. Is there a worse way to die than to be eaten alive? Having your limbs torn from your body as you lay there, helplessly watching the undead feed upon your arms and legs. Being witness to them dragging your liver and intestines out across the ground as they feast.

Some, crazily, embraced the hordes and ran willingly to their deaths. As if Judgment Day was upon them and whatever deity they believed in was going to save them from the undead rapture.

Then the strays came. The dogs, the cats, the carrion, everything that was not dead would show up to feed on the remains left behind by the roaming dead.

There were swarms of flies large enough to block out the sun. Similar to a squadron of World War Two bombers headed to their target, they buzzed through the air that was thick with the stagnant stench of death. Nature cleaning up for us, I guess.

You cannot begin to realize how much damage the human body can do until you have been to a city where the hordes have roamed through. Whole blocks destroyed by bare hand! Like all the kung-fu masters of the world having a break block competition, their prize being you.

Everything crushed as millions of lost souls shamble over, trampling it. Mailboxes, cars, fences, lawn furniture, anything on the ground, flattened. The streets flowed with rivers of blood. Do not forget the body parts, and skeletal remains—everywhere.

The military, having too many flu victims within their own ranks, were virtually powerless. A few large-scale attacks were coordinated but at that time, it was still unknown that in order to defeat the undead hordes, you must destroy the brain. With the lack of manpower, many vehicles and weapon systems became useless as they sat idle and in disrepair.

One such assault took place somewhere on the east coast of the United States. The actual account of what the total amount of units, manpower and horde strength, along with the final numbers of casualties from both the undead and the living were sketchy at best.

The story, watered down as the few survivors repeatedly told it, had several different locations as to where the battle actually did take place.

The numbers of the undead ranged anywhere from five million to ten million. The quantity of defenders usually started at three hundred, which referred to the amount of Spartans that had fought in the battle of Thermopylae and stopped at around one thousand.

Most people, upon hearing the tale knew that there had been more troops involved than what the teller was relaying. Nonetheless, they would let them tell their story, knowing it gave hope to the few remaining survivors.

The closest telling of the truth that I heard went something like this. The military, mobilizing all the resources they could, attacked an oncoming horde that swarmed over the countryside after wiping out a major city. The battle would take place over a ten-mile front line pitting twenty thousand men and women against over three million undead. The assault was to take place in four phases.

First, came the air strikes, consisting of everything from F-14's, F-16's, A-10's, F-22 Raptors, and even one B-2 Spirit called in to carpet bomb. They were to soften up the oncoming horde.

The second wave would be from the air also but in the form of Apache attack helicopters and Cobra gun ships. They would be next in unleashing their arsenal on the undead.

The next wave would take place after the air power had finished unloading their ordinance onto the masses of walkers. The ground artillery was to open up a barrage with everything they had and destroy what remained of the advancing horde. Six M777 Howitzers and two M270 MLRS (Multiple Launch Rocket System) would pound the undead into the earth and back to the grave.

The fourth and final defense sat in the form of fifteen thousand Army and Marine personnel perched on high ground. Some combat trained, some not. Cooks and clerks picked up arms and stood beside Special Forces soldiers to await the oncoming entourage of evil.

None of the soldiers actually thought that they would even have to fire their weapons. Nothing, not even the millions of undead, could withstand the firepower of the mighty American war machine, even in its decrepit state.

Ten miles from the frontlines, the horde attacked a small farmhouse, adding the half dozen occupants barricaded inside to its numbers. At the five-mile mark, the battle against the undead was to begin. The officers wanted the ground troops to witness the destruction of the oncoming monsters in hopes of raising moral if in fact they did have to fight.

As the demons of the flesh passed the mark, the B-2 appeared high overhead in the sky. It slowly swept over the mass of walkers dropping its load of bombs. Following closely behind, the jetfighters flanked the Spirit swooping down to fifty feet, streaking over the troops. The Riflemen let out cheers of excitement as the fighters hurtled towards the horde, the rings from their afterburners blazing in the twilight of the night sky.

The earth shook as the bombs from the air strike came crashing down onto the crowds of the undead, smashing them into pieces, sending them through the air and lighting them ablaze. The jetfighters swooped in for the first prong of the attack. The shockwave of the falling bombs, fanned out across the horde, knocking the walkers to the ground like blades of high grass blown over by the wind of a powerful hurricane. Giant fireballs and mushroom clouds of black smoke filled the sky as the glowing afterburners of the jets streaked off.

Yet, the dead still advanced, their burning bodies, glowing in the night like human candles. But they continued. The parts of the crumbled ones crept closer, using whatever limbs or pieces of limbs that remained to drag themselves across the blackened scorched earth. They continued towards the soldiers, crawling over the gore of the destroyed creatures that the first onslaught had left behind.

The jetfighters, having expended their ammunition, cleared the skies to make way for the second wave as the Apaches and Cobras took the fight over. The attack helicopters hovered over of the oceans of undead, thrashing at the dead with their rockets and machine guns. Battle cries squawked across the comms as the flashes of flame and streaks of smoke filled the dark sky.

The war cries fell silent as a call for help screamed through the pilots' headsets,

"Mayday, Mayday—Crazyhorse-1-2,
going down—going..."

Enemy machinegun fire or missiles did not cause the helicopter to come crashing down on that day; there was none, just a simple mechanical failure in the tail rotor.

The screams from the cockpit filled with panic as they watched the tides of flowing undead spin towards them. At first, it was fun, sitting there, hovering over the waves and waves of unarmed monsters that accepted all the ammo that they had to offer—with no resistance. Now, as the pilots swirled through the air towards the earth towards the sea of hungry demons, they wanted no part of it.

The soldiers on the ground and in the sky watched helplessly as the Apache slowly yawed to its side and began to drop out of the sky, spinning wildly. The pilots' cries for help turned to static as the chopper hit the ground.

Disappearing into the horde, the helicopter landed on its side, its blades thrashing at the dirt and grass as it spun like a child's top. The blades of the crashing 'copter chopped into the swarming masses of undead, sending limbs and hunks of burnt flesh flying through the air as the walkers encircled it.

It was unknown whether the pilots were lucky enough to die in the crash or if the undead had eaten them as they lie there still buckled into their seats —alive, recruiting them unwillingly into their masses.

Seeing the walkers swarming over the wreck of their downed comrades' Apache, the helicopters surveyed the battlefield. With their empty guns still smoking, the spinning of their rotors whipped away the dust and smoke as they flew. As the remaining attack choppers skimmed across the top of the remaining multitude of the undead, they looked down onto the carnage of death and destruction below and saw that they had made a sizable difference. However, was it enough?

Missing limbs and blackened from fire, the charred half-naked corpses of the dead pressed on. Stumbling over the fallen and crushing them, not caring if they themselves were on fire or split in half. The flesh ripped and torn from their bodies, the grotesquely disfigured horde moved on. They had come for one reason—to feed on the living.

The barrage of artillery opened up with thunderous claps as if god himself were striking down upon the advancing swarm of unholy ghouls. The salvo of massive shells tearing into the demons, returning some of the death and destruction that the undead themselves had brought to so many places. The shockwaves liquefying the internal organs of the ones near the blast, knocking them to the ground. Yet they arose, their innards dribbling down the back of their bare legs as they slowly resumed their advance.

Everything seemed to be going according to plan as the numbers of walkers slowly diminished. What was once three million, now stood at less than five hundred thousand as the arty walked with the horde as it still slowly advanced. There were still plenty of animated pieces of ghouls left behind on the ground. However, with no arms or legs, they were not going anywhere anytime soon.

The mass of resisting troops set up firing lines to deal with the remaining oncoming creatures. Surrounding themselves in sand bags and razor wire, they would be the ones to finish the job.

Fifteen thousand armed men and women and not one knew you had to kill the brain to dispatch a walker. Hundreds of thousands of empty wasted shell casings littered the ground before they did finally figure it out. But it was too late. The death of the walkers had made it to the wire.

Only about two thousand of the undead stood as they breached the wire, crawling over it as if it were not even there. Some, tangled in the razor wire, pulled the wire, dragging it with them. The wire shred their scorched flesh and snagged any soldiers that became cornered, adding to the pain and misery of being eaten alive.

Many of the less seasoned troops, and even some seasoned combat veterans, having never seen the gore of a walker up close and personal, turned and fled as the monsters made their way into the base camp. The circular defense of the razor wire trapped many inside. Some of the fleeing soldiers snared themselves in the razor wire. As more fled, they climbed over the snagged ones, not caring as it pushed their comrades further into the wire. The screams of pain and agony rang through the still air. The moans of the undead became deafening.

Some soldiers sat on the ground, placing their hands over their ears to block out the thunderous noise of the remaining horde. Even as the demons of the flesh began their feast, they continued to cover their ears. The horrific groans of the undead were worse than being torn apart. The rest of the soldiers stood fast to fight in one of the bloodiest hand-to-hand struggles in human history.

Empty rifles now became bludgeoning tools instead of firearms. For once, the living outnumbered the dead and the dead were going back to where they came from. With entrenching tools, knives and even helmets, the remaining soldiers defended their camp from the inside.

In the end, the soldiers were victorious since all of the walkers met their doom. Unfortunately, there would not be many battles such as this to take place. No one knows exactly how many soldiers stayed and fought that day or how many of them made it out alive.

If you look hard enough you might find one. He is usually the guy wandering outside alone, with no weapons. His hands and his brain are his weapons. He is not afraid of being out in the open. He makes you think of a homeless man but he does not push a shopping cart. His appearance looks disheveled as he wanders around muttering nonsense. You might wonder how he has managed to survive all this time in the chaos of the walkers. Why have the demons of the flesh not eaten him? Believe me when I say, they try and try again but as crazy and as weak as the tired and shabby man looks—he is a survivor.

The multitude of undead was still rising and the ways to exterminate them was dwindling. The more their numbers grew, the harder eliminating them had become.

Aside from other small pockets of military resistance here and there, it became every person for themselves. Trust no one and watch everyone.

Groups of military deserters banded together to form their own little "hunter" teams. Like they were super soldiers from a movie, all gung-ho and ready to deal the shit, they roamed the countryside looking for fights with the masses of wandering undead. They were going to save the world. They were going to be the heroes of the planet like the scientists were.

The majority of them, never even having killed a human in combat before, found out how hard it really was to hit a moving target in the head. How fast the ammo ran out. How much faster the dead seemed to move as they struggled to reload empty magazines. How quickly the food and gas diminished and how futile it was to hole up somewhere for any extended period of time.

The dead always found you and eventually found a way in. The only way to survive was to run—and keep running. Always stay one step ahead of the masses. Just then, you might have a chance. Nevertheless, how do you stay one step ahead of something that was everywhere, surrounding you like a thick blanket of creeping deadly fog?

I can still vividly recall seeing a family of skeletal remains hanging from a makeshift rafter in the living room of what was once a luxurious multi-million dollar domain. Mother, father, and three children, maybe young teens; they had hung themselves in a group.

The long wooden mahogany bench tipped over to the floor as the dead burst through the large opulent double doors that once prevented admission. The odor of death gaining access as the evil poured in behind.

The family's bodies, still warm and twitching, dangled from the tightened nooses that wrapped around their necks as the creatures began their feast. Feeding off the flesh from the fresh corpses as they sway back and forth, the rafters creaked under the weight of the ghouls tugging at the newly dead. Finishing their feast, the monsters moved on, leaving the once lavish furnishings in a reddish-brown fright.

As the walkers wreaked their havoc, many buildings and houses, destroyed to the point of collapse, caved in around them and the living. The fallen structures seeming to have a life of their own, as buried beneath the rubble are the dead and the undead. Their bodies tattered, their bloody arms and legs still struggling, their fingers reaching at your ankles as you pass, attempting to get free, to find that next meal.

I remember watching a television show on Hiroshima once, thinking that that was the most destructive thing I had ever seen. Until the day I witnessed what a few million walkers could do.

The dead feel no pain, sorrow, or pity. They never tire or need to rest. They just keep coming and coming, pounding, clawing, ripping and tearing until their limbs are bloody stumps and yet they persist. They do not stop—ever. My worst fears had come true. The demons of the flesh were outside the body—and they were now at my front door.

FIRST ENCOUNTER

I still remember the first time I saw a "walker." I will never forget that day. It sticks in my mind like a horrific car accident or maybe when you see some kind of catastrophic disaster like a plane crash. The stench of the dead, the blood, the corpses, the bits of bodies, and torn flesh that lay strewn across the ground like discarded refuse. Everything mangled beyond recognition. You just cannot seem to shake it. I guess that is what they call posttraumatic stress disorder. That was when the dead—stayed dead.

Anyways, back when things were "normal," before all the walkers came, I used to drink my fair share of beer. One of the "useful" skills I learned from when I was in the army.

Spending six years in the armed forces, I had always wished I had stayed in. It would be close to retirement for me now. The military was my passion. It may sound crazy but I did not want the typical nine to five job. I loved being in the army. I was an infantry soldier with a mechanized unit. I carried the light machine gun and was always the first one out of the Armored Personnel Carrier.

The life of a Combat Infantryman in a mechanized unit came with all the exciting things a young guy wants. You got to go four by fouring in APC's. You had plenty of machine guns and explosives to play with. It also came with the added bonus of not having to walk anywhere. The vehicles drove you right up to the battlefield.

Life in the military was exhilarating. Hearing the crack of a bullet as it broke the speed of sound and whizzed by your head might scare some, but to me it was adrenaline pumping. And that was what I craved.

The down time sucked though. With nothing to do on the base at night, you hit the mess and drank until you were either drunk or it was time to leave. When you were out in the field, they would even truck cold beer in for you to enjoy. Trying to numb our senses, I guess.

They even had beer machines sitting side by side with soda machines. It cost one dollar and fifty cents for a can of soda and a dollar for a can of beer. When you only have two dollars in your pocket, it's easy to choose. At a buck a beer, twenty dollars went a long way.

You did not dare pass out in the mess hall either. If you did—I remember this one guy from a visiting unit passed out. A bunch of guys went into the washroom and filled a hay box, which is a large metal food warmer, with piss. They slowly walked back in being careful not to spill the warm golden liquid on themselves. They crept over to the sleeping soldier and screamed the guy's name to wake him.

"Finch!"

As Finch's tired eyes began to open, they dumped the container of piss on him. I will never forget the look on that poor soul's face as he sat there dazed and licking his lips. I will also never forget the ear-shattering shriek that Finch let out once he did finally realize what it was that he tasted. Finch's mouth hung open and round for a good ten seconds as his shrill girlish squeal echoed down every corridor of the building.

The mess hall went silent. The talking, the laughter and the socializing all ceased. Everyone turned and leered at Finch with hatred in their eyes. There was no laughter. Just silence. Everyone knew better. This was where we came to relieve stress and enjoy ourselves—not nap. If you were tired—leave. You did not doze off in the mess hall.

The hay box clanged off the reddish brown tiles of the mess floor as the group turned and walked back to their beers. A single soldier stood in front of Finch. The lone soldier leaned in and stuck his finger in Finch's face. Once Finch had finished his cry of despair, the soldier screamed at him,

"Don't you ever fall asleep in our
fuckin' mess again!"

Finch jumped up and ran down the hall to the head. As Finch scooted out the door, everyone in the mess went right back to where they left off. Drinking, and laughing as if nothing had happened.

It wasn't so much that Finch fell asleep in the mess that everyone hated. It was the fact that he was from a visiting unit. It all came down to respect—or his lack of it.

My girlfriend at the time gave me the boo-hoo story of how we were to be married and how we could not have a normal functioning family if I was a soldier. No way was she going to live on a military base. What kind of life would that be for her? What would happen if I went to war? What would she do? Yeah right, Canada at war? PFFFT! I just kept thinking to myself,

"Isn't that why I joined the army in
the first place?"

Well, that was that, and no re-enlistment.

Before enlisting in the military, I had gone to college for graphic arts. It was more of a hobby when I was young. It was before I knew what I wanted to do in life. So after leaving the forces, I took the boring job of a graphic artist. At first, it did feel somewhat nice not having to pull all-nighters on observation post, or digging trenches in the rain or the hurry up and wait that was involved with being in the military. The only thing I really did miss about the army was the guns.

For the life of me, I could not see how any of those people that bitch about gun ownership could hate military weapons. Had they ever tried firing one? They made you feel like you were the ruler of the world. Mind you, it was your own little world, but you were the king.

Being a graphics artist was not all that bad. It was sometimes interesting. Walking down the street or opening up a magazine and getting to say,

"Hey, I did that."

The pay was good also. So I stayed.

I never did end up marrying my ex-girlfriend. She decided later to go to college—to improve herself. While there, she went out partying one night and got drunk. That night she cheated on me. Yeah, big improvement. Funny thing, I knew exactly what had happened right away.

So that was the end of her and five wasted years of my life. I had always wondered what might have been had we married, until I recently saw her in a picture. Whew, I dodged a bullet there.

My wife's mother and mine worked together and that is how I met her. We spent twelve years together and were still going strong.

The two things that I did keep from my past are my love for the brew and guns. My head also still sported the close-cropped haircut that the military requested.

When I bought beer, I would always buy tallboy cans because they fit perfect in the fridge on our boat and I could use one of those drink cooler things to keep it cold.

Our boat was a thirty-five foot Cabin Cruiser that could sleep six. Two 7.4-liter engines made it really move for a sizable vessel, giving it a cruising speed of about thirty-five miles an hour.

During the summer, we docked our boat in a slip at the local marina. Nothing was better than being out in the blazing sun, anchored off a sandy beach, sitting on the boat, listening to the stereo blasting, and drinking a few beers.

I hated carting the empties around. At the marina, I would toss them into the recycling bin. At home was another story. Being too lazy to take the beer empties back, I would end up with an entire basement full. Week after week, my wife—yes, she is still alive—would be continually harassing me to get rid of them. I cannot call it nagging but she would casually mention the empties that were piling up in the basement at least once a week.

One day, while around the corner having a beer with a friend, I met this boy, Ethan, who was, what is the correct term?—mentally challenged.

Ethan was a lanky kid who was in his mid-teens. He was very excitable but well mannered. He would come down that part of the street and harass everyone for his or her empty beer cans. Ethan would gather up the empties that he had collected and return them giving him a little bit of spending money to buy some candy.

After a few beers, I became generous and knowing that I had a crap load of empties, I told Ethan to go down to my house and that my wife would give him all the beer empties I had.

Calling my wife on my cell phone, I explained to her that Ethan was coming to pick up the beer empties. It was a good cause and it would make her happy to get rid of the stacks of cans that kept growing in the basement.

What a sight it was, watching Ethan coming down the street grinning from ear to ear. He came wobbling slowly down the street on his bike. Two giant plastic bags with over two hundred empty tallboy cans dragged on the ground as he rode. There was over twenty dollars in those bags for him. It made his day.

The problem was that Ethan started coming by and banging on my door everyday looking for more empties to return. He would bang there nonstop for at least half an hour or until someone answered.

Now, I did drink quite a bit but not so much where as I could supply Ethan with beer empties everyday. Eventually I would just try to ignore the insistent knocking on the door by turning up the television or putting on a pair of headphones. Then that dreadful day came.

The pounding started at about 6:30 PM one Saturday night. It was right on time for my little friend.

Normally, we stayed on our boat during the weekends but my wife, being in the retail business had to put in her one weekend of work a month. She worked at a lingerie store selling women's undergarments. They were not the trashy looking stuff that hookers wore, but the sexy, classy, matching undies that you might find on a model.

For a woman of forty, my wife still looked great. She was fit, toned and had long golden hair that highlighted naturally in the summer sun. Offsetting her hair was the bronze tan of a goddess that she received from being out on our boat. The set of 34D breasts she inherited, pressing out against her spandex tops, still sat high and pert, making all the girls she worked with jealous.

The beating of the portal continued. Bang, bang, bang, on the door for an hour. We had one of those steel doors with the small reinforced-glass windows, so I was confident the door was going to stand up to the barrage of fist thumping it was taking.

Then one hour turned into two hours. The sun began to set and still, bang, bang, bang on the front door. I could faintly make out the sounds of moaning. It did not strike me as odd because I could never really understand anything the kid was saying to me anyways. I just always nodded and said yup, yup whenever Ethan talked.

We sat on the couch watching the television, attempting to ignore the noise. My wife turned to me. Her annoyance of the constant banging was quite clear as she said,

"Maybe you should just go and tell
him we have no empties this week."

With a sigh, I dragged my ass off the couch and went to into the hallway. As I neared the door, the never-ending pounding became much stronger and angrier. The moans became louder and more disturbing.

I ripped open the door to say,

"Enough is enough, you little
bastard!"

There standing in the doorway was a hulk of a man, about six foot four and two hundred seventy-five pounds. This was not Ethan.

Two bloody stumps hung where the man's hands might have once been, as if a couple of pit bulls had devoured them. The shredded flesh that dangled loosely from beneath his torn sleeves dripped pools of blood at his feet. The behemoth stood there motionless, his mouth agape, and oozing with a slimy black froth. His wild eyes, fixated on me, looked lifeless. Shocked at the sight of this poor soul, I thought to myself,

"Holy shit! This guy needs some
help!"

As I turned to yell to my wife to dial 911, I paused. Without turning back, I slammed the door closed, rocking the door jams. The beast of a man, his bedraggled limbs outstretched, lunged at the entrance with a thud. From beyond the shut door, I could hear the blood squeaking as he tried in vain to claw his way through with his chewed up stumps. It was the stink.

It had been quite a few years since I had recognized that smell but it is something that you never forget.

About ten years ago, we lived in a house downtown that had an apartment building across the street from it. One hot, summer, long weekend, a guy jumped, or so that is what they said, off the twenty-sixth floor. On the way down, he hit a tree, severing his leg and landed in the buildings playground. Being a long weekend, it took until after dusk for the authorities to find someone to remove the body.

The corpse lay there decomposing from nine in the morning until nine that night, stinking in the sweltering heat. The light summer breeze brought that sickly sweet odour right into our windows. It is a stench I will never forget—the stench of death—that's what was not right about my visitor. I could smell the death wafting from him like a cheap perfume out of a sick twisted joke.

My wife stared at me wide-eyed and panicky. I turned, quickly walking down the hallway past her. My wife's eyes followed me, searching for some kind of explanation, some sort of comforting.

I continued down into the basement. My wife stood, frozen by fear at the end of the hallway. I returned carrying an old piece of galvanized gas pipe that I had removed during renovations the year before. The pipe was about two feet long and still had a ninety-degree elbow attached to the end. I had always wanted to buy a gun but she said it was a waste of money. It would have been handy to have one now.

As I passed by my wife the second time, she could see the look in my eyes. A glare she had not seen in years. Not since I beat the two teens who tried to mug me for some spare change while we were shopping downtown. The look that meant someone was about to get hurt in a bad way.

I stood in front of the door, pipe in hand, listening to my flailing friend on the outside. I bowed my head and gripped the pipe tightly. Without turning, I spoke in a deep authoritative voice,

"Go to the bathroom and lock the
door."

The calmness of my voice reassured my wife somewhat as she quickly made her way up the stairs. I slowly reached for the doorknob and prepared to greet my guest.

In one motion, I pulled the door open with my left hand and swung the pipe ferociously with my right. The first swing hit the ghoul on the left elbow, breaking it. Amongst the spray of blood, I could see his bones protrude from the joint as they stabbed through his flesh.

With his arm dangling down, the monster continued its assault. The hulk lunged at the door once more. Pushing on the door, his left forearm tore off, sending it flopping to the porch floor. I backed off giving the demon entry into the foyer. The monster lunged into the doorway, sending the door crashing open, the knob punching a hole in the drywall.

Grabbing the pipe with both hands, I continued my attack, striking grisly horror on the left side of the head. The pipe came down at a forty-five degree angle just above its temple. The thud of the pipe and the crack of splitting skull echoed off the narrow walls of the corridor. The monster's blood sprayed across my face and the ceiling in a red gooey cloud. The hulk faltered back into the open doorway.

With the ghoul's gore dripping down on me from above, I then planted the hardest straight kick I could muster into the horror's sternum. The decaying demon stumbled backwards out onto the porch. Tripping on its discarded arm, the monster fell. Skidding on its ass, the demon landed with its back up against the porch railing.

The monster sat against the rail, its one and a half arms outstretched, still trying desperately to reach for me. I stepped out onto the porch. The walker looked up, its teeth snapping at me, spitting a mist of black froth into the air. My knuckles turned white from gripping the pipe. I stood in front of the walker knowing well what I was about to do. I then quoted Oppenheimer, the guy who built the bomb.

"I am death—destroyer of worlds."

—then swung the pipe.

THE NEIGHBORS

I stood there, spattered in blood, staring down at my first dispatched walker. I then realized that I had been oblivious to what was happening outside all around me.

There were sirens off in the distance, loads of sirens. Maybe they were coming from downtown. Far off, I could hear the faint thumps of explosions, and the cracks of gunfire. I had served in the Armed Forces for a few years; I knew what they sounded like. My eyes slowly scanned the horizon. Downtown was aglow with fires, the plumes of smoke rising up against the backlit sky like the icy fingers of death that they brought.

I could hear a frantic woman down the street. She was screaming for her husband to stop. Terror filled her voice as she yelled at him. Stop what? What was happening to her? I did not know and was not in the mood to care. I had my own problems. I had just killed someone on my front step. Sorry about your luck lady.

Suddenly, to my left, my neighbor's door came bursting open. They were an older retired couple named Walter and Beverley, their son, George, came pouring out onto the porch. Holding a shotgun in one hand, George clutched at his neck with the other. Blood gushed through his fingers and ran down his shirt as he grasped at the wound on his neck.

George lived downtown and after witnessing the chaos there, he decided to rescue his mom and dad. It was too late. With tears running down his cheeks, George grabbed the shotgun in both hands. Vital fluids spurt out onto the front of the house covering the grey vinyl siding in gore as George pulled his hand away from his neck.

George held the gun up to his right shoulder, pumped the action and fired one shot into the open doorway before him. He then spun the weapon around and shoved it into his own mouth, breaking out several of his teeth. The top of George's head disintegrated in an eclipse of reddish gray mist mixed with hunks of bone and hair as he squeezed the trigger. George crumpled to the porch floor. Blood and brain matter leaked from the cavity that was once the top of George's head.

I ran down the steps and across the front yard, over to George's fresh corpse. Kneeling beside his lifeless body, the rest of him cascaded down on me from the porch ceiling. Picking up George's shotgun, I peered into the open doorway. There in the darkened hallway looked to be what was left of Walter. He lay in the hallway on his back. As I stood up, I could see that Walter's body was intact. Everything was there minus his face, so I could not really be sure if it was Walter or not.

I pumped another round into the chamber of the shotty, stuck the pipe into my belt, and stepped into the murky darkness. The blood drenched carpet squished under my shoes as I made my way down the hallway. Stepping on something soft, I paused. Picking my foot up, I glanced down at my shoe. Mashed into the treads of my sneaker was what looked like a chunk of flesh. I put my foot down and twisted my shoe into the carpet to free the human hunk of beef. Out of the darkness of the hall ahead of me came a thump. I lifted the shotgun up to my shoulder and continued down the hall and into the kitchen. I reached over in search for the light switch. I flicked the light switch on to find Beverley near the back door, wriggling face down on the bloodied tile floor.

Walter had died that day and returned from the dead to eat Beverley, who was handicapped, so there was no real chance for her to get away. Strange thing that. For some reason, when they came back from the dead, they all had the basic instinct to feed.

Maybe Beverley did not want to get away since I had heard no commotion earlier. On the other hand, maybe Walter got her from behind. However it happened, it did not matter.

Beverley's wheelchair lay tipped over near the fridge, and a bag, of what appeared to be George's belongings, rest on the small round table that sat in the middle of the floor.

I walked over to the wiggling creature on the floor and with one hand placed the shotgun to the back of her head. I squeezed the trigger. The slug smashed through Beverly's skull. Damn, that made a mess.

Bits of bone and brain stuck to the floor and walls. A mat of bloody hair slid down the wall slowly like a wet rag. Beverly's blood soaked me from head to toe leaving my shirt warm, damp, and sticky. I had thought about turning my head away before I fired but I wanted to make sure I did not miss.

I walked back to the table to check out the bag. Opening up George's bag revealed that he was planning to come prepared. The bag that George had packed held hundreds of rounds of shotgun ammunition. Unfortunately, George was not prepared to kill his parents.

I grabbed the ammo bag and headed back down the hallway and out the front door. Stepping over George, I crossed the yard back to my house and over the dispatched walker. Grabbing the cordless phone from the living room, I dialed 911. The signal was busy. I headed upstairs to my wife, dialing once more on the way. It was still busy. Hearing my voice call to her from the other side, my wife unlocked the bathroom door.

She stood in the doorway to the bathroom, visibly disturbed by the events that had taken place. I sat my wife down on the side of the bathtub and explained to her as calmly as I could,

"Walt and Bev are dead, and George
just killed himself."

My wife responded with a quick blurted reply of,

"What! What's happ...?"

Grabbing my wife by her shoulders, making her look directly into my eyes, I cut my wife off in mid sentence, saying,

"Just listen."

I went on,

"I am not sure what in the hell is

going on but everything will be ok."

"Trust me."

As I said the last two words, I tried to make them as believable as possible. I knew I was lying but if she did not know what my true thoughts were, then all the better. I would never admit to my wife what my exact thoughts were,

"We were going to die."

The last two words that I uttered to her had always made her listen to me. Every time we had ever been in some kind of jam, I had managed to make good when I said those two words...

"Trust me."

One weekend, we took our boat on a two-day trip. We were to spend one night at a nearby island marina and then one night on the way back at another marina. The winds had been out of the east for the past few days and that usually meant that the lake was going to be rough. We were meeting several other boaters and the winds had been relatively calm that day so off we went.

Leaving on our journey just after lunch, we decided to take our time and enjoy the ride since even though the water was a bit choppy; it was still a beautiful sunny day. What would normally take us one hour, took us two and a half.

Our ride to the island marina was enjoyable as we drank our beer and listened to loud music, while laughing and joking the whole way. It was not until our backs began to burn under the hot sun that we figured it was best that we make up some time and head inland.

As we pulled up to the marina, the boat engines slowed suddenly, almost dying. Glancing down at the gas gauges, I said,

"Uh, oh! I think we are out of gas."

My wife blurted,

"You've got to be kidding me?"

We were running near empty. Our plan had been to fill up at the island marina before the second leg of our trip. I figured we had enough gas to get there easily. Maybe I was wrong. Maybe we took our time a little too much.

Putting the gearshifts into neutral, the engines responded, roaring back to life. Whew! We had just bottomed out on a sandbar.

"No we're ok."

I said, as I chuckled, wiping the beads of sweat that began to form on my forehead.

"We just hit a sandbar."

My wife, smacking me across the back of my freshly sunburned arm, yelled,

"Don't do that to me!"

Our friends met us as we docked our boat. That night at dinner, they informed us that they would be joining us on the second day of our trip.

The next day everyone left for the next marina in his or her respective boats at their own leisure. We were the last to leave since we were the only ones of the group that had a powerboat and had to make a stop at the next island over to fill up with gas. The sailors would have to leave early in the morning to make it there. We would leave in the afternoon.

Right away, we should have known to turn back. The water had become so rough over the course of the day that we barely made it into the gas docks. We were out on the water already, so what was the point in going back? It really was not that far for us and if the waves were not too big it would only take us about fifteen minutes at cruising speed.

Pulling away from the island, the lake seemed rough but bearable. The waves had only grown to be about three feet high and our boat could handle these no problem. The farther we went the larger and more frequent the waves became.

I turned into the waves to make the ride more comfortable for my wife. The waves quickly grew in size and intensity reaching up to twelve feet in height. They came at us from two directions as they bounced of the shoreline and became relentless in their pounding assault.

The waves began to thrash the back corner of our craft one after another tossing us from side to side. The thunderous crashing waves lifted the back of our craft tossing us forward. The boat's drives whined loudly as they raised high out of the water. The bow of the boat dipped forward into the lake as the water crashed over the front.

The VHF radio began to crackle with the calls of Mayday. Repeatedly, the cries for help came as vessel after vessel sank on that dreary day. Without glancing down, I reached over and turned off the radio. The less we heard the better.

Ducking down below, my wife grabbed our life jackets and put hers on. I had never once put my life jacket on since I had always felt safe and comfortable that our boat could handle almost any kind of weather. But this was a tough drive and it was taking everything I had to keep us upright.

Mother Nature was testing all of my seamanship skills on that day as all of my concentration poured into piloting the watercraft. In the distance, I watched as the white crest of a wave formed. Then the water seemed to fall away into a giant pit as the wave approached. I miscalculated the oncoming wave and yelled out,

"Hang on!"

The wall of water came crashing over the side of the boat, sending us keeling over to an almost ninety-degree angle, leaving the water just mere feet from my face. It sent my wife skidding across the fiberglass deck, almost throwing her overboard into the churning waters below. The souls of her running shoes squeaking like a dying mouse caught in a trap as she slid across the deck.

After a few seconds, which seemed like an eternity, the hull dropped back into the water with a thud.

"Put your life jacket on!"

My wife screamed at me. I replied, my heart pounding with adrenaline and fear,

"Don't worry, we'll be ok."

"Trust me."

I did not tell her at the time I was thinking to myself,

"Oh shit, we are going over."

Panicked, she screamed again,

"Put your life jacket on!"

I yelled back,

"I can't!

I'm driving!"

My wife did manage to get the life jacket on me that day and we did eventually make it to our destination. Even though, the rest of the way she refused to lift her head up out from its hiding place in her arms.

Now, when we talk about our harrowing experience she can laugh about it. So ever since that day, she has trusted me with her life. If I were right then, I would be right now. Ever since that disastrous trip, she had always trusted the way in which I handled a bad situation. However, this time I knew it would be different.

Handing my wife the phone, I told her to call her mother. My wife's father died when she was a child. A drunken snowplow operator crashed head-on into his car while he was on his way up north with a couple of friends. They never did make it to their hunting trip. All in the car died as the plow ripped it apart, casting their smashed bodies into the air and leaving them sprawled across the snowy road amongst the pieces of broken automobile.

My wife pushed the numbers on the phone and waited—no answer. She tried again—still no answer. Looking up at me, she said,

"She's not answering."

Reaching out, I asked,

"Let me try mine."

I dialed my parents' number and listened. There was nothing, not even a dial tone. Then the phone went dead. I dropped the phone on the bathroom counter,

"It's dead."

My wife followed me as I went into the bedroom to look for some fresh clothes. I pulled out my old pair of combat pants. I was sure the extra pockets would come in handy. I grabbed a handful of shotgun shells out of the bag of ammo and began shoving them into the shotty. With the shotgun now reloaded, I filled the pockets on my legs with extra shells. Leaving the bag of ammo with my wife, I told her to get my backpack and fill it with food and water. Having changed out of my ghastly blood soaked attire; I said that I would return in about five minutes. Bewildered my wife asked,

"What are you going to do?"

I replied,

"I am just going to "check" on the
other neighbors."

Passing through the living room, I paused in front of the television. The coloured bars of the Emergency Broadcast System were on the screen but there were no instructions. Picking up the remote, I flicked the channels a few times but it was all the same. I threw the remote on the couch and went to the kitchen.

Opening up the fridge, I grabbed a can of cold beer. Popping it open, I quickly swigged half the can and slammed it down on the counter. I then turned and headed outside.

I made it to the front lawn when I saw, coming down the walkway between our houses, our neighbour, Gail. Right away, something was not right. Gail was an agoraphobic; one of those people who are afraid to go outside, leaving the comfort and safety of their homes behind. Yet up the walkway she came, trundling slowly towards me in the floral moo-moo that she wore everyday while peeking from her window.

Aiming from the hip, I fired a slug into her grotesquely obese belly. Fat cells spewed everywhere. It left a hole in her blubbery stomach about the diameter of a soda can, revealing some of her innards and dripping cellulose. She did not even pause. If anything, she started to come at me quicker.

Beads of sweat dripped down my forehead, one rolling into my right eye. I swiped at my eye with the back of my hand. This time I brought the gun up high to my shoulder, pumped in another round and fired a twelve-gauge slug aimed right at her nose. Whoa! That shot pretty much caved in Gail's entire face.

No nose, mouth, or functioning eyes remained on Gail's face. You could see clear to the backyard through her head. Nonetheless, she still stood—walking. Gail's eyes dangled from her skull, swaying back and forth—getting closer.

Pumping in yet another round, I stepped forward quickly, shoving the shotgun's barrel into the gaping hole I had blown into her face. With the war cry of,

"Die, you fat fucking bitch!"

I let off a shot that took what remained of the top of her head off. Gail crumpled like a beached whale at my feet—no more movement—just a slab of lard, rotting on the walkway.

You had to destroy the brain to stop them! I wondered how many people, if any, had figured that out yet. Wiping the sweat from my brow, I chambered another round.

Wait a minute. If Gail was outside, where was her scrawny ass husband, Stanley?

I hated Stanley. He was one of those neighbors that everyone has. The one you cannot stand. A skinny little ass weighing in at about one-hundred and ten pounds, Stanley once had his roofers put their trailer in my driveway while I was out boating.

I came home to find the roofers had backed the trailer into my porch, damaging it. There was a note on my door that looked like it was written on a piece of cardboard ripped from a Twinkie box. The note said that they were leaving it there overnight and that it was ok with Walter and Beverley.

Funny, last time I checked I was the one that paid the mortgage on my house. The guy had not said boo to me in the three years I had lived there and thought it was all right to do this. Moron. I could have choked him there on the spot. The trailer got tagged and towed.

I was actually hoping that Stanley had become re-animated just so I could kill him. Is that wrong? As I stood there contemplating on whether I was fucked up for thinking this, I was alerted by the shuffle of slippers on the cobblestone walk behind me. It was Stanley.

He always wore those cheap ass slippers, and his little shorts and nothing else. Without turning, I looked over my right shoulder, lifted the shotgun behind me, and blew off Stanley's right kneecap. He fell; face first, to the ground, reaching for me.

I was going to enjoy this one. I threw down the shotty and pulled my pipe from my belt. I beat the back of Stanley's head, counting the swings as I went. I counted at least fifty, when I heard the pipe clang off the cobblestone where his head once lay. I knew I was done.

The scrawny runt's head, now just a mound of pulped tissue, looked like an eighteen-wheeler had run over it a few times; smashed beyond recognition. I stood up, breathing heavy and covered in sweat, blood, and brain matter. I kept thinking how good it felt to destroy that skinny, ignorant fuck's skull. Was I losing it? Was I some kind of deranged lunatic? I did not care if I was—it was going to keep me alive.

Wiping the blood from my face, I went back home to see how my wife was coming along with the supplies.

That lady screaming down the street—it turned out her husband was a newly risen walker and was feeding on her. She showed up at my door a while later. There was not too much left of her, and I had never met her before so she was no big deal to kill. Or should I say—re-kill.

Her beloved had eaten most of her legs, right shoulder, and neck. She came up the porch slowly in a trail of blood. Pulling herself with her good arm, her head flopped around, hanging by just a few tendrils of flesh. I was not about to waste a round on this lame creeper and the pipe split her head nicely like a ripe melon.

I called to my wife,

"We are leaving."

She questioned,

"Where are we going?"

I answered,

"We're gonna try to make it to the boat."

Our boat had a VHF radio, a generator, two hundred litres of freshwater, and close to one thousand litres of gas. We could live on it for quite some time—if we could get it out of the marina.

As my wife approached the front door she winced, and turned her head at the sight of the first corpse. The loud burp of a dry heave she let out almost made me puke right there. She could not handle the smell of rotting death as I could.

Placing her hand over her mouth and nose, she recovered and headed outside. Following behind her, I muttered under my breath,

"Ah, shit."

This was the end of humanity, as we knew it.

OUTSIDE

We lived in a small city of approximately five hundred thousand people. Our house, a three-bedroom two-storey detached home, sat about a third of the way from downtown. Just far enough away from the core that we were free from all the crime, drugs, and vagrants that resided there.

Three Police Stations, none of which were near us, watched over the entire city. I did not expect to see any law enforcement come to our aid on this night. They were probably off guarding our househusband of a Mayor. Why anyone would ever vote for a stay at home dad with no job or political experience is beyond me. I just think the people that are qualified to run the country are smart enough to stay away.

Opening the car doors, I threw the ammo and pack of supplies in the back seat of our Ford Taurus. It was not a great car but it was the SHO model so it had some get up and go. Being all black, complete with ground effects and illegally tinted windows, it looked like a racecar.

As we backed out of the driveway, it became obvious that the chaos was escalating rapidly. People ran from their houses screaming strange things about the dead. Others packed their vehicles with whatever they had, preparing to flee the oncoming carnage. As they packed their cars and mini-vans, others attempted to come and take what they wanted by force. The living fought each other in the street as the demons of the flesh went unchallenged. Everyone was too worried about his or her own skin. The monsters began to roam freely amongst the living.

I live by the rule,

"Only take what you can carry."

If you cannot carry it, it is a waste and a burden.

Half-eaten corpses wandered the streets here and there, their clothing saturated with fresh blood. Tattered limbs hung from the half-naked bodies of those that still stood. Hunks of gnawed flesh and chewed entrails dropped from their torsos to the pavement like breadcrumbs. Those that could not stand—crawled—dragging themselves towards their victims. They silently approached as they smeared the ground with their innards like a snail.

The ghouls began their hunt as they slowly staggered through the darkness of night that fogged the streets. They stalked their prey as they crawled across the grass and into the shadows that blanketed the ground. Sliding along side the panicked people, the demons of the flesh tracked down and attacked the living.

All down the road, spouses were eating their mates, parents eating their children, children eating their parents—even children eating children. The screams of the dying filled the night air as the dead stalked the living and the living ran from the dead.

Approaching the main street, cars sped past in either direction, the roofs of the autos packed with belongings. None of the drivers looked like they knew where their destination lay. They were going anywhere—away from the carnage. Away from the hunters that were the demons of the flesh.

On the sidewalk, across the street, a woman ran. She pushed a stroller, her baby crying at the top of its lungs. The wails of the infant attracted the undead walkers like a dinner bell. Attempting to stay ahead as she fled the monsters, the lady managed to exhaust herself until the point that she could no longer continue.

The soldiers of the dead quickly swarmed her and her small child. Tearing the stroller from her weak arms, she screamed in horror to fight them back. The ghouls quickly silenced the toddler. The young woman reached for her baby as the dead feasted upon it. The remaining demons plucked the woman's arms from her body like wings from a chicken.

Tads of flesh hung from the mother's shoulders, flapping in the air as the ghouls pushed her to the ground. Her skull slapped the sidewalk with a crack. Blood gushed from where the woman's limbs once belonged. The deep red liquid sprayed into the faces of the decaying pack of demons as they tore into her flesh with their teeth. They chomped at her, pulling out strips of meat and tissue. The doomed mother lay sprawled on the sidewalk. Kicking her feet instinctively, she tried to defend herself from the hungry monsters, her blood drained down the curb and into the sewer. The woman's blood curdling screams of death echoed off the buildings, tearing through our ears.

There was no way we could have made any effort at a rescue. There were just too many of those—things. They were slow but gathered quickly. They came from every direction, attacking with steady, relentless force, without tiring.

Another guy, about the same age as me, was standing on a corner making his stand. With a pistol clutched in his hand, he fired into a crowd of about ten of the undead monsters.

I guess he had not resolved the problem of how to dispose of them since he just kept unloading magazine after magazine futilely into the creeping crowd of carnage. As the man stood there reloading the last mag into his pistol, he reminded me of this guy, Richard. Richard was my ex-roommate in Graphic Arts College. What a dick!

Richard, who was dating a female friend of mine, kept cheating on her with several other girls. If it was Richard, he deserved it. I kept this thought in my head as the last bullets spewed from the barrel of his pistol, the slide locking back to signal his doom. We did not stick around to see the aftermath of what we were certain was going to happen.

As we raced down the street, the hoots and hollers of what sounded like a party bellowed from a ramshackle two-story house.

The dwelling's decrepit appearance made it look like a crack house with its pealing paint, graffiti, and porch leaning to one side. Thick plywood and two by fours sealed the bottom floor windows. Heavy rap music blasted from loudspeakers that rested in the upper windows. Atop the porch and house roof sat young men, all wearing gang colors. Half wore red and the others in blue. The strange thing was that they were from two different gangs.

Normally they would be out protecting their turf from each other. No longer doing drive-by shootings on one another, they had pooled their resources. They sat atop their perch firing down into a crowd of undead that had gathered from the noise. The gang bangers had taken this disastrous situation and had made a sport out of it. It is just too bad that it had to take a global catastrophe to bring them together as brothers in arms.

The gang members sat, drinking beer, rapping to the music, smoking reefers and shooting the dead. It was as if they were playing video games and having a great big LAN party. They took turns at the roof's edge, urinating down onto the heads of the ghouls as they laughed hysterically, high-fiving each other.

As we passed the house, one unlucky gang member, his balance unstable from alcohol, blacked out. He keeled over, falling into the growing mass of undead. With his prick still in his hand, the dead shredded his body. The way the demons of the flesh ripped him limb from limb reminded me of a pack of hungry gators. There was not even a scream. Who knows if any of the others even saw or noticed? It did not matter.

The porch teetered under the weight of the partiers. It slid off the house with a crash, sending the youngsters cascading down into the swelling horde of undead. The gang bangers' screams and shrieks terrorized our ears as the carnage left our view.

I slammed on the brakes locking up the car's tires as I entered the next intersection. I braced myself against the steering wheel for an impact. My wife jammed her right hand up against the car roof and her other onto the dash, also bracing for a crash. The loud squeal from the skidding tires deafened us and the smell of burnt rubber filled our noses. The car shuddered, sliding to a stop. A police car and paddy wagon streaked into the intersection in front of us, screeching to a halt.

We stopped in time but our car stalled, leaving us stranded in front of the intersection. I tried to restart the engine. The engine answered back with a whir and nothing else. I turned the key again and again. There was no way in hell I was getting out here. As I kept trying the engine, I said to my wife,

"Any of those fuckers comes near;
you blast 'em!"

My wife sat ready with the shotty watching the battle that took place out in the streets. I was going to keep trying until I had no other option but to abandon my vehicle. I knew it would start. It would just take time. Time I was not sure that we had.

Two uniformed officers popped open the doors of the squad car. Flicking open their batons, they rushed to deal with a group of four walkers. The rear doors of the paddy wagon opened up and six heavily armored riot police scrambled out with their shields and clubs at the ready. Two more exited the front. Grabbing their gear, they ran to join the others to tackle a larger mass of the monsters. The officers moved in to retaliate against the demons' rage of violence.

We spotted a news van idling on the side of the road near the corner. The reporter and his cameraman tried to set up a live shot of the ongoing carnage not knowing that the television stations were no longer on the air. A man and a woman in their mid-thirties ran towards the reporter. The woman's flowery sundress was thick with blood. The liquid gushed from a gaping wound in her neck. The man had the woman by the hand, dragging her along. She stumbled with exhaustion and near death. Her one flip-flop slapped the bottom of her dirty foot as she made every effort to keep up. Behind them, a group of four walkers gave slow chase.

The bright light of the camera lit up the darkness. The cameraman pointed it in the direction of the reporter, giving him permission to proceed. The newsman began his report.

"This is Dan Mayweather reporting
live for channel twelve."
"Behind me, chaos is erupting in
our streets."

The reporter turned towards the man and woman running to him. In an attempt to get some answers, he stuck his microphone in the air in front of the running couple. The newsman reached for the man's arm to stop him, inquiring,

"Sir, can you—?"

The running man barreled into the newshound and shoved the cameraman, knocking them both to the ground. He dragged his female companion behind, giving the reporter nothing more than a,

"Get the fuck out of my way
asshole!"

The couple disappeared as they rounded the corner.

Picking up his microphone, the newsman stood up, brushing off his suit jacket. Looking over to the cameraman, who was already up and checking to see if his camera still worked, the reporter asked,

"Harry, how's my hair?"

Not looking up from his camera and replying as if he had been asked the same question many times over their years together, Harry gave him what he wanted to hear,

"You look great as always Dan."

"You're the man, Dan."

Still combing his hair with his hand, the newsman said quietly, loving himself,

"Yes I am."

Lifting the camera onto his shoulder once more, Harry began filming as Dan began narrating about the ongoing carnage in the background.

In the distance, over the reporter's shoulder, the two uniformed officers confronted the stalking walkers. The cops attacked fast and furiously, whipping the demons repeatedly with their batons. It had no effect as the undead continued their course. One officer screamed to his partner,

"Back up!"

Pulling his pepper spray from its small holster on his hip, he quickly gave the tiny bottle a shake and hosed the small group of walkers. Squirting it into the monsters' glazed lifeless eyes, the cop emptied the bottle. It also had little effect.

The pepper spray did not stop them but it did partially blind them as the ghouls staggered into each other. The two officers used their batons once more, this time thrashing at the monsters' legs. The four demons tumbled to the ground as the two cops continued to beat them.

Two of the undead horrors slowly arose, advancing towards one of the officers. The cop backed off still whipping them frantically. He did not realize they were forcing him away from his partner and up to a wall.

A downed walker grabbed hold of the other cop's ankle. Pulling him to the ground, the ghoul dragged the officer tightly into its icy grasp. The policeman lay on the pavement kicking at the monster.

The demon tugged at him, crawling slowly up his leg, pulling him closer. Panic set into the officer's face as he tried desperately to escape the ghoul's unforgiving grip. The undead horror sank its teeth into the cop's thigh. Tearing through his trousers, it ripped out a slab of fabric and flesh. The policeman screamed in agony as the monster went in for another taste, this time tearing out hunks of muscle and bone.

Cornered, his partner pushed at the demons upon hearing his friend's shrill squeal. He tried to shove his way through. He was desperate to help his wounded friend. The two walkers tackled the frantic cop to the ground biting him on the back of the neck and shoulder. He lay on the cool pavement, his blood streaming freely before him. The dead weight on the officer's back pinned him down as the demons of the flesh groped at his arms.

The cop lay, helplessly watching as the undead ghouls fed on him and his partner. He made no sound. He gave no scream. He just watched as the monsters continued to feast. The cop closed his eyes. Tears began to flow from the corners in his eyes. He knew his time was up.

The riot police formed a line in front of a horde of about twenty walkers. Holding their shields high, they clanged their clubs off them in unison not knowing if the monsters would respond. When the demons did not waver, the riot cops advanced towards the pack of ghouls. Both sides advanced slowly until they met face to face. It became a medieval battle of good versus evil. But evil had the edge. They were already dead.

As they met the walkers, the riot cops tried to push them back using their shields as a wall. The crowd of angry undead grabbed at whatever they could, tearing some of the shields from the cops' grasp. The line of police retaliated by swinging their clubs. Two of the creatures crumpled to the ground. The repeated blows to the head sending them back to the grave. The riot cops continued swinging their clubs at the pack of undead. The monsters fought back, clawing at the officers. The policemen had no option but to retreat. The demons of the flesh did not stop.

The army of undead managed to tackle three of the riot cops to the ground. Pulling at their equipment and armour, they wanted it to release the flesh that they so hungrily desired. Two officers dropped their clubs in the fray. They quickly drew their sidearms and opened fire. The bullets punched into the undead without effect. The remaining three riot cops ran to the aid of their tackled comrades, smashing wildly at the demons with their clubs, beating them off their buddies.

One of the two officers emptying their ammo into the army of walkers noticed it did not stop them. As the two backed up, reloading fresh magazines into their pistols, he yelled out,

"Shoot the fuckers in the face."

Hearing the command, his partner began firing towards the heads of the monsters. Some of the rounds smashed into the lower part of the ghouls' faces, tearing apart their jaws as they still advanced. Others bullets found their mark, taking down the demons of the flesh.

Regrouped, the riot cops seemed an even match for the twenty walkers as they battled it out in the street. As the group of undead attacked, the officers fought them off. Neither group was making any headway but the cops were beginning to tire. Once they figured out the only way to stop them was to shoot them in the head the cops started to get the upper hand. They had disposed of eight of the monsters now. Two more of the ghouls lay on the ground immobilized and posed little threat.

The odds were now almost one to one as the riot cops continued to fire at the walkers, backing up slowly in the direction of the news van. One cop barked out,

"Ammo! Ammo!"

This cry sent another officer running back to the paddy wagon to re-supply the officers' quickly diminishing ammo count.

The riot cops had now retreated to the news van. Hearing the reporter behind him, the commanding officer turned back, looking over his shoulder. The light of the camera flashed into his eyes as he saw the reporter. He screamed angrily at the news crew,

"Get the fuck out of here!"

The newshound was determined to get his story and jammed his microphone into the officer's face. The riot cop grabbed the microphone out of the newsman's grasp and threw it to the pavement, yelling,

"Are you fucking nuts?"

A sinking feeling rose up from the pit of the riot cop's stomach. He thought he was going to be sick as he watched another mass of walkers round the corner behind the cameraman. One of the demons still munched on the lower leg of a female as a flip-flop dangled precariously from the foot attached to it.

Feeling the doom creep in around him and his squad, the cop let out a sigh of,

"Shit."

Shoving the reporter to the side, the cop pointed his pistol at the cameraman and began firing past him into the crowd of creeping carnage.

The officer pointing the firearm towards him did not faze the cameraman. He had done two tours in Iraq taking combat footage so it was hard to startle him. Watching the muzzle flash from the cop's pistol light up the darkness, the empty shell casings fly into the air and the rest of the officers in the background still firing towards the oncoming dead all seeming to happen in slow motion, he thought only one thing. This is gold! It was not until the horde of demons drove him to the ground from behind that he realized the danger he faced. By then, it was too late.

Harry the cameraman still held the camera in his grasp as the dead fed upon him. The camera continued to film, catching all the sights and sounds of the losing battle. The riot cops now fired in all directions, their shots slowly petering out, their guns running dry. The carnage continued in the viewfinder of the camera as Harry's blood slowly spattered the lens until it coated it in a deep red. Just the fresh blood streaking down the camera lens was visible now. The screams of the dying and the growls of the hungry undead feeding on the still living shrieked into the microphone as the camera finally went dark.

Having gathered up extra ammo, the last remaining officer in the back of the paddy wagon jumped out. A mass of more than fifty walkers now surrounded the news van. He could not see any sign of his fellow officers. He did not know what to do. He was now alone. Looking around quickly, searching for some way out, the last cop climbed back into the rear of the paddy wagon and closed the doors.

My efforts finally paid off and the car's engine responded, roaring to life once more. The tires squealed with the burning of rubber as we raced away from the legions of undead that had begun to amass around the police van. We did not stick around to find out if the last remaining cop made it or not.

Continuing down the street, we could see that the carnage was widespread. On every corner and down every street, the demons of the flesh gathered. Some sat on the ground in small clusters feeding off the fresh corpses of the newly departed. Others attacked the homes of the living that had barricaded themselves inside. The rest roamed the streets, looking for a shot at some poor soul caught in the open, searching for the feast of flesh.

Farther down the street, columns of smoke rose up with their fingers of fumes reaching high into the sky. As we drove closer, we realized the towers of black came from the mall. Several hundred people ran to the mall in hopes of finding shelter or supplies. It was after hours, so the mall's doors were locked. The people used there vehicles to smash through the glass doors as they flooded to it. Passing along side the mall's parking lot, we saw a pick up truck that smashed through a glass display window. The display and the mall were now ablaze.

Out in the parking lot and inside the mall, people fought each other over the precious items found inside. The army of the undead stormed in uncontested. The survivors that made it to the guns first shot the others to preserve what they had. The monsters had little work to do to take control of the mall. The humans had eliminated each other and any resistance they might have formed against the demons of the flesh.

The mall burned in several spots as fire crews sent to put out the blazes no longer concentrated their streams of water on the fires. The accompanying police officers overrun and dead, the fire hoses now acted as water cannons. The firemen sprayed the masses of undead that congregated towards the mall. Shooting them back across the pavement of the parking lot, the firefighters bought themselves some more time. At least until the water ran out.

We concluded that going deeper into the city would be a bad idea. That was the most direct route to where the marina was located but highly populated and with narrow streets. We decided to take an alternate but longer detour and headed for the industrial area of town. With wide roads and hardly any people, we figured there would be less action and an easier travel route. We came across a mini-van parked off to the side of the road. Dark green and complimented with its faux wood paneling, the cargo door sat open.

Inside the van, a soccer mom struggled to get out, her arms and legs flailing wildly. The team of young girls making her an after game snack. The woman swatted at them in vain, calling out to the girls by name as if they would recognize her voice and stop their terror. The woman's shrill screams of agony bubbled past the mouthfuls of blood filling the air. The team of young girls gnawed off hunks of flesh, their teeth scraping deep into the bone. Their tiny white instruments of death ripped and tore at the soccer mom's tissue that was soft and supple from all the years of the moisturizing creams that she used.

The woman lay on her back, arched halfway out of the cargo door, her head near the road. Her arms dangled motionless onto the street below. Gushes of vomit poured from her mouth at the intense pain as it coursed through what was left of her body. The flow of liquid sickness streamed out onto woman's face, cascading up her nose and into her eyes.

The hungry little demons sat perched overtop the motionless lady, feeding on the woman's lower torso, satisfying their thirst for the flesh. The soccer mom's blood arced up, squirting the inside of the windows, painting them a deep red as we sped past. I guess they didn't like the oranges.

A lone helicopter flew by overhead, heading in the direction we had just left. Its searchlight scanned the ground as it passed. The beating sound of its blades thumped in our ears. At that moment, I wished that we were in that helicopter and getting away from all of this.

The rest of our journey to the marina was quiet. The ever-glowing fires of the steel mills had gone out. Now the city burned instead, the fingers of smoke emerging from the palms of death. The streets, usually full of big trucks hauling various goods, were now barren. Only the sound of our speeding car and the far off explosions from the now ruined city sounded in our ears.

Neither of us said a word to each other the whole way. The belief of what was happening still tumbling through our minds. The shock of what we had just witnessed leaving the images imprinted in our brains.

Was this the end of the world? I had always believed that humans were just another stepping-stone in the short history of planet Earth. We too, like the dinosaurs, would one day be extinct.

THE MARINA

We pulled into the marina parking lot at about eleven that night. Tires screeching to a halt, I immediately thought, it might have been a bad idea to come here. The lights were on but it was still too dark for my liking. There were only twenty or so walkers wandering around aimlessly. Perhaps they were other boat owners that had the same idea as us and did not make it.

Examining the Yacht Club, it was clear to see; the large glass doors and windows that adorned the front of the building were now shattered and destroyed. Fifty's music chimed from the opening where the doors once stood. That's right; they were having a Fifty's Murder Mystery/Dance tonight.

Exiting the vehicle, my wife carried the shotgun. I grabbed the backpack and ammo from the back seat. I could see that the security gate to the main dock remained locked and secure. Good, that would help keep any of those bastards out.

We managed to get halfway between the car and the security fence when the first demon of the flesh began to threaten us. It was a teenaged boy of about seventeen. A few small childlike bites decorated his forearm. A large chunk was missing from his neck causing his head to droop to one side. Dressed in his "gansta" outfit with wide brimmed baseball cap on sideways, blood drenched his dress length t-shirt. His pants that were usually around the bottom of his ass were now around his ankles. It was comical.

I always hated seeing those kids walking around holding up their pants with one hand. Bobbing as they walked they would strut around as if they were the shit. Who in their right mind would take to wearing a fashion that originated in prison all because belts were off limits to inmates?

Still wearing his MP3 player, the young ghoul came closer. As he neared, I could hear some kind of rap music blaring out of his headphones as they dangled by his side. I hated rap.

I said to my wife in the most serious voice I could muster, trying to contain my giggle,

"Shoot it in the head."

She raised the gun, aiming down the barrel at the ghoul. Lowering it again, she turned, looking at me.

"I don't think I can."

I told her the monster was not alive so it did not matter, to;

"Pretend its head is a can of
tomatoes and pull the trigger."

The undead demon continued to slowly advance towards us.

She lifted the shotty once again and squeezed the trigger. My wife had never fired a gun before in her life let alone something that gave the kick of a shotgun. She yelped from the roar of the shot. The recoil sent her to the ground, the shotgun spiralling into the air. She had missed.

Eyes wide, adrenaline rushing through my veins, I pulled the pipe from my belt and charged the closing creature. Raising my arm over my head to begin my assault to the undead, I felt the wind and heat of the twelve-gauge shot as it passed by my left ear. Instinctively, I ducked and grabbed at my ear. The slug smashed into the walker's head, tearing open the top left side. A plate of skull spiraled off into the distance. The "gangsta's" ball cap popped up in the air like a cork from a bottle of New Years Eve champagne as his head tilted over leaving what was left of his brain, to slop out onto the pavement.

Still cupping my left ear, I turned back to find my wife standing there. Her eyes squinted, staring down the still smoking barrel of the gun, she released,

"Punk ass wigger."

Our commotion brought the attention of a few other walkers, which slowly began to turn and make their way towards us. It was only a bit farther to the gate and once inside we should be safe.

As we ran towards the security gate, I could feel dampness on the hand that covered my ear. Shit, she shot me. Pulling my hand away, I checked for blood. Good, it was only sweat on my hand and not blood. I looked to my wife saying in disbelief,

"You almost shot me!"

Rolling her eyes and shaking her head as if it was no big deal and I should stop being a baby, she replied,

"But I didn't."

I argued back,

"But you did."

My wife ended the conversation with,

"Shut up and quite whining."

I fired back quietly under my breath one last time, making sure I got the last word,

"But you did."

She, of course, did not hear.

Reaching the gate, I dug out my keycard for the electronic lock when I spotted a few half-submerged bodies that bobbed about in the water. My wife pointed to some other floaters and commented,

"It looks like they are trying to
swim."

Swimming? That is ridiculous. I searched the darkness for them and sure enough, they looked like they were swimming all right.

There in the water, the half-submerged "floaters" bobbed up and down as they slowly swung their arms and kicked their legs. A few lay on their backs as if to do the backstroke.

I turned back to the gate to swipe my card. That is when the lights went out. Standing there in the pitch black about to swipe the keycard, one word came from my mouth—

"Shit!"

My wife replied,

"What's wrong? You didn't forget
your card, did you?"

She then realized why I had said what I did. No power—no card reader—nothing but the shuffle and the moans of a few closing walkers.

With the new additions to the gate after vandals broke in, there was no way in hell we were going to get around it. We just had to stop to watch the swimmers. We could have been on the other side already. Damn! The fifty's music had also stopped. Along with the noise cover that had been hiding us from the party guests.

Through the silence of the eerie blackness came the greenish glow of round orbs. They slowly floated towards us as a mass of about one hundred undead came rambling out of the broken doors of the Yacht Club entrance. Our eyes slowly adjusting to the darkness of the night, we could see that they were all dressed in fifty's garb.

A female ghoul with a fake rubber knife protruding out of her chest was the first to appear. The artificial blood looking more like ketchup trickled down her front. She must have been the murder mystery victim. The blood staining her sweater and poodle skirt was real. Her pale, dried up skin confirmed she was definitely dead now. The woman's lips, which had now drawn tightly back, revealed the grisly flesh of others that hung from her teeth.

The creeping shadowy figures of the revellers, their torn clothing now all covered in real human blood showed the signs of the brutality of the attack. From the fashion in which their flesh now hung in tatters from their limbs, it was evident that they were all victims.

It was like having front row seats to some low budget fifty's horror flick. Except, this B rated movie was deadly and was now between our getaway vehicle and us. This time we had no choice but to abandon our car. It looked like we would be on foot for now.

We made our way west through the children's waterfront playground. It was a typical kiddy land with swings, water park, wading pool, and jungle gym. The meat chunks hanging from the monkey bars, and the blood red water in the wading pool, however, were not of the standard norm.

The land that the playground occupied arced around the main dock out into part of the harbor. From there we could see the docks and our boat.

Several walkers stood on the docks, staring in the water. Perhaps they too were perplexed with the swimmers that floated around helplessly in the water. Shopping carts, duffle bags, and whatever else people could stuff their belongings into, littered the docks. It seems we were not the only ones to try to get out on a boat. None of them made it very far.

At the mouth of the marina entrance, a flotilla of boats sat jumbled together, rocking in the gentle waves at the break wall. They were all sizes, both power and sail, most of them streaked, and smeared in blood. The arms and legs of their crew, now partially devoured, hanging overboard, splashing the water, and bumping the sides as the waves rocked their floating tombs.

Once the first boat sank, the others became hung up, one at a time, creating a beaver dam. I am sure some made it out but these poor souls did not. Even if we could get to our boat, there was no way of getting it out of the harbor. I had absolutely no idea where to go, how to get there, or what we would do when we did finally arrive—wherever it was that we were headed.

It did not take us long to find our next ride. We could hear the music from the playground. The

"Doot, doot, doodle, oodle, oot, doot,
doot,"

of the Ice cream truck, its engine still running.

As we approached the truck, it was obvious that it was not going to be a free ride. Two small child walkers, a boy and a girl, about the age of seven or so, were milling about the truck with a male adult. Maybe they had come down to the waterfront for a treat with their dad. Mr. Ice cream was on the ground chewed to the point that you would not know it was he if it was not for the hat that lay on the ground beside him.

As the Yacht Club goers closed in on us, we knew we had to make this getaway rather swiftly. The three ice cream patrons, noticing our arrival, began to near. Wearing his green golf shirt, khaki shorts, and brown leather sandals, the dad led the trio. Behind him, teetering in front of the Ice cream truck's side window as if still waiting for their cold creamy treat were the two kids. The boy, with his long baggy t-shirt and knee length shorts turned to follow. Dressed in a yellow sundress with her hair pulled to the sides and hanging in pigtails, the sister tagged along. A stream of dark feces drained down one of the young girl's bare legs and into her white patent shoe as her feet slid slowly across the pavement.

My wife aimed the shotgun at the father of the three. Leaning forward, bracing for the kickback of the shotty this time, she blasted a shot into the head of the undead horror. At close range, her aim was dead on. The slug punched a hole through the ghoul's head, coming to a halt in the side of the Ice cream truck. In a red mist of blood, bone, and brain, he crumpled to the ground. Red specks surrounded the silver dollar sized hole in the truck. Gravity slowly pulled the spatter earthward as it dribbled down the truck. I turned to my wife and ordered her,

"Go check the inside of the truck."

Glancing over to the staggering pint sized demons, I said flatly,

"I'll take care of the kids."

I did not want my wife to have to live with the image of killing a couple of kids.

Gripping the pipe tightly between my fingers, I walked over to the two small creatures. Their high-pitched little squeals pierced my ears as they raised their tiny arms. They drew back their lips to reveal their pearly white baby teeth that hungered for a taste of my flesh.

I did not really care for kids but I was no monster. I would never consider hurting a defenseless creature. I tried convincing myself that it was an ok thing to do. They were already dead—right? Nevertheless, I could still feel a small amount of guilt wash over me as I raised the pipe.

It was an easy dispatch with each of the half-pints getting a good hard whack to the head. As the pipe came smashing down on each of the miniature demons, in all honesty, I did feel bad for them. It just did not seem right that these little kids should die like this.

I am not sure if my wife heard the cracking of their tiny underdeveloped skulls. Or the squishing of their little brains as the pipe split both their small heads with ease. Unbeknownst to me, as my wife searched the vehicle to see if our newfound ride was clear of any undead, were her true thoughts,

"Boy, I hate other people's kids."

THE GETAWAY

The stragglers from the parking lot were now joining the collection of revellers. Making it look more like a "no more nukes" demonstration was approaching. The sonance of moans stemming from the converging undead assembly sent chills travelling up my spine. If it was not for that, I might have stayed my ground.

With the ok from my wife that our ride was clear, I shuddered as I turned. Bolting to the treat truck, I ran as if I were a little boy going for a chocolate dipped cone, all the while screaming,

"ICE CREAM!"

With the parade of walkers hot on my heels, I climbed in through the back door of the vehicle.

Spying the candy sprinkles, I took a handful and crammed them into my mouth, ignoring my blood soaked hand. At the helm, my wife put the ice-cream truck in gear and gave the beast all the gas it could muster. With a puff of black smoke, the truck lurched forward. I turned and reached for the handle to close the back door. Ragged hands thrust towards me sending me to the floor of the truck. They stretched in grabbing at my legs. I whacked at the hands with my pipe, beating them back. I could hear the bones of their fingers snapping as I smashed at them. As the heap sped away, the pack of undead attempted to hold us back, their bloody hands pawing at the vehicle and my body. One by one the hands slowly disappeared as the demons of the flesh skidded and rolled across the pavement.

I stood up and watched the monsters slowly fade in the distance. Then, out of the corner of my eye, I caught a glimpse of the chopped up peanuts. I reached in and grabbed a handful. Continuing to stuff my face with cone toppings, I watched out the back. Beyond the thick black smoke that spewed from the sputtering piece of shit van, the gathering of walkers fell slowly behind and then slowly got closer.

My wife yelled back to me,

"We are out of gas!"

Spitting chewed cone toppings through stuffed chipmunk cheeks, I spewed,

"For fuck's sakes!"

That was my favourite saying when things in life went wrong. Things in life went wrong for me so often that I used that phrase daily.

I used to joke with my wife saying that I was going to change my name to Murphy Law. Anything that could go wrong in my life—did. If I was to do a simple task such as make toast; you had better believe that I would drop a piece of bread onto the floor.

One time before a barbeque, I attempted to break apart a pack of frozen hamburger patties with a knife. As I stuck the knife in between the slabs of hard meat, the first patty broke away and shot across the counter. I saw it fly but I could not find it. I searched for the hamburger for fifteen minutes. All over the kitchen, I searched. There was nowhere for it to go—except for the one-inch gap separating the fridge from the countertop. Looking down into the space with a flashlight, I could see the elusive hunk of frozen beef. Sure enough, it landed down in the tiny space.

"For fuck's sake!"

What were the odds? If it were not for bad luck, I would have no luck at all. I had to move the fridge out to get access to the missing meat and ending up wasting more time than it actually took me to cook the hamburgers.

So here we were, out of gas and getting another healthy dose of bad luck. What else could go wrong? I guess our good luck was in the fact that both of us were still alive.

I grabbed one last mouthful of chopped up peanut bits and candy sprinkles as we departed from the truck. It had about as much life in it as the small horde behind us. Trying not to choke on the gob full of goodies as I ran, I began to think that the last face stuffing was not such a good idea.

We ran along the newly renovated waterfront. There was no time to smell the flowers as we jogged along the shrub-lined pathway. Passing the sandy-beached swimming area, a few of the swimmers had made it to shore. Their soggy footsteps sloshed against the ground under the weight of their bloated bodies as they rose. Our breathe come out hard like the panting of dogs. We dodged in and out of the picnic tables towards the end of the park. From there we could see the train repair depot.

Spotting the rail station, we hurried towards it, hoping to find some kind of shelter and maybe a bit of rest. A ten-foot chain link fence ran the length of the tracks to keep people from wandering into harms way. Pushing my wife up onto the fence, I looked back to see the small horde advancing. It was a good thing that they were slow. Scaling the wire barrier, I followed my wife up and over. Crossing the tracks, we searched for a way in.

The giant three-story structure sat nestled into a small hillside. The main road ran along the top of the hill. The depot's walls, constructed out of rusty sheet metal siding, had been painted an olive green to try and spruce it up. The paint, now bubbled and peeling, flaked of in various places. By its appearance, if you were unaware that the building was in use, you would have believed it to be abandoned.

There were three ground level entrances complete with shatterproof glass windows, the ones with the wire mesh in them. Up the left side of the building, rising to the top, was an old metal staircase. The staircase came to a stop at another door. Several repair sheds, large enough to fit a locomotive, sat at the ends of the turn-off tracks. Trying each of the three doors we spied, we became desperate. Locked, locked, and locked!

Looking over my shoulder, I could see the mass of undead creeping closer as their moans became louder. The pursuing horde trampled over the ten-foot fence like it was not even there, pushing it into the dirt as they continued their hunt for us.

I turned to watch the monsters' advance, the weight of the

backpack now wearing on me as I bent over to try to catch my breath. The demons of the flesh were gaining ground now as they began traversing the tracks like slow charging bulls.

I nearly shit my drawers from the wailing whistle of the oncoming train. Screaming like a banshee from the depths of Hades, the speeding locomotive plowed the track. Barreling into the mob of ghouls, it sent them, and parts of them, in all directions. One flailed at me as the top half of its body passed over my head. Blood spurted from were the legs once hung, the intestines flying behind like a kite tail.

I could see some of the dead in broken pieces, trying to hold onto the train as it passed, trying to claw their way in. Mashed bodies lay scattered across the ground still wriggling towards us. Some still standing—walking.

The blast from the shotgun awoke me from my daze. Hearing the words,

"Hey pretty boy, you done sight-
seeing?"

Shocked at the fact that she had just called me pretty boy, I spun around. Yes, I was good looking. Yes, I took care of myself. And yes, I always had the girls chasing me. Was I a pretty boy? I don't think so. I once had a bodybuilder friend, who was quite large; tell me that he thought I was the most macho guy he had ever known. I was a good-looking, well built, ex-military man that, when confronted, could give the biggest guy a serious beating. Talk about head swelling. I never really noticed. I just did what I liked and what I thought was necessary. But I was no fucking pretty boy.

My wife was at the top of the metal staircase and had blasted the lock out of the door to gain access. My boots clanged up the metal treads as I ran to join her, the remaining undead closely in pursuit. As I joined my wife at the top, I shot her a stern look saying with disappointment,

"Huh, pretty boy my ass."

She fired back with,

"Just get that tight little ass in the
door."

Nosing the creaky metal door open with the end of the pipe, we stepped into the dimly lit depot.

The little bit of illumination in the depot came in the form of emergency lights. Weird shadows dancing on the walls by the flickering of the lights toyed with our wild imaginations as we proceeded inward. We walked along an overhead catwalk peering down into the darkness below. The shop machinery was quiet and unattended. The monstrous overhead cranes that loomed high above were still. The massive metal lathe, still holding the shaft that awaited repair, sat idle.

Making our way along the catwalk, we continued to scan the inky black that rest below. We approached some offices as the walkway opened up at the end. There were no visible walkers but we could hear the unmistakable drag of their feet and smell the piercing stench of their decay.

As the walkway opened up in front of us, I handed the pipe to my spouse. Grabbing the shotty from her grasp, I quickly refilled the weapon. I told her to place one hand on my back and stay close as we crept farther into the dimly lit building. Rounding the corner of what looked like the foreman's office, two close range stalkers staggered out to greet us.

Both walkers wore dark blue work uniforms, their nametags illegible with the brownish staining of dried blood. One walker was missing a sizable portion of the left side of his neck. The liquid of life dribbled onto the hard concrete floor marking his path of death as he shuffled towards us. The other had most of his nose and underneath of the right eye socket gnawed off, showing bare bone. Crimson fluid ran from his ears and down into the collar of his shirt. Saying aloud to the two walkers,

"Break time's over."

I began to raise the shotgun.

A scream from my wife sent me reeling to my left to see the attacking monster in mid lunge. With its arms outstretched towards me, the smell of rot seeped from every orifice.

Knowing the gun was not high enough for a kill shot, I did not care as I sent a slug flying into the ghoul. I popped the guy right above the "Jim" nametag on his uniform. Stopping him dead in his tracks, the buckshot blew his left collarbone in half, leaving the clavicle protruding from his shirt. The beasts' left arm swung down, dangling low.

Without hesitation, I stepped forward, saying,

"Heads up!"

I thrust the shotgun forward, smashing the deceased demon on the chin with the rifle butt. As the undead creature staggered backwards, I spun the shotty back around and fired into his forehead. The shot sent the top of his hair rearward like an unstuck toupee flapping in the wind.

Yelling at my wife to,

"Get back!"

I turned to the other two walkers and blasted buckshot at them until the weapon was dry. I stood there staring down at the bone, blood, and wriggling body parts on the floor. The mess made it obvious that they were not getting back up. Scanning the dark for other threats, I quickly reloaded the slug thrower.

The pack of remaining party revellers clambering up the metal staircase began to ring in our ears. The fleet pushed through the slow-footed sending them tumbling over the railing, thumping to the ground.

It did not appear that we would be finding any survivors as we passed through the foreman's office. Flesh, bone, and blood littered the cheap, grey speckled linoleum floor. The spatter continued across the old metal desk and onto the flaking beige paint of the filing cabinets. The off white drop ceiling and concrete walls, sprayed and streaked with blood, looked like a slaughterhouse. Several deep red handprints swiped down the walls into smears. They adorned the room like a hellish finger painting of death. An assortment of papers and files lay scattered about the blood soaked floor.

A low-back brown leather computer chair still sat in front of the desk. Green duct tape patched several wear spots in the chair. Dirt and grease blackened the arms over time. The user, sat lifeless like the blank monitor in front of him. As if waiting to enter the next command. His right hand still held the mouse tightly, crushing it with the icy grip of death. His left arm lay on the floor beside him with hunks of flesh torn out. The wedding band was still visible on his ring finger. The computer geek's head and left shoulder were missing. The demons of the flesh ripped open the man to devour his innards leaving several openings in his chewed up ribcage.

Handing the buck blaster back to my wife, we continued through the depot to the front of the building. The path of death and destruction ran through the entire building. Passing the closed doors of the washrooms, we heard the growls of the undead as they feasted on a victim inside. The crunching of bones and the slurping of bodily juices came from beyond the closed portal. We stepped over the pool of dark liquid flowing from under the door and crept past.

We snuck up to the receptionist's desk and ducked behind. A female ghoul sat in the middle of the floor. Even dead, her ass looked shapely in her tight fitting skirt. A bloodied bra covered her top. Hunched over a man who was partially clad in a suit, the demon fed on the man's throat. Beyond the monster were the front doors—and the street.

Seeing the doors wide open, I said to my wife,

"We are going to run for it."

I waited for the walker to bend down for another bite, whispering,

"Get ready."

As the beast dove in for another mouthful of flesh from the dead man's neck, I whispered again,

"Go!"

With a tug on my wife's arm, we made a b-line for the outside. We slid, skidding in the pools of blood that dotted the white ceramic tile flooring as we ran. The monster looked up as we ran by. Then bent down and bit off more of her victim.

Heading out to the street, we discovered it was relatively quiet. When I say relatively, I mean there were not any of the ghouls chasing us at that moment. They were still there but scattered about and fairly easy to avoid. The group behind us would hopefully take a while to get through the depot.

The street remained mostly blacked out from the lack of power. Some lights were still on but not many. It reminded me of the time the whole east coast was in a massive power failure and you could not see your hand in front of your face. Of course, everyone blamed it on us Canadians.

We could faintly hear the thumping blades of the solitary helicopter that was still buzzing around. Also, there was still the shooting off in the distance.

Heading west and traveling one more block, we came upon a police barricade with five cops. They were fighting off a small group of approximately twenty or thirty walkers. They had three squad cars set up as a wall and were behind it. They fired their pistols at the closing creatures. The muzzle flashes lighting up the night.

We crouched behind a concrete flower box to rest before making our way over to them. From behind our cover, we watched the battle unfold.

They had the oncoming dead down to about a half dozen or so when one of the officers began to cough uncontrollable. The choking cop fell to his knees as the others stared in disbelief. The four remaining constables shared a quick glance with each other, all knowing what they had to do. They then quickly targeted their fallen comrade with their weapons.

Before the first shot was fired, the kneeling officer fell forward clenching his teeth into the closest cop's leg. The bitten man screamed in horror as the toxic saliva made its way into his veins. He wildly discharged his weapon in desperation at the monster tearing his tissue from the bone. The bullets ricocheted off the pavement in puffs of concrete dust as they punched through the officer's own thigh. Total chaos ensued.

The three surviving policemen began shooting at the standing victim and the hungry attacker on his leg. They killed both monster and victim with another officer taking friendly fire.

We tried to warn them that the remaining swarm of undead they had been in combat with earlier was still closing. Either the officers could not hear us or their panic was too great to bother.

Wounded and dead lay on the ground as the last two cops tried to help their wounded buddy. They never even noticed the creeping crowd of carnage as it stormed through their barricade and on top of them to commence their feeding frenzy.

The group of ghastly ghouls pushed the officers to the ground as they tore into the survivors with their teeth. The dead ripped off limbs and chewed at their throats until almost severing the cops' heads. Trying to block out the screams of the dying officers, we ran to steal the cop car farthest from the feast of flesh.

Quietly opening the doors of the car, we gave a sigh of relief. The keys were still in it. It was one of the newer Chevy Impala models, which I thought looked smart for a cop car.

I started the car. Hearing the engine, the police picnic dispersed and made their way to us for dessert. Slamming the door, I hammered the gas as an undead hand slapped the window leaving a streaky palm print of fresh blood. As we accelerated away from the carnage, my wife grabbed the shotty. Leaning out her still open door, she fired. Dropping one of the demons to the ground, my wife grinned and yelled,

"Booyah! Who's my bitch now?"

I looked over at her and her smile drooped,

"What?"

I said with some concern,

"You seem to be enjoying this a little bit too much."

Her reply was a simple,

"PFFT!"

Closing her door, we both buckled up, not knowing what kind of ride was in store for us.

Driving through the outskirts of the city, the flashing lights of the squad car attracted survivors trying to escape the ever-growing masses of undead. Believing we were cops, the survivors ran down the street after us frantically looking for help. The wave of creeping death that followed behind quickly washed over them.

The impact to the rear passenger side from the Nissan Maxima sent our car spinning out of control. With the deafening crunch of fibreglass and metal and the shattering of glass, the Impala swung around twice. The tires' squeals echoed through the deserted street as they rubbed the pavement, skidding. Jumping the curb and backing into a street lamp, the car came to a rest.

Neither of us had seen the oncoming vehicle. As we regained our senses, we exited the now destroyed pursuit car. Looking over to the Nissan, we could see that there were four people in it. The impact crumpled the car's front end. It sat shrouded by a smoky haze, the auto's fluids leaking out onto the pavement.

The driver of the Nissan was quite dead as his corpse hung through the front window and out onto the hood. The hair from his scalp matted around the hole punched into the windshield, his blood seeping out over the hood. The passenger sat trapped from the collision and two people stirred in the rear. The couple in the back seat climbed out still shaken from the impact.

The two survivors were a petite couple of around the age of forty. A man and a woman dressed in business attire. As they turned and waved to us to suggest they were uninjured, the Maxima burst into flames lighting up the night sky with an eerie glow. A plume of black acrid smoke rose skyward. The fire quickly crept up towards the passenger compartment of the vehicle. The couples' trapped friend cried out for help as the flames licked up her pinned legs.

There was really nothing that the couple could do, except to watch the flames slowly engulf the trapped woman. We watched and I wondered. How long does it take to burn to death? The woman's flesh blistered as she thrashed about. She let out a piercing shriek as her skin darkened. Her cries fell silent as her tissue began to peel off.

As the couple stood helpless, the woman buried her face in the petite man's shoulder. They listened to the final screams of their companion fade as she died, her corpse leaving behind the stench of her burnt flesh.

The burning woman's shrieks told me it was a horrible way to die. But I guess it is still better than to be eaten alive.

The crash survivors ran over to us as we began gathering our gear from the wreck that was once our ticket out. Searching the trunk of our wrecked cruiser for useful items, I came across an eight-cell flashlight, one of those long metal ones and a police duty belt, complete with forty-calibre Glock pistol.

The small woman was still crying over the death of their companion. I think it was more of the shock of witnessing such a disturbing event that had gotten to her. All of us agreed that it was not a good idea to be caught hanging around out in the street. So the introductions would wait. We were on foot—again.

THE BAR

Making our way a few blocks from the collision site, we came across an old bar with the front door open. Ducking inside, we shut the door. As I entered, I bumped into a thick wooden table. Looking to the petite man, I said,

"Give me a hand."

Lifting the heavy table, the two of us propped it up against the door, blockading it.

It was a small, seedy looking bar. One that you would think you might find a group of bikers hanging out in. Against the one wall were a Jukebox and a pinball machine. A pool table, balls still scattered about, sat in front of them.

Several round wooden tables dotted the floor, each surrounded by rickety wooden chairs. The tops adorned in condensation rings, the odd coaster, and a glass jar holding a candle.

Multiple neon beer signs, now blackened with the loss of power, hung from the walls. Two long rectangular windows set up high, flanked the doorway. A dusting of empty peanut shells acting as a rug, crunched under the soles of our feet as the four of us made our way in.

In front of the bar sat half a dozen tall stools with black vinyl cushions. Three small wicker baskets of peanuts sat on the bar as well as three of the candle jars. The bar was dotted with the black spots of cigarette burns. The initials and names of several previous patrons scratched the bar's top. Behind the bar, two well-stocked beer coolers stood. Bottles of half-empty liquor lined the shelves on the wall. On the left side of the bar was a doorway that led to the back storeroom. I lifted my shotgun to my shoulder and slowly walked over to the opening. The others followed closely behind.

Upon entering the storeroom, I noticed a staircase heading up to a second floor. A trail of fresh blood ran the length of the stairs. Passing my wife the shotty, I took off the police belt and put it on her. I pulled out the Glock, checking to see if it was loaded. Quickly showing my wife how to use it, I handed it to her and took back the shotgun. I put my arm around my wife and asked,

"I need you two to check the back
door. Make sure it is locked. Can
you do that for me?"

My wife nodded.

Looking over to the diminutive guy in his flashy suit, I said,

"Let's check the upstairs."

The small man reached into his waistband. He then pulled out this huge fifty-calibre, nickel-plated, Desert Eagle with rhinestones in the grip. The fucking gun looked bigger than he did!

Holding the gun in two hands, he pushed passed me to be first up, his bloody shoe prints remaining on the stairs as he rose. I stared in amazement. Raising my eyebrows, I said,

"Well ok then".

—At least he wasn't a chicken shit.

Before clearing the top of the stairs, I heard the roar of the big bore pistol the Lilliputian carried. My first sight upon gaining access to the upstairs was this tiny little man dressed in his snazzy duds. He stood holding the Herculean pistol out in front of him, wisps of smoke still rising from the barrel. A single empty shell casing, the size of a lipstick tube, lay on the floor. The small man's gun glowed in what little light there was as if it was an angel sent down from the heavens.

On the floor lay one of the rotting creatures. A waitress in tightly fitted jeans, the pants left her pink thong visible, the order pad still sticking out from her back pocket. Her snug spandex top, now ripped, revealed her cheap floral thrift store bra. Draped over a fat smelly looking bearded man, who was probably her boss, I could see the giant hole the massive bullet had crudely punched into the back of what used to be her head.

It was quite clear the fat man was not getting up. The server had helped herself to the majority of the top of his skull, leaving only his beard.

The upstairs was a small bachelor pad adorned with the usual dressings. The torn up old sofa and chair looked like they came from a second hand store. An old TV, missing the knobs sat on a cheap particleboard stand. The woman's brains and shattered skull streamed down the front of the blank television screen. The floral patterned throw rug in the middle of the floor where the bodies lay was dirty and stained. The sink sat full of dirty dishes. Empty pizza boxes littered the counter.

The room smelled of old food and musty furniture. A faint hint of B.O. floated about the air, along with the sickly-sweet stench of death. The last remaining feature of the room was a door leading out to a small rooftop patio. Having cleared the building of hostiles, we regrouped at the bar. All was safe—for now.

As the others pulled stools up to the bar, I went around the tables and lit the candles to give us a little light. That was one time that I was glad I was a smoker. In fact, I thought, I could go for a smoke right now. I pulled my squashed pack of cigarettes from my shirt pocket and offered one to everyone.

Lighting our smokes, we made our introductions. Mike and Billy were their names. It was obvious that Mike was not a smoker from the cough he let out on the first drag he took and by the way he held his cigarette. I think he only took one out of courtesy as a gesture of friendship.

Judging by the way Mike talked and acted, he was either very feminine or very gay. The nickel-plated pistol with the rhinestones in the grip was not working in his favour either. It really didn't matter since Mike seemed like a solid guy who loved his cannon of a gun and knew how to use it. I thought I even caught him talking to it once. I was glad to have the help and the company of others did not hurt as well.

Billy, even with her face spattered in blood, was a hot little number. Her small perky breasts poured out of her ripped low cut dress. She also had a set of legs that did not stop. I could not help but stare.

As we rested, I opened the beer cooler and took beers out for each of us. The PSHT! sound coming from the uncapping of the bottles was like a church choir singing a hymn. Placing the bottle of brew up to my dry lips, I took a long hard swig. Ah, still cold—and free! I chugged down the first beer and opened myself another as we began to share our stories.

Although it had only been a short time, it felt good to sit down, have a cold beer, and chat with someone, even if Mike and Billy were strangers. A little bit of normality in all this chaotic carnage—until I heard their tale.

Mike and Billy had been having dinner together when the anarchy ensued. He and Billy were not married, only business partners. Mike sold lumber and Billy was a purchaser for a major home improvement store. They were in the middle of eeking out a lucrative deal for both parties when it all spiralled out of control.

During their elegant dinner, a file of Police cars passed by the windows of the restaurant, their sirens wailing and lights flashing. As Mike and Billy headed out into the street to see what the disturbance was about, a lone walker confronted them.

A bloated East Indian man, his once bright white robes hung ragged and blood soaked. His forearms, stripped of their flesh, hung in hunks, tattered like his traditional garb. His turban, once neatly coiled about his head, now dangled down. As he approached, it unravelled, revealing his long scraggly hair.

The demon dove at Mike. Falling on top, the monster pinned him to the ground. The monster leaned in trying to get a taste of Mike's flesh. The meat from previous encounters still dangled in its hungry grin, suspended from the creep's teeth. Gasps of rotten air bearing the soul of the ghoul's last meal flowed from the walker's mouth forcing its way into Mike's face. The stench of death and curry flooded into Mike's nostrils as he struggled, fighting for his life.

Mike and the undead horror grappled on the ground. Panicked, Billy pulled off one of her high heels. She wore the expensive kind, the ones where the spikes have metal on the inside. Using the makeshift stabbing weapon, Billy beat the corpulent creature about the head. The demon turned its head, attempting to get an easier meal from her. It left itself vulnerable to Billy's repeated attacks.

The tip of Billy's spiked heel jabbed deep into the beast's eye socket stabbing into the monster's brain and shutting it down.

I sat at the bar tracing Billy's legs up and down with my eyes. I could see the dried blood caked on one of her stilettos from the brawl.

The ghoul, now motionless—the way it should be—lay still on top of Mike. Rolling the lifeless beast away, Mike grabbed Billy by the hand and they ran to get Mike's car. He owned the Nissan Maxima that would later plow into us.

Upon entering the auto, Mike unlocked the glove box and reached for his Desert Eagle. He grinned as he stared down at the gleaming gun. Purchasing it on the black market, Mike had always kept it there for,

"Just in case."

Well, that time was now. Grabbing the extra magazines, Mike stuffed them in his jacket pocket.

Starting the vehicle, Mike gazed at the reflection of himself in the rear view mirror. Blood and sweat streaked his forehead and cheeks. He and Billy both breathed deeply. Charged with adrenaline, Mike's hand shook as he adjusted his mirror. He looked into it seeing the back window of his car. A demon of the flesh staggered towards the rear of the vehicle. Deep scratches lined the monster's bare chest. The ripped, and shredded tan khakis he wore, showed the bones of his thighs. Barely able to stand, the creature teetered closer.

Slamming the transmission into reverse, Mike floored the engine. A grey smoky haze and the smell of burning rubber filled the air. The screeching tires carried the makeshift battering ram backwards. Slamming into the shambling corpse, the car crushed its pelvis. The fiend lay squished between the back of Mike's Maxima and the car parked two spaces behind, the undead ghoul's bodily fluids leaking out onto the trunk of Mike's car.

The jarring pressed Billy back in her seat as the rear of the vehicle crumpled from the impact. Looking through the haze of dissipating fumes to his right, Mike lifted the behemoth of a gun and squeezed the trigger. With a thunderous boom, the passenger side window exploded, showering Billy in shards of tempered safety glass. Billy screamed but could not hear it over the ringing that droned in her ears from the blast.

The round smashed into the neck of a female animated dead, decapitating her as she reared her arms to begin her ghastly assault. The ghoul's body fell back. The head bounced off the hood of the Nissan, its eyes still searching for the feast of flesh.

Behind, the crushed creature flailed wildly in its desperate attempt to feed. Mike put the car in drive and stepped on the gas. The Maxima sped off dragging the mashed monster until it lie on the ground, its legs twisted oddly from the collision. Yet, the creep still pursued.

Racing from the parking lot of the restaurant, Billy began to sob uncontrollably. Mike looked around at the growing carnage in the street. He could see that other diner's were not as lucky as they had been. The newly arriving demons overpowered the fleeing restaurant patrons with ease.

Once Mike thought they were clear, he pulled the car to the curb. He hugged Billy, trying to soothe her pains. It was not what was going on around her that was upsetting. It was the fact that all she had worked so hard to accomplish in her life was all for shit. All of Billy's years of laborious work were for naught. That was why she cried. Her expensive condominium overlooking the lake, her flashy jewellery, and her designer clothes, all gone. After a few minutes of not being able to manage her tears, Billy finally accepted the fact that she would never see those things ever again. Bringing her tears under control, Billy said sadly and without lifting her head,

"Just drive."

Grabbing the shifter to put the car in gear, Mike glanced across the street. The flickering lights of a bowling alley's sign had caught his attention. Shutting off the engine, he stepped out onto the road.

Standing in the street quietly with his pistol at his side, Mike strained his ears to hear what was happening. Billy leaned over to the driver's side window. Raising her eyebrows, she looked out at Mike and said impatiently,

"Let's go!"

Without moving, Mike gave her a soft,

"Shhhh—Listen."

Billy replied,

"What? I don't hear any..."

Billy never finished. The doors of the bowling alley burst open, tearing off their hinges. Wave after wave of the walking dead flooded out into the street. Simultaneously, Mike and Billy both yelled,

"Shit!"

Lifting his Desert Eagle, Mike fired into the encroaching entourage of evil. The first shot ripped a walker's arm off as it turned the bone to pulp. The next two rounds slammed into the same decaying demon.

It was a skinny teenage monster carrying a bowling pin. Maybe he worked there clearing the machines. Mike did not care as he repeatedly squeezed the trigger. With each thunderous boom, the muzzle flashes lit up the darkened street like lightning. The big bore bullets blasted into the kid's torso and continued through the crowd. The bowling pin tumbled across the pavement as the teen doubled over, his body peeling in half and falling to the ground. As the fiend's legs lay still, the top half of the creep resumed its course towards Mike.

Panicked, Billy tried to yell over the roar of the gun,

"Mike, get in the car!"

She yelled again frantically, beginning to sob again,

"Please Mike, please!"

Deep in concentration, Mike ignored Billy's cries.

Exiting the Nissan, Billy ran to Mike. Grabbing at him, she tugged at Mike's arm, urging him to get back into the car. Turning to enter the vehicle, Mike and Billy heard the pleas for help coming from the alleyway beside the building. A man and a woman in their fifties emerged, stopping at the corner. They stood in amazement as they watched the demons of the flesh pour out of the bowling alley.

Billy waved at the couple wildly to get their attention,

"Over here!"

Mike covered the couple by blasting away at the group of ghouls with his big bore pistol.

Mike was not a stupid man and could see that the decimation he was delivering into the undead crowd was having little effect. Reloading his pistol with a fresh mag, Mike took careful aim at the closest walker's head and squeezed the trigger.

The deep growl from the barrel, the blinding flash, the action of the slide gliding back to chamber another round, the spent casing ejecting up and out into the air, all seemingly to happen in slow motion. The bullet raced towards the monster's face.

The round slammed into the monster's forehead. The demon's

head folded in on itself like a deflated balloon. The creature fell back and lay there, unmoving. That was the trick. Mike muttered under his breath,

"Destroy the mind and the body will
follow."

Running past the group of ghastly ghouls, the older couple made their way to Mike and Billy. Mike stood fast, falling the ever-nearing mob of death one at a time.

Down to his last magazine, Mike handed the empties to Billy, ordering her to,

"Get in the backseat and reload
these."

"The bullets are in my briefcase."

Mike kept a box of ammo in his briefcase in the backseat of his car. As the older gentleman ran past, Mike said to him,

"Get in and drive."

The older woman climbed in the front seat next to her husband.

As the last remaining bullets travelled down range leaving the slide of the gun locked back, Mike knew it was time to leave. He turned and jumped in the backseat beside Billy. Their newly arrived chauffer put the car in gear and accelerated away from their would be attackers.

Excited about the fact that he had figured how to take them out, Mike thought to himself,

"There are just too many."

Racing along the darkened street, the older man at the helm told his tale. He and his wife bowled every week. It was obvious to Mike and Billy since the couple still had their bowling shirts and shoes on. Now soaked with deep red stains, their names, "Phil" and "Loise" were barely visible on their jerseys.

Phil continued his story. The shoe rental guy, being a heavy pot smoker, used to frequent the alley outside to have a toke. While out soothing his need for a quick high, the dead paid him a visit.

Decaying death came spilling into the alley as the shoe guy, eyes closed and head back, took a long haul off his joint. The smoke expelled from the top of his neck as the undead pulled the low-wage worker's head from his body. A slight high-pitched squeal rose out of his tearing voice box as he died.

Inside the bowling alley, the living failed to see the walkers filing in the open side door. The pandemonium of the bowling balls smashing into the pins masked the ghouls' entrance. The screams of the first victims being drown out by the hoots and hollers of the excitement over spares and strikes.

About to leave after a fun night of bowling, the two survivors had made their usual journey to the restroom before the drive home. As the dropping of the pins became less, the cries of the prey became more.

Phil ran from the Men's room to the Lady's to retrieve his wife. The older man saw the brutality of the carnage as the few defenders made a futile attempt for their lives. Throwing bowling balls and bashing at the undead with pins, the bowlers' blood flowed over the floor like the surf hitting the beach. It was too late as the tide of undead washed over the rest of the patrons.

Sliding out of the bathroom window head first, Phil and Loise landed on the remains of the shoe rental guy. They made their way to the corner of the alley and that is where they saw Mike and Billy.

Having finished his narration, the man behind the wheel turned, sticking out his hand.

"I'm Phil and that's Loise."

Phil smiled lightly and pointing to the woman accompanying him. Mike reached out to shake Phil's hand. Then came the impact. Mike was always meaning to get the airbags replaced after his small fender bender. But you know how it is. Things always manage to get pushed back and delayed. He never did do it.

As Mike finished his chronicle of events, I handed him another beer. I tried to lighten the mood a little. It was almost 3 AM and as a joke, I blurted out,

"Last call!"

We all laughed and deciding to hunker down for the night, continued to drink our freebies.

Considering that we were all strangers and the current events that were unfolding around us, the four of us had quite the party. Entertaining Mike and I, the girls at one point got up on the bar to dance, singing their own rendition of Michael Jackson's Thriller. Unfortunately, Mike and I, no matter how much booze we plied them with, could not coax the girls into stripping.

As the night progressed, it was clear that Mike was straight and that he had a thing for Billy. She definitely had the physical attraction and I guess for a guy Mike was ok looking too.

We continued to help ourselves to the plentiful bounty of our hideaway, filling up on peanuts and beer with total disregard about the amount of noise we made. If the dead came streaming in through the door at that moment, I am sure we would have just offered them a drink and went on partying. If we were going to die, we were going to die having fun.

We passed out from over consumption, the effects of the alcohol eventually taking its toll on us. The girls slept up on the bar and the men at a table with our feet up.

The crashing of the table that acted as a doorstop awoke us as it fell to the ground. They had found us. The doorframe cracked and creaked as the demons of the flesh tried to push their way in. Their moans sounded like a fiendish alarm clock from the depths of hell in my ears. Light beamed in through the small windows on each side of the door. It was morning.

Trying to right myself from my makeshift bed, I tipped back in my chair. Spilling myself onto the floor in a puff of peanut dust, I realized,

"Oh, shit! I was still drunk."

With the room spinning as I got to my feet, I looked around at the others. I could tell we were all in rough shape. Mike staggered over to the bar picking up his gun. Putting on the police belt, I handed the shotgun to my wife.

We headed for the backdoor. Billy stopped mid-way and threw up. The lust I had for her suddenly disappeared as I watched the beer and the chewed nuts from the night before spew out of her mouth and nose out onto the floor.

The top corner of the backdoor began to push in as we neared it. The rotting, blood-covered hands of the decaying demons came reaching in at us, clawing madly, desperately trying to feed. Remembering the door to the roof, Mike yelled out,

"Upstairs!"

It is a good thing that someone in our group was thinking straight. My wife pushed Billy up the stairs as Billy continued to vomit.

Rushing up the now puke and blood covered stairs, our heads pounded from hangovers. We could hear the splintering of wood as the door bust in behind us. Smashing bottles and glasses, the dead flooded in.

Opening the door to the roof, the morning light blinded us. We exited as Billy made a feeble attempt at swiping the sickness away from her face. The thumping of the walkers' shoes came up the stairs, the mangled digits of their fists clawing at the walls. The groans poured from their stinking orifices as the creatures hunted us.

Up on the roof we all saw the sizable force of our foe as they continued to pile in through the rear entrance of the building.

The rooftop joined to the next series of buildings. It appeared to be our only chance away from the frightening flesh feasters. Hopping from roof to roof, we made our way as far as we could. As we ran and jumped, I was quite impressed at how agile Billy was in her spiked shoes. On the last roof, a rusty steel ladder led down to the street below.

The demons of the flesh followed out, creeping after us. Some falling off to the pavement below as they crowded the roof. The girls climbed onto the ladder to begin their descent. Mike and I stood with our pistols, firing at the advancing assembly of undead.

Holstering my weapon, I climbed off the roof and onto the ladder. With Mike in tow, only his shoes were visible to me. With the sharp outcry of,

"Nooo!"

Mike's feet lurched up and away from me. Instinctively, I jumped up and grabbed his ankles.

Hanging from Mike's heels, I craned my neck to see the animated bodies of the deceased pulling Mike back up to the roof by his wrists. One of the creatures snapped its broken teeth. Its mouth just mere inches from Mike's head, the stinking spit of the dead seeped into his hair.

Wrapping my legs around the outside of the ladder, I pulled as hard as I could. Just arriving on the ground, the women would have had no idea what was transpiring above if it was not for Mike's cry.

Shotgun in hand, my wife fired slug after slug into the attacking monsters. Bits of bone, brain, and hair showered down on Mike and me. The threads from Mike's jacket tore. He came catapulting down at me, landing between me and the ladder. The collision jarred the retaining bolts loose. Nearly ripping the ladder from the wall, it knocked me to the street below.

Dropping down, I landed hard on my back, the wind escaping from my lungs as I gasped for air. The girls ran to help me up as Mike finished his descent of the now unstable rungs. With the women practically carrying me, we ran up the street. The frenzy of hungry demons continued to grow behind.

We did not make it far when we spotted an SUV. With the doors open, it sat parked in an alley. We headed over to the SUV. Mike saw the lower half of a torso lying in front of the car and walked over to it. A blood trail led away from where the top used to be. Mike followed the path of death with his eyes until it disappeared up the alley.

Dried blood spattered the driver's seat and the inside of the windows of the vehicle. Grisly streaks and smears led out to the victim's remains in front. A case of bottled water sat in the back along with some foodstuffs consisting of breads and cereals.

Checking the ignition, we discovered—no keys. Having gained my wind back, I walked over to Mike and the torso. The victim was a female, or what remained of one, wearing a short jean skirt.

Standing over the partial corpse, I said to Mike,

"That's too bad. She had nice legs."

Mike agreed,

"I'd fuck 'er."

I bent down to check her for the keys. I struggled, pushing my hands into the pockets of her tight fitting skirt. I should have let Mike do it since he had the smaller hands between the two of us.

Feeling the keychain, I blurted,

"I got the keys!"

Then under my breath, I muttered,

"I hope."

As I yanked at the keys, the dead girl's legs fought back. Swinging around on the ground, the legs flopped like a dying fish. Kicking off the one pump she still wore, the shoe nearly hit Mike in the head. Tugging one last time hard, her skirt came off in my hand with the keys. Leaving the legs wearing only panties, they looked like a half mannequin from my wife's lingerie store.

Heading back to the blood soaked vehicle, I managed to rip the skirt off my hand. Piling into the car, the men sat up front, and the women sat in the back.

I turned to Billy,

"Pass me a bottle of water."

Billy handed everyone a bottle, saying

"That's a good idea."

"I could use a drink to wash the taste of puke from my mouth."

Opening the bottle, I poured it onto the dead girl's skirt.

Wiping the blood from the windows with the wet skirt, I said

"Let's get the fuck out of here."

Through the partially wiped window, we saw that down the alley a band of undead had formed in front of us. The demons of the flesh now blocked the exit ahead. I had had enough!

Turning the key, the beast roared to life. Slamming the transmission into gear, I stomped the gas pedal to the floor. Speeding down the alley, the SUV hurtled towards the blockade of demons. The big car plowed into them, knocking them over like bowling pins, the whump, whump, whump, of the bodies as they bounced off the hood, the tires of the vehicle skidding as they ran over the fallen.

A few managed to hang on but we lost them rather easily after bouncing up and down a couple of curbs. One with a loud clang as it lost its head to a parking meter.

As we left town, the hot sun cascaded in through the windows of the vehicle, warming us. Occasionally, the sound of a helicopter could still be heard. Was it the same one?

I cannot remember enjoying the heat or the light of the sun as much as I did that day. Unfortunately, it also let us witness how badly things had progressed.

THE DINER

Driving out of town, we could see the results of the mayhem of the night before. Buildings burned on every street. An empty fire truck sat in front of one with its lights still flashing. The hoses, hooked to the hydrant, sat dry and unattended. Automobiles sat vacant in the streets. With their doors pulled open, some of the engines still idled. Bodies and parts of bodies lay scattered, strewn across the streets. Some still surrounded by the demons of the flesh, the monsters feeding on the decay.

The dead seemed harmless if they had food. They completely ignored you—as long as they had food. The sporadic gunfire and explosions that had filled the air the night before had ceased. The city was devoid of every living thing but us, the only movement being that of the undead.

The masses of walkers could be seen everywhere and as far as the eye could see. The death and decay they wrought, melting everything in their path. As we hit the on-ramp to the highway, it would appear to be smooth sailing from here. Then the traffic jam of abandoned vehicles showed up.

The first vehicles we saw were just the occasional burning hulk of a car here and there. Soon, the road was crammed with cars, trucks, vans and anything you could use to make a getaway.

Some, the automobile's paint blackened and peeling, smoldered from fire. Black smoke still billowed out from the windows, and the corpses of the burnt sat charred in grotesque poses.

Others were up-ended onto their sides or roofs, the vehicle's cargo spilling across the road, their human contents stripped out. They sat, smeared, and streaked, inside and out with the dried blood and vital organs of their owners. In one car, its driver's hands still clutched the steering wheel. The pink nail polish that dotted the fingertips sparkled in the daylight. The rest of her was nowhere to be found.

The demons of the flesh wandered in and out of the abandoned autos. They staggered aimlessly as if they were lost. A semi-truck parked on the shoulder had one of the undead monsters pinned beneath the truck's tires. The ghoul thrashed about, trying to free itself. I wondered—how long had it been under there? How long would it remain there? I was sure it would be there a month from now, still flailing its arms.

Slowly cruising along the shoulder of the road and sometimes into the grass, we bounced from the occasional whump of a body hidden amongst the tall hay. Making our way along, the odd ghoul harassed us as we went. A blast from the shotty or Mike's cannon took care of them.

Seeing a gas station farther down the road, we decided to make that our next stop. The area looked to be fairly devoid of the walking dead, other than a few stragglers. If we were to keep moving, it was best to have a full tank of gas.

The gas station sat off to the side of the main road. Its two repair bays were empty and available. Attached to the gas bar was a small diner. An island of four gas pumps was in front. The lot teamed with abandoned vehicles. Parked in lines, the derelict cars waited in front of the pumps, the hoses still hanging from the previous patron's tanks.

There was no way to get our vehicle near the pumps without pushing some of the existing line up out of the way. Our first order of business was to make sure the area was secure. The last thing we needed was to get into a dangerous situation and to be boxed in while filling up with gas.

Leaving the SUV running, we grabbed our belongings. Exiting the vehicle, we stepped out into the hot sun. It would have been a beautiful day to be on the boat right now. My wife walked over to me and grabbed the pack on my back, stopping me. She unzipped one of the side pockets and searched inside. I strained to look over my shoulder to see what it was that she desired. Hearing the pocket zip back up, I turned to face her. My wife unfolded a pair of sunglasses and put them on. Sarcastically, I said to my wife,

"Where's mine?"

"Oh, that's right; you borrowed them
and broke them."

Annoyed, she replied,

"Geez, are you ever gonna let that
go?"

"That was like three years ago."

With the sun blinding me as I walked, the four of us began to scout out the building and its surroundings. Junked cars littered the grass along one side of the building. A heavy metal door rest on the ground in front of the dirty dingy washroom it once hid. A piece of paper reading

"Out of Order"

was still taped to it. I walked over to the doorway.

I stuck my hand inside the open doorway and reached around the corner for the light switch. I fumbled about, searching. I felt the switch touch my fingers. Flicking it up and down, I was not surprised when it did not work. I stepped back and pulled the maglight from its ring on the holster. Turning the flashlight on, I cautiously entered the washroom.

I flashed the beam of the light slowly around the room. Ceramic chunks littered the tiny black and white tile floor of the washroom. Hooligans had smashed the sink and urinal. Colorful graffiti covered the one stall in the corner. I drew my pistol and walked over to the stall.

With the barrel of my gun, I nudged the stall door open. It was empty. The toilet was dry and caked in feces. The floor was wet and smelled of urine. On the back of the wall behind the toilet, someone had crudely scratched a poem into the wall. I shone the light on it and began to read.

"Here I sit broken hearted, paid my
dime, and only farted. Yesterday I
took a chance, saved my dime, and

shit my pants."

Giggling to myself, I left the dingy washroom to join the others. I found them around the back of the building already. Behind the gas station, a short field stretched back to a large forest. The four of us continued around, circling the remainder of the structure. One could not help but notice the far off plumes of black smoke that rose from the cities afar.

Our reconnaissance of the outside showed no signs of activity barring a couple of distant walkers. We made our way back around front noticing the stippling of the diner's windows from the impact of gunfire. Bloody specks ran down the inside of the glass.

Mike opened the front door to the diner slowly, being careful not to ring the two little bells fixed to the top. The stench of decaying death blasted our senses and it became apparent that not even this remote place was immune from the butchery that was running rampant.

The pages of an order pad sitting beside the open cash register fluttered in the slight breeze as Mike opened the door. Crimson stains and shattered dishes covered the cream-colored ceramic floor tiles.

A chocolate cake with two triangular slabs cut from it looked out at us from under its glass dome on the main counter. Two fingers lie in a small pool of blood beside the cake dish.

At one of the booths that lined the windows, a plate of French fries slathered in ketchup still sat on the table. The plate hurriedly shoved forward, tipped the glass of soda in front, the contents spilling out over the table and onto the floor below.

Three walkers lay motionless on the floor. Flies buzzed the air around the rotten corpses. One of the dispatched dead had its head smashed in. The demon wore a set of greasy coveralls with the top half pulled down and tied around his waist. Grease and dried blood covered his arms like sleeves. Stabbed with a tire iron, it remained sunken into the ghoul's chest.

The second monster, a waitress, lay on her back. Exhibiting a distinct gunshot wound in the forehead, the creature's peach coloured uniform was dotted with burgundy bullet holes.

The white shirt worn by the last fallen walker contrasted sharply against the cherry blossoms that filled his chest. He sat slumped in a booth, a void where the top of his head once was.

Ejected shell casings sat scattered through out the diner. A spent pistol magazine lay discarded on the cream-colored tile. Footprints leading from the gore on the floor made their bloody way into the gas bar. Whoever was here last at least put up a fight.

Entering the diner, Mike followed the trail of death. It stopped behind the cash desk that belonged to the gas bar. A man sat dead on the ground. His pistol, the slide locked back and empty, rest on the floor beside him. The blood spray from the bullet piercing through the top of the man's skull coated the panelled wall behind him and streaked down to the floor. Wrapped tightly around the dead man's left hand, an oily rag doubled as a bandage.

Heading into the repair bays, we could not see any sign of trouble in here. All looked like it should be. The tools still hung on the walls above the workbench. A disassembled carburetor, in mid fix, occupied the bench. The stains on the concrete floor were not blood but from oil and grease—as they should be.

Backtracking, I dropped my backpack on the counter as we headed for the kitchen. A charred hamburger sat waiting for its place on the garnished bun beside it, never to be eaten. Once again, everything appeared, as it should, minus the unattended burnt food.

If it was not for the stink of death and decay from the rotting corpses, I am sure that the four of us could have sat down and had a feast. Besides the peanuts and beer, none of us had really eaten anything since the day before.

My head still pounding from a hangover, my back still aching from the fall, I searched for some orange juice and some painkillers. Maybe that would help me a little. Digging out some orange juice from the walk-in fridge in the kitchen, I now needed the pain pills. The waitress! Didn't they always have headaches from dealing with customers? She had to have some.

Walking over to the waitress' foul smelling remains, I bent down. Holding my breath, I swatted away the steady stream of flies that had come to claim her corpse as theirs. I began to rummage through the decomposing woman's pockets. Billy looked at me as if I was molesting the dead girl. Disgusted, she said,

"What the hell are you doing?"

Ahha! With a pill bottle in my grasp, I raised my hand in victory. Shaking the painkillers back and forth in a teasing motion, I asked,

---

"Anyone got a headache?"

I have never seen people line up with their hands out so fast, except for the introduction of DRED-not. It was as if I had the magic pills to make everything that was now happening, go away. Doling out the pain dope, if anything, it made us feel mentally better. Now we needed gas. It was going to be dark in a few hours and this place, with all its large glass windows, was definitely not safe.

Turning to look at the gas pumps outside, with the rows of abandoned cars lined up in front, I knew we would be in for a great deal of work. Standing there, staring outside, I suddenly felt old and worn out. How much more of this could I take? How much could any of us take?

Looking at the rest of our small group, hoping that the others could not see how tired I was, it was plain to see that this was taking its toll on all of us. The four of us did not look much better than the rotting bodies sprawled out across the floor.

Mike sat at the counter. His hair still matted with ghoul spit, his face covered in blood and the sleeves missing from his flashy suit.

The girls stood behind the counter gabbing with each other. They looked like a couple of raccoons with their make-up smudged around their eyes and their disheveled hair.

Just then, my wife reaches into my pack and pulls out her brush. She proceeds to brush her hair as if she were going out for a night on the town. Once done, she hands it off to Billy. Who begins to brush her hair. Shaking my head in disbelief, I catch the dirty look from my wife. She blurts at me.

"What?"

She always travelled with a brush. I would not be surprised to find a hairdryer instead of food in our bag. A hairbrush, hairdryer, and make-up seemed to be the necessities of a woman. If they were going to die, at the very least, they could look their best. Laughing, I said to Mike,

"Let's do this."

Mike slowly rose from his seat at the counter. Staggering over, Mike resembled a demon of the flesh. Mike reached out and pulled on the diner door. Its bells chiming as it swung open. Stepping out onto the hot pavement, Mike squinted and looked up at the sun. He stood there basking in its glow as it warmed his face. Mike took a deep breathe and stepped forward.

Suddenly, Mike's body spasmed violently, his back erupting in geysers of blood showers as the thump, thump, thump of bullets hit his chest. The rounds continued to tear through him, exiting out the back of his suit jacket. The multiple missiles of death tumbled out Mike's back and smashed through the diner's glass door. Showering me in glass and hosing me in a mist of reddish gore, I felt the crack of the bullets as they zipped past. Mike fell straight back, crashing through the diner's door. He landed on the floor in front of me, his feet still outside enjoying the warmth of the sun.

Dropping to the diner floor, I could see the Humvee that had snuck up on us parked across the road. The diner's windows shattered as more rounds came streaming downrange. With glass raining down on me, I peered up as far as I could.

Taking cover across from the diner was a band of hunters that had deserted from the military. With their Hummer parked across the road, five ex-soldiers peppered the diner with their automatic rifles.

The women screamed diving for cover behind the counter. Mike lie on the ground. A stomach churning flopping noise hissed from his lungs as they collapsed. His life fluids draining like someone had kicked over a wash bucket of crimson water.

Were these guys fucking nuts! They had to know that there were not many survivors. We should be helping each other, not killing. Maybe they thought we were some of the roaming dead. Maybe they just did not care.

Knowing that we did not have the firepower to deal with this new threat, I yelled to the girls,

"Get to the back door."

I crawled over to where Mike lay. I could see the blood bubbling from his chest. I said,

"I'm sorry."

It was not really my fault but it was the only appropriate thing that came to mind. What else do you say to a dying man? It is not as if I could voice my true opinion.

"Better you than me."

Shucking her feet out of her heels, Billy kicked open the back door of the diner and ran out. She raced over the grassy field without even turning to look back to see if anyone else had made it. As she ran, the sticks and rocks dug deep into the souls of her feet.

Self-preservation was now all that she thought about. It was even more important than the pain of Billy's now cut and raw feet.

Billy disappeared into the tree line behind the diner. Panicked, she continued to flee down into a small shallow creek. Still running for her life, Billy slipped on the slick surface of the slimy moss covered rocks that lined the creek bed. Tumbling face first into the cool water, she caught a quick glimpse of the walker standing in front of her.

A few feet from Billy stood an old hairy man wearing a mustard stained wife beater tank top and plaid shorts. Dark blue socks and sandals complimented his outfit. The monster stopped in mid bite and dropped the leg of a soldier that he had been feeding on. The demon of the flesh began to advance towards Billy.

Billy's wet hair dripped down into her face as she climbed to her feet to escape. Billy turned and ran into the waiting arms of another of the undead ghouls. The hulk of a creature bore the arms of a power lifter. Draping its massive gory arms around her, she did not have time to scream. The first bite tore into Billy's throat.

A third walker attacked Billy from behind. The young woman was dressed in a pink tank top stained brownish red and a pair of denim Capri pants. The monster's boney fleshless arms latched onto Billy, pulling her down into the stream with the icy grip of death.

The last sound Billy heard was the gurgling from her windpipe. Her life force washing down the stream as it escaped, leaving her body an empty lifeless shell.

With the cries from across the street of,

"Get some!"

I began to back away from Mike's cooling corpse. The military "hunters" continued to spray the building, the rounds smashing into the diner sending everything skyward. Chunks of plaster, napkins, lights, and stuffing from the booth cushions all cascaded into the air.

Pushing myself backwards across the floor, I watched in horror as Mike's now dead body began to slowly rise. Shit! He had the DRED-not in him.

Letting out a bellowing moan from hell, Mike sat up. I quickly drew the forty-calibre Glock from its sheath at my side and pointed it at the back of his head. Mike's skull split open as the bullet raced through, ricocheting off into the ceiling. I had not fired a shot. Even in death, Mike had saved me from the soldier's bullet that was sure to punch into my face.

Sprawled out on my stomach, I could see the hunters across the street. I trained my pistol towards them. If I could just hit one of them, maybe I could give Mike some small piece of justice. Slowly, I squeezed the trigger.

Watching my target as the round from my pistol travelled down range, I could see it smash into the soldier's right cheek, tearing off a hunk of flesh. The empty bullet casing tinking off the floor beside me as it tumbled around. Got him!

Instantly, the whole area around the group of deserters erupted in a whirlwind of smoke and dust. Large calibre projectiles strafed the ex-soldiers. Shredding them, the rounds sent their lifeless bodies crumpling to the ground. The growling chatter of the chain gun filling the air a second later. Explosions punched into the Hummer, the blasts sending its doors outwards, bucking the vehicle into the air.

The helicopter that had just executed the hunters came screaming in at low level. Just clearing the burning wreck of the Humvee, a swirling black dust storm that resembled the face of Satan himself formed behind it as the blades thumped past. Smoke trails filled the air from the helicopter's spent rocket ammunition. The deafening roar of its engines shook my chest as the chopper whipped past.

Watching the 'copter, it swung high up into the air. It turned in a wide arc, preparing to make another pass. Was I next? Not thinking twice, I turned and ran. I holstered my gun and grabbed my bag from the counter. I ran through the kitchen looking for my wife. She sat crouched down, waiting by the back door with the shotgun in her hand. My wife looked at me saying,

"Billy ran."

I only had one reply,

"Crap."

I knew this was going to be bad. I really had no desire to go out and search for Billy. I just wanted to get away from that demonic helicopter. But I could see in my wife's eyes that she wanted to go and that the company of another woman gave her some comfort.

Dashing out the rear of the diner to search for Billy, I realized I was going to hear about it later for leaving the hairbrush behind on the counter. The sun that was shining brightly earlier was now gone and a slow drizzle began to come down on us.

Rushing across the field towards the tree line, the helicopter turned towards us. I screamed,

"Run faster!"

The urgency in my voice made my wife begin to whimper as she ran. Damn! I had to be more careful. I knew this time that she was aware that we were in deep shit. The confidence and reassurance she had had in me that everything would be fine—was now gone. She was as sure as I was that this was it. We were going to die.

Ducking into the trees, we heard the clatter of the chain gun come from high above. Hitting the dirt, we could hear the rounds striking down the embankment in front. They missed! Hurrying down the hill and into a shallow stream, we saw that the helicopter did not miss its target. We were not the intended path for their bullets.

In the creek bed, lay three walkers and Billy. Well—what was left of her. The monsters chewed off Billy's once luscious lips. Her sexy legs now just stumps of flesh, Billy's torso bobbed in the shallow stream. Her nearly severed head rolled gently back and forth in the current. The ghouls lie there smashed to pieces by the high calibre projectiles. Only one of the creatures still had movement, an old guy in a stained tank top. Missing most of his torso as well as both arms and legs, he was not going anywhere in a hurry.

Pulling my pistol from the holster, I watched the monster's mouth open and close in the rain. It was as if he were trying to catch the raindrops on his tongue like a kid attempting to quench his thirst. I wondered about this guy. Who was he? What did he do before he started roaming the hillside like a dead fuckstick eating people? Where was his family? Where was my family? Did the bastard eat them too? There were too many questions and not one answer.

Blasting the ghoul's brains onto the rocks, I replaced my weapon to its resting place by my side. Staring into the sky, my wife and I watched the helicopter. Making one last quick pass above us, the chopper left just as quickly as it came. Looking to me with bewilderment, my wife said,

“Did that guy just wave to us?

The Woods

Following the creek bed, we wound our way through the trees. The rain filled the air with an eerie mist. Our feet were wet and cold, the water squishing out from the sides of our shoes as we trudged along. The fallen twigs that lay scattered and strewn over the forest floor cracked loudly. Out of the corner of my eye, I caught a glimpse of something moving. It was to our left and over a small hill. Grabbing my wife by the arm, I whispered to her,

"Stop!"

I crouched down, pulling on my wife's arm. She crouched alongside of me wondering why we had stopped. I drew my pistol and pointed it towards the shadowy figure staggering towards us in the rainy mist. Seeing the darkened form of a body, my wife asked,

"Is it one of them?"

The black shape crested the hill. Shaking my head, I replied,

"I can't tell."

The rain began to fall heavier now, obscuring my view even more. I struggled to see the cloudy figure that came towards us. The rain ran down my face and into my eyes. My vision began to blur. As quickly as I could swipe the water away, the rain filled them again. The shadowy figure slowly made its way towards us. Weaving in and out through the trees, it closed the distance between us.

My wife whispered to me, this time with urgency in her voice, repeating her question,

"Is it one of them?"

I answered back, the frustration mounting in my voice,

"I said I can't tell."

As the shadowy figure staggered closer, the rain intensified once more. The constant pelting of the drops stung at our faces like angry little hornets disturbed out of their nest. The wanderer in the woods was now only about twenty feet away. His pace began to quicken. The rain turned into a downpour, the huge darts of precipitation falling from the sky like spears of water, obscuring our view. My wife had to yell to me over the roar of the deluge as she asked,

"What do we do?"

I could barely make out her words over the constant barrage of the torrential rainstorm. The only sound that filled my ears was the eerie hissing of the monsoon and the crackling of the leaves as the rain tore into them. Using the deafening downpour to my advantage, I answered quietly, half muttered,

"I don't know."

Watching the staggering form close in on us, I did not even turn my head to see if my wife had heard me. I did not want her to hear the uncertainty that once again filled my voice.

From behind our cover of a giant Maple tree, we watched. The shadowy wanderer was now ten feet from us at the next tree. The trespasser's boots kicked up plumes of water as he staggered, splashing through the puddles that had formed on the uneven ground. I clicked the safety off my pistol. I readied myself to stand up from behind my cover and begin blasting away at the invader.

The dark figure was now five feet from the other side of the tree when the cloudburst ceased as if the well had suddenly run dry. The ghostly silence that followed, although only a second or two, seemed to last an eternity. Through the eerie dead silence, I could hear my heart thump. The blood rushed to my ears as the beat of my heart quickened. At that moment, I was actually scared. I had not felt an ounce of fear up until that point. It was the fear of the unknown. I had no idea whether the figure coming towards us was dead or alive. I needed to be sure before I squeezed that trigger. If I hesitated too long it could spell our doom. I looked at my wife as I contemplated on what to do. Do I get up and blast away regardless? Or do I wait until I am sure?

The tiny rivers left from the flood flowed through the woods, trickling between our feet. The water droplets that had once clung to the leaves above cascaded down. It was as if the trees were spitting on us, wanting us to leave their peaceful domain, to take our bloodshed elsewhere. Well, too bad, it was going to happen here and it was going to happen now.

With the shotgun in her hand, my wife sat facing the tree we used for cover. She removed her right hand from the trigger of the shotty to swipe her wet hair away from her face. I readied myself to kill the invader in the woods. The slosh from the heavy wet foot that crashed into a puddle sent me spinning on the ground to look behind. I managed to fire one shot off as the grotesque monster lunged at me, aiming for its forehead. I missed...

The shot crashed into the demon, harmlessly blasting off the creature's left ear. My wife dove to her left to avoid the pouncing beast's attack, the shotgun spinning out of her wet hands and landing in the undergrowth of the woods. My gun landed in the mud beside me as I dropped the pistol to catch the ghoul in mid-lunge. The smoke ring from my attempt to kill the monster still hung in the humid air.

I lie on my back in the mud holding back the ghoul on top. The backpack pushed over to the side restricting my movement. Pain shot through my body as the roots of the tree stabbed into my lower spine. The demon of the flesh bore down on me with all it had, grabbing my right hand at the wrist, trying to push it into the mud. I pushed back equally hard.

The walker's right hand pinned me to the ground by my left shoulder, the agony gripping me. It felt as if he was going to tear it from its socket. The triceps in my arm strained as I grabbed a fistful of shirt and pressed my left hand into the ghoul's chest.

As the demon leaned in for a taste of my flesh, the smell of putrid wet dog came from him. I turned my face to the right in an attempt to avoid his bite. My wide panicked eyes met my wife's as she helplessly searched the underbrush for her lost weapon.

Giving the monster one last push with my left hand, I felt my fist sink into the ghoul's rotting ribcage. His bodily fluids leaked out, dribbling down my arm. As the undead beast closed in again at another attempt to feed, my arm began to cramp and I knew that I did not have the strength left to fend him off. The creature just did not tire.

I watched, powerless to respond. My arm began sliding further into the demon's decaying chest. He sank down on me, his entrails slowly tumbling out on top of me. Strangely, I almost enjoyed the sensation as the monster's insides warmed my chilled wet body. Still filled with the flesh of others, the walker's yellowish teeth came closer. The ghoul's brownish tongue lashed out, the tip nipped off by self-mutilation during a previous feeding frenzy.

My wife let out a loud bellowing scream that sent shivers up my aching spine. A giant boot kicked the undead demon in the head, lifting both the creature and myself off the ground. The attack left the muddy imprint of the sole on the monster's face. The animated corpse fell back, splashing into the puddle that had alerted me earlier.

The demon of the flesh lay on its back in the mud puddle splashing around lethargically, struggling to get to its feet. The wearer of the boot walked over and stomped at the creature's head. From behind, my saviour looked like the first walker I had encountered on my porch. He was about six foot four and two hundred and seventy pounds. He definitely was a much larger man compared to my five foot nine and having a hundred less pounds on my frame.

The big man continued to stomp on the beast's head. The splashing murky water of the puddle mixed with the deep red liquid that spewed from the undead horror's head. The boot pounded repeatedly against the demon's head. The monster's skull sank farther and farther into the muddy earth, the crunching of its bone breaking the haunting silence of the woods.

I lay on the ground, exhausted, a steaming pile of internal organs resting on my stomach. Covered in gore, my arm felt as if it were broken. Watching as the hulk of a man finished his kill, I glanced over to my wife. She continued digging through the weeds that blanketed the forest floor, searching frantically for her shotgun.

Breathing heavy, the big man turned to me. His small potbelly quivered as it pressed against his wet t-shirt. His balding scalp glistened from the dampness of the rain and the goatee that covered his broad face dripped with sweat. He spoke,

"Are you ok?"

Sweeping off the stinking pile of death left by the monster, I replied unsure whether I was actually injured or not,

"I'll live."

The heap of decay slopped to the muddy ground as I brushed it off.

My saviour turned to my wife. Still pawing the ground, she finally found her prize. She grabbed the shotty out from under the brush and weeds that had concealed it. Whimpering, my wife shakily raised the weapon and pointed it towards the big man. She squeezed the trigger. The big man instinctively raised his arms to fend off the shot.

"Click!"

The chamber was empty.

Panicked, my wife attempted to pump the slide to chamber a round. Reaching forward, the hulk of a man hurriedly snatched the gun from my wife's grasp. The big man then grabbed her by the shoulders.

"It's over now, you can relax."

Still shaking, my wife slumped down into the mud, sobbing. The thought of what she had just done raced through her mind. She had almost killed this poor man. Was she to make these kinds of hastily life or death decisions over and over? If so, she wanted no more part of it.

With the shotgun still in his hand, the stranger helped me to my feet. He introduced himself,

"I'm Dave, I believe we met briefly."

I exchanged the greeting and thanked him for his help. Shaking his hand, I could see the gashes that tore across his knuckles from another encounter. Turning his large hand over to reveal the cuts, I asked,

"How about you? Are you ok?"

Dave replied sheepishly,

"It's nothing."

Dave was unaccustomed to people worrying about him since he was a big man and everyone assumed he could always take care of himself. It gave him a sense of belonging when someone was genuinely concerned for his well-being.

I walked over to my wife and wrapped my arms around her. I rubbed her arms, attempting to sooth, and warm her. She had stopped sobbing and calmed down but her shivering was uncontrollable. The three of us stood in the woods, wet, cold, and shivering. The quaint silence of the forest slowly came back as Dave explained how he had seen the walker sneaking up on us and was hurrying to help.

I thought to myself how close I had come to dying. If his timing had been off, I might have shot him or have been bitten by the monster's relentless attacks. I bent over and searched through the mud. Picking up my pistol, I replaced it in its holster.

It would be dark in a couple of hours. We needed to find some shelter and warmth for the night. The three of us headed off deeper into the woods. As we walked, Dave told us his story.

Dave was a truck driver who hauled long distance loads back and forth across the border. His cargo—was DRED-not.

The night before, Dave pulled his Freightliner into a local truck stop to get some rest and relaxation after a long sixteen hours on the road. Maybe he might find a bit of "fun" also.

He knew his type of "fun" was the wrong thing to do since he had a wife and child at home. But it was difficult being on the road constantly and he figured what his wife didn't know would not hurt her.

Dave made his way down into the basement of the truck stop. They kept the showers down there for the truckers that stayed overnight. He was tired and was not really in the mood to shower. Taking a whiff of his armpits, Dave knew he needed one. He spent the first part of the evening having a shower and cleaning himself up.

Dave then headed to the restaurant for a big all night breakfast. The "big breakfast" consisted of three pancakes slathered in syrup, three eggs sunny side up, three strips of greasy bacon, golden brown home fries, and two pieces of thick Texas toast dripping with butter. The only thing that Dave did not order was the large greasy thumbprint on the edge of his plate.

Looking down at the gooey impression left on his plate, Dave glanced up behind the counter to the kitchen. The fat cook worked feverously on his next order. His brownish grease stained apron also served as a sweat rag as the fat unshaven cook wiped the moisture from his brow. An open pack of raw wieners stuck out of his upper shirt pocket.

Dave watched the slob of a cook. The fat man threw the next dish of greasy spoon food on the counter, ringing the pick-up bell and yelling,

"Order up!"

A petite waitress hurried over to grab the plate of grub from the counter. As she shakily picked up the plate, the cook snapped at her,

"Before it gets cold, Abbey!"

Abbey wore a short little one-piece dress that showed off her shapely legs very nicely. Her tan pantyhose swished as she quickly walked.

Dave's eyes followed the small server as she delivered the meal to her customer. Why was Abbey not his waitress? Dave's server was a chunky older woman who was in a bitchy mood.

Abbey leaned over to place the food onto the table. Her chestnut coloured hair fell to each side of her shoulders. Abbey's breasts overflowed her bra, almost falling out of her half buttoned dress. The cleavage stared straight at Dave. And Dave stared back.

Man, would he like a taste of her. I guess that is how she made big tips. Dave wanted to give Abbey a big tip all right but it was not money.

Abbey continued about her work serving her customer. The pudgy bitch waitress that Dave was blessed with, looked to Abbey, and said,

"Can you take my tables for me?"
"I'm done for the night."

Abbey nodded to the chunky woman and went about her business.

Cutting off a hunk of pancakes, Dave crammed the forkful into his mouth. The fat food preparer coughed and hacked away in the back of the kitchen. Dave's taste buds danced with delight from the forkful of skillfully cooked batter. He thought to himself,

"The man is disgusting but boy can
he cook."

These were the best pancakes that Dave had treated his palate to in a long time. Maybe the food tasted better because he had been on the road for so long—who knows. Right now, it was great.

As he ate, Dave watched the sexy waitress hurry around the diner, fantasizing about an evening with her. After having his fill of the heart clogging diner food and downing a few quick beers, Dave left the dining area. Making sure to leave a big tip for the cute little waitress, he decided to retire to the bunk in his rig. Dave walked away from the table. Abbey hurried over and picked up Dave's generous tip. She shot him a quick smile then hollered to the grimy cook,

"I'm going on break, Bill."

Maybe there was more money to be made.

Bill nodded without looking up as he took a wiener out of the pack and tore off a mouthful. He knew that Abbey doubled as the local "lot lizard." Because he let her go whenever she wanted, Abbey gave Bill a portion of the proceeds from her services rendered.

Abbey's smile made Dave blush. Not even thinking that she could possibly be a prostitute he sauntered slowly through the parking lot and back to his rig. Dave had no sooner closed the door to his truck than there was a soft knock. He looked out the window to see who had followed him. You could never be too sure.

Dave had heard the stories of guys getting truck jacked for their loads and always made every attempt to be careful. To his amazement, it was Abbey. This would complete his perfect night. A nice hot shower, some good food, a couple of beers, and now his fantasy girl had come a calling.

It is a good thing that he took that shower. Abbey was not as colourful as the usual "entertainment" that Dave was used to. He wanted to treat his dream girl right, although he was sure she would not care if he did or did not. None of the local hookers ever did. They just wanted their money.

Abbey grabbed hold of the handle to climb in. Her long pink polished nails glinted in the tower lights of the parking lot. In a sultry voice, she asked,

"Is there room for one more?"

Dave hurriedly grabbed Abbey's other hand and helped her into the cab of his truck.

Pulling the keys out of his pocket, Dave stuck them in the ignition. He turned them to the accessories position. Reaching over to the stereo, Dave turned on some soft music. He loved the way any type of music sounded in the surround sound stereo of the truck. It was money well spent.

Kicking off her sneakers, Abbey climbed into the back bunk. She began to unbutton her waitress uniform from the top exposing her ample perky bosoms. Pressed into a cherry red micro-fibre bra that hugged them tightly, Abbey's breasts began to pop out.

Dave climbed in the back with her, asking,

"What about your pantyhose?"

Abbey replied playfully,

"They're crotchless."

With those words, Dave almost finished the deed right there.

Abbey said to Dave as if she was reading a menu, her being the dish,

"Fifty bucks for bed and twenty
bucks for breakfast."

Dave knew, by "bed," Abbey meant intercourse and that "breakfast" was an oral snack. He knew before she even finished the sentence that he wanted the whole package and quickly replied,

"I want it all, baby."

No sooner had the words made their way from between Dave's lips than he thought of how cheesy that it must have sounded. Dave stripped as if his clothes were on fire, ripping his underwear as he frantically yanked at them. Abbey pulled a condom from her uniform pocket and tore open the wrapper.

Dave kneeled beside her, ready for action. She placed the condom on Dave and leaned over, saying,

"This is for free."

She rolled the condom down onto him using only her lips. Dave fought hard not to fill it right then and there.

Abbey liked to do this to all her customers for two reasons. One reason was that it might speed up the process with the added excitement. The other was that she wanted them to come back for more. The more visits, the more money.

Not being able to contain himself any longer, Dave mounted Abbey. After a few quick strokes, Dave began to pump furiously. Abbey moaned loud as he continued. Dave was sure the whole parking lot could hear. It excited him even more as he continued to thrust deep into her.

As Dave released his tension into Abbey, she began to get a deep phlegmy cough. The cough did not last long. Abbey then stopped moving and lay there—still. A quick thought darted through Dave's head,

"I killed her!"

Dave lay on top of Abbey holding her. Tears formed in his eyes. What was he going to do now? His wife would surely find out. There was no way of hiding this. Wild visions of a lengthy court trial and his wife storming out of his life flashed through Dave's mind. Suddenly, he felt Abbey stir beneath him.

"Whew, she was still alive."

Dave cursed himself for having those kinds of thoughts as Abbey's lips came slowly up to his neck. The touch of her lips against his sweaty skin made Dave think about spending another fifty bucks.

Dave's eyes flashed over with a blinding white light as a searing pain shot through his neck.

"Son of a bitch!"

Dave screamed, pushing Abbey back away from him,

"What the fuck? You bit me! Are
you fucking insane?"

Looking down into Abbey's eyes, Dave saw that they no longer had the sexy bedroom squint that they did when she first entered his truck. Her eyes were now wide open staring madly at him with a white frosted look to them. Abbey's mouth hung open, her tongue flailing wildly from side to side. Her lips, lined with Dave's blood giving the impression of freshly applied lip-gloss. They drew back tightly, revealing Abbey's bleached white teeth. The flesh from Dave's neck fluttered in between Abbey's sharp little weapons as she rustled beneath him.

With her legs still wrapped around Dave's torso, Abbey tried to lean in for another bite. Her fingers dug deep into Dave's back, clawing and ripping at his flesh. Dave pushed Abbey back into the bunk of the truck holding her down with his left hand. He lifted his right arm into the air. Balling his giant hand into a fist, Dave muttered,

"God forgive me."

Dave's tightened knuckles smashed into Abbey's face with the force of a mallet, breaking her nose. Abbey's blood sprayed the light-blue carpeted walls of the bunk. The haymaker of a punch that would have stopped any normal man did not even faze her. Abbey continued to buck beneath Dave. He swung repeatedly, her teeth shredding his knuckles as Dave slammed his giant war hammer of flesh into Abbey's gapping mouth.

The continual thrusting of her hips strangely excited Dave as he pinned her down. Letting go of Abbey, he pounded his big fists off her forehead until she stopped moving. At the same time, Dave got another fifty dollars worth. The sweat dripped off Dave's forehead and onto Abbey's still body as he tried to catch his breath. Abbey's once beautiful face was now unrecognizable to Dave.

Staring down at her broken and bloodied face, he expressed his disbelief in what he had just done,

"Jesus Christ!"

Prying Abbey's tightly wrapped legs from around his body, he dismounted her. Sitting on the edge of the bunk, Dave pulled of the well-used condom.

Looking down at his now bloody tattered knuckles, he winced from the pain, his hands beginning to throb. Reaching over his shoulder Dave tugged out a fingernail that Abbey had left lodged into his back. Dropping the nail onto the floor of the cab, he plucked his pants from the bunk and slowly pulled them on.

Grabbing the keys out of the ignition, Dave dropped them into his pants pocket. Slipping his feet into his boots, he reached for the driver's door. Opening it, Dave began to step out.

As he opened the door, a shadowy figure came into Dave's view a few feet away. Standing there sideways, the black form did not move. Dave's foot hit the metal step-up of the truck sending out a slight clang into the quiet night air. The darkened shape turned towards him bellowing out a loud monstrous groan.

Startling Dave, the demonic roar cast him back, sending him leaping into the cab of the truck. Quickly, he turned and stretched out. Dave slammed the door shut, locking it. Jamming his hand into his pants pocket, Dave fumbled around for the truck keys, the pain coursing through his shredded hands.

Dave frantically looked for the ignition key in the dark. A pair of fists smashed into the passenger door, bowing it in. The echoing boom it emitted made Dave jump and look to his right, causing him to drop the keys on the floor. He stared at the passenger door in fear, waiting for it to come crashing in as his fingers searched the floor blindly for his keys. What in the hell was happening?

Turning on the interior light of the truck, Dave found his keys. He picked them up and stuck them into the ignition. The truck shook and roared to life as Dave turned the key.

Putting the big rig into gear, Dave looked up over the dash. A large shadowy group of figures slowly closed in from the front of his truck. He could see the green glowing eyes dotting the mass of darkened forms as they closed in. Dave floored the gas pedal. Plowing into the crowd of black shapes, the truck bounced as it ran them over.

As the rig heaved from side to side, Dave glanced over his shoulder to make sure Abbey was dead. He could see her lifeless corpse bouncing slightly into the air from the motion of the truck. Dave raced through the parking lot smashing into the back bumper of a car, tearing it off as he sped away. Dave turned the semi onto the main road sharply almost flipping the trailer load of DRED-not that he hauled behind him.

Shifting through the gears like a racecar driver, Dave tore down the street. Out of the corner of his eyes, Dave saw that people ran in all directions screaming. The slow staggering figures that stalked them gathered in every street. Some of the demonic forms pooled around the victims as they devoured them wherever they fell. Up ahead, a Police roadblock covered the street—and Dave's path.

Police in riot gear fired their teargas and small arms into the growing hordes in an attempt to take control of the growing disturbance. Dave's truck barreled straight for the blockade.

Racing for the barricade of cop cars, Dave's eyes only saw one thing—the other side. The bullets from the Police firearms punched through Dave's windshield showering him with glass shards. The cops ran, spreading out away from the roadblock as Dave plowed into the blockade of cars.

The wave of destruction from the impact sent the Police cars spinning away in a shower of scattering glass and metal. The leaping of the truck shot Dave forward onto the steering wheel. His palms, wet with sweat, released their grip, letting the wheel spin out of control to the left.

The truck jackknifed tipping over to its side, the trailer's doors crashing open. It slammed to the pavement throwing its contents of the DRED-not into the street. The big rig slid down the road leaving a trail of debris until it smashed into the wall of a corner building, finally coming to a rest.

When Dave came to, it was daylight. The sun's glare blinded him as he tried to look around. Abbey's cold corpse lay on top of him.

Her hand lay across his chin, the flesh from his back still lodged under her fingernails.

The way she laid seemed as if she was trying to apologize for the night before. Almost as if, she was hugging him. Whew! She was starting to stink. Dave rolled Abbey off as he struggled to get out of the wreck.

Kicking out the front windshield, Dave climbed out into the street. He was lucky, just a few cuts and bruises from the accident. Reaching into his back pocket for his wallet, Dave pulled out one hundred dollars. Throwing it in on top of Abbey, he said,

"Thanks for the fun—bitch."

Dave stood straight, stretching his stiff spine. He paused, looking around at the carnage that lay before him. Fires burned out of control all over the town. There were no people to be seen anywhere. Debris and glass littered the sidewalks as almost every building had the bottom floor windows smashed. Papers fluttered in the gentle breeze that blew down the street. Light standards lay toppled into the street, blocking the road. Suitcases lay here and there, yanked open during struggles. The clothing that they once held was now no more than mere garbage strewn across the land. Broken shovels, baseball bats, bent golf clubs, pipes, and anything that might be used as a hand-to-hand weapon were dropped in the streets, the remnants of dried blood caked on them.

As Dave slowly walked away from his wreck, he found out where all the people had gone. They had not gone anywhere. They were still everywhere. But now it was literally—everywhere, pieces of them—everywhere.

Half-eaten bodies lined the streets. Some of the bodies almost completely eaten and picked clean until their bones looked bleached. Devouring every part, the skin, the muscles, the tendons, even the internal organs, and the eyes were gone. There was still worse. They were the ones that no longer looked like bodies. The ones that the bones had all but been eaten. Or the bones broken in half and the marrow sucked out.

Dave continued to walk, his eyes taking in all of the carnage of the mass extermination that had taken place. He approached a pair of the human carcasses and stopped beside them, looking down. It was a young mother and her daughter.

The mother's head, torn from her body lay cracked open like a coconut, now empty. Her daughter, a small girl of about ten, was nothing but a head and torso. Her one arm lay beside her still clinging to her dolly as if afraid to let go. The doll's open eyes stared up at Dave.

Dave bent down picking up the girl's arm. He placed it on the young girl's bloody body. Dave squatted beside her. This could be his wife and child. The girl's head slowly turned towards him. Dave saw the glazed look in her eyes. Abbey had the same hazy look when she attacked him. The young girl's mouth opened and closed slowly. Her torso began to wiggle as her lifeless eyes fixated on Dave's warm flesh.

Startled, Dave jumped up and stepped back. Disgusted by the whole situation, he turned and bent over. Dave then vomited onto the street. He thought about his own family as the gushes of sickness poured out. Were they still alive? Did they suffer the same fate as those that lay strewn at his feet?

The sounds of shuffling feet approached, invading Dave's ears. Wiping his mouth, Dave looked up. A wall of tattered bodies came towards him, closing slowly. As they neared, the horrific noise of the oncoming undead filled the air. Dave clamped his hands over his ears, the moaning, and groaning from the advancing entourage of evil ringing through his skull.

Looking around in a panic, Dave ran to the only place he knew in the area that might be safe. He ran for his life to the nearby creek and away from the city. Dave ran until his chest felt as if it would explode. But he kept going. His throat hurt from the continual gasps of air rushing past into his lungs.

It began to rain as he finally reached the edge of the woods. Spotting a payphone on the side of the road, Dave staggered over to it gulping for air and nearly exhausted. Dave dug a quarter out of his pocket. He dropped the coin into the phone and dialed his home number. Placing the receiver up to his ear, he discovered there was no dial tone. Panting into the phone as he held it, Dave pushed the zero button. Maybe an operator could put him through—still no tone.

Slamming the phone down, Dave slumped to the ground and placed his face in his hands. Every inch of his body hurt. Pulling his hands away from his face, he looked at the dried blood that caked his shaking palms. Dave slowly turned his hands over to examine the damage that his knuckles had sustained. As he sat looking at his tattered hands, his face twisted, wincing from the pain. Then that dreaded noise pierced Dave's skull once again. It was the far off moans of the undead floating through the air towards him. Dave knew what that meant—time to run.

Picking up his weary body, Dave tumbled down the embankment and into the woods. Off in the distance, he just barely saw the man and the woman. They walked in and out through the trees as the rain began to intensify. What Dave did see, was the walker following closely behind, stalking them. Out of breath, he hurried through the forest as fast as his tired legs would carry him.

Dave could barely walk, his body shaking from exhaustion. He struggled through the undergrowth, pushing his way past the hanging branches of the trees. Staggering closer to the couple, he lost sight of them in the heavy rain that now came down even harder. However, Dave could still see the demon of the flesh that wandered towards the unsuspecting pair. Then suddenly the creature disappeared from his view. Dave headed towards where he last spotted the monster and the couple as fast as his tired legs would carry him.

Cresting the final mound of earth, Dave found the undead horror in the middle of its assault on the man. The man lay on his back in the mud with the monster on top of him. Dave's adrenaline took over. With the force of a sledgehammer, he put his massive boot into the demon's face, returning some of the terror and violence that they had earlier bestowed upon him. Now—he walked through the woods with his new companions hoping to find out what in the hell was going on.

Dave asked,

"Do you guys know what's
happening?"

I replied,

"No—I don't think anyone knows."

I continued,

"All I know is that the dead are
coming back to life and eating other
people."

Dave responded as I thought he might,

"That's fucked."

I agreed,

"Yes—yes it is."

As I finished the sentence, a run down shack emerged from its hiding place amongst the trees. It wasn't much but right now, we did not have much of a choice other than to check it out. It was going to be dark soon and it was best to get inside.

THE CABIN

The cabin was more of a shack than anything else. As much as the three of us hated to, we had no choice but to make this our home for the evening. The black of night had already begun to shroud us in its darkness. Nestled between the trees of the forest, the cabin leaned horribly. Its walls sloped to the left side. A porch ran across the length of the front. The roof overtop of the wooden porch lay half on the ground covering the left side of the porch floor. The roof's tree trunk pillars still stood upright at attention. A large vine like tree wrapped around the back of the cabin and over onto the roof. The branches grabbed at the tiny decrepit shack as if to cradle it in its palm, holding the cabin up. Large gaps in the thick unevenly cut barn board that made up its walls allowed the wind to howl through freely, mimicking the demonic moans of the dead. The windows of the cabin sat at odd angles. Covered with criss-crossed pieces of lumber the wood blocked our view of the inside. The cedar shake shingles that once lined the roof planks had all but blown away over the years leaving just a few dangling precariously here and there. Large holes dotted the roof, exposing the inside of the cabin to the elements. A stone chimney sat perched atop the slanted roof, its missing stones scattered around its base.

Slowly walking towards the creepy cabin, the three of us

---

exchanged glances. The look on each of our faces asked the other,

"Who was going first?"

Dave and my wife both stood staring at me. Apparently, I had volunteered.

Drawing my pistol from its sheath at my side, I slowly walked over to the sloping cottage. Cautiously, I stepped up onto what remained of the rickety-planked porch. The floor groaned under my weight as I stood in front of the cabin door.

Placing my hand up to the door—I knocked. It seemed only right. I stood waiting. My wife whispered over to me,

"What the hell are you doing? Just open the door!"

Turning back, I replied,

"What? It's not our house—and why are you whispering?"

My wife looked at Dave and shook her head in disbelief, saying,

"Dumbass!"

Dave stared back at my wife perplexed and shrugged his shoulders. He could not believe that the two of us were even having this absurd conversation.

I turned back to face the door. I reached out to grasp the old iron door handle. It squeaked as I began to turn it. Nothing! I looked back to the others.

"It's locked."

I twisted the doorknob jiggling it back and forth. It came off in my hand.

"For fuck's sake!"

I kneeled down and quietly placed the doorknob on the porch floor.

Hearing my troubles, Dave and my wife began to walk over to me. As my hand let go of the knob, the door in front of me let out a creak and slowly opened up a crack. The odor of damp moldy air flooded my nostrils, choking my lungs. I stood up, sliding the flashlight out of its ring on my duty belt. I pointed it at the door and pushed the button, turning the light on.

The manmade torch came to life. Its beam cast a circle of light, illuminating the door before me. Reaching forward, I nudged the door open the rest of the way with the end of my flashlight. The old door moaned as I pushed it opened, revealing the interior of the cabin.

Shining the flashlight into the darkness of the inside of the cabin, I paused. I awaited the man in the hockey mask, who I was certain would appear with the desire of hacking me to bits with his machete. Of course, the masked man never showed.

Raising my pistol, I quietly stepped forward towards the open doorway. I inadvertently kicked the doorknob I so careful placed down on the porch. I closed my eyes, wincing. As if closing my eyes would make me invisible to any dangers that lurked beyond, I stood still. The doorknob rolled across the floor sounding like a ten-pound bowling ball thrown down the alley and crashing towards the pins. It effectively eliminated my stealthy entrance.

I opened my eyes and looked around. Searching the room with my light, my eyes first spotted a huge stone fireplace. Its face blackened from the years of soot of the numerous fires that had once burned, it was now cold. A cord of wood sat stacked beside the fireplace. Covered in spider webs, it waited for the next visitor to come and build a fire. As the light scanned the room, the beam dimmed then went out. I whacked the flashlight against my leg bringing it back to life.

Taking the light, I once again shone it into the darkness of the cabin. A large wooden table, two of its legs broken, lay toppled on the floor. The table was simple, made out of heavy wood as if it had been hand made long ago. Two handcrafted wooden chairs still sat facing each other across the heap that was once a table. Against the back wall rested a bed of planks. Its legs still showing where the limbs had been cut off of the small trees used to make them. Beside the bed was another smaller handmade table with a candle perched on top. A blob of melted wax acted as the candle's holder. The large tree that cradled the cabin from the outside, its vine like branches twisting through the cracks in the walls, claimed the bed as its own. The large holes in the ceiling still dripped from the earlier deluge, the water cascading down onto the rough wooden floor.

The porch behind me creaked and cracked as Dave and my wife joined me at the doorway. The three of us entered. The dust and dirt on the floor kicked up into the flashlight's beam dotting it with tiny particles. The howling of the wind passed through the large gaps in the ramshackle structure giving us the eerie illusion that the dead surrounded us. The small shack teetered, moaning, and groaning as the blowing gusts outside rushed over it. You could almost feel the walls of the cabin moving as if it were alive.

Dropping my pack on the floor, I went to investigate the fireplace. Surprisingly, the fireplace looked well-taken care of over its years of use. Holstering my pistol, I lifted a log from the pile, the spider webs stringing off it as I pulled. Ripping the dried bark from the log, I tossed the hunk of wood into the fireplace. I repeated the process twice more. Arranging the bark around the logs, I took out my lighter and lit the bark.

Dave walked over to the doorway. Taking one last look outside at the diminishing daylight, he shoved the door closed. My wife, pulled aside one of the dusty chairs, using the end of her shotgun to tear away the cobwebs. Brushing the seat with her hand, she plopped down onto it, wiping her dirty hand on her thigh.

As the light of the fire lit up our temporary shelter, it cast strange shadows across the walls. The tree branches flickered in the light like giant fingers motioning for us to enter its grasp. Switching off the flashlight, I placed it on the floor beside me as I grabbed another log for the growing fire.

I yanked the stump free. A large black spider scurried from the safety of its nest, scuttling in front of me. Its shadow danced on the floor in front of me making it grow to the size of a hedgehog. Startled, I yelped reeling back on my heels and falling on my ass. Sheepishly, I looked behind me to the others to see if they had heard my girlish squeal. Thankfully, they were both preoccupied as my wife searched through my backpack for something for them to eat, her shotgun laying on the floor beside her.

As my wife explored the pack, Dave tipped the collapsed table on its side. Sticking his hand out to me, he said,

"Pass me the flashlight."

Picking up the maglight, I headed over to the others and handed the light to Dave. Using the metal cased light as a hammer, he pounded the crude nails back into the table legs. Up righting the table, Dave handed the flashlight back to me with a,

"That'll do."

Dave's handiwork was enough to make the table stand and hold food but that was about it. My wife placed a squashed loaf of bread on the table and opened the end of the plastic bag in which housed it. Reaching into the bag, Dave took a slice of smushed bread. He bit off a wad as I put forth the option,

"I guess we can sleep in shifts."

My wife quickly blurted,

"I'm not sleeping!"

We all knew that none of us would actually get any sleep. The shack that we now inhabited did not afford the adequate safety for us to rest. Dave nodded, saying through a mouthful of dry bread,

"I'll take first watch, if that's ok?"

I replied,

"Yeah, sure."

Dave bit off more bread. A deep-throated roar from outside the front of the cabin made him cough it out onto the table. The chewed up hunks of dough sprayed across the wooden surface of the table. Dave dropped the half-eaten slice of bread and spun towards the door. My wife jumped up from her seat tipping it over, sending the old chair crashing to the floor in a cloud of dust. Bending down, I picked up the shotgun and threw it to Dave, alerting him to my intentions with,

"Here!"

Shooting his eyes quickly in my direction, Dave caught the shotty in both hands and pumped a round into the chamber. I pushed the button on the flashlight—nothing happened. I repeatedly pushed the button, jiggling the light and whacking it on my hand—still nothing but darkness.

The three of us looked at the flashlight then to each other. Our thoughts merged into one as we all said simultaneously,

"Crap!"

In any other situation we would have all laughed but that small bulb encased in metal that I held in my hand could very well hold our life in its little beam.

At least there was still the dim lighting from the fireplace. Looking around the one room shack, the tightly boarded windows meant that there was only one way in—and one way out. Handing the maglight to my wife, I drew my sidearm and took a spot beside our newfound friend.

Dave and I stood side by side, pointing our firearms at the weak wooden door that filled the void between the three of us and the terrors that lie beyond. My wife remained behind us still wiggling and smacking the flashlight, trying to get it to come to life.

Another heart-pounding roar came from outside the walls of our meager shelter—as did the moans of the newly arriving walking dead. Dave and I remained motionless, listening, pointing our weapons towards the door.

The sounds of horror suddenly stopped. Only the crackling of the fireplace and the gusts of wind whistling through the gaps in the small shack now filled our ears, along with the jiggling of the batteries from inside the flashlight as my wife continuing to coax it to work.

A heavy footstep hit the porch step from outside with a loud thump. The jiggling of the light batteries stopped and my wife stood silent, staring at the door. From beyond the thin wooden door, came the drag of a shoe. It rose up over the first step, followed by a clump. Another clump as the footfalls from outside struck the porch floor. Accompanied by more dragging and a final whump, the footsteps came to a stop. The terror now stood in front of us, on the other side of the door.

Our hearts pumped furiously. Our blood raced through us pounding into our eardrums as the adrenaline kicked in. The sudden quiet from the woods erupted with an earsplitting howl. We did not hesitate—we opened fire.

Dave and I blasted round after round into the thin door. It cast off sharp splinters of wood into the air as the bullets slammed through it. Behind us, my wife stood, still holding the flashlight. She jammed her hands up to her ears trying to soften the deafening blasts of our gunfire.

As the last empty shell casings dropped onto the dusty floor of the cabin, Dave blurted,

"I'm out!"

As I dug into my pocket and handed Dave a fistful of shotgun shells it became evident that we had just wasted our precious ammo.

Past the smoking barrels of our guns, out through the haze of gunfire that still hung in the air and beyond the holes in the door that our barrage had left, the creature stirred.

I quickly replaced the spent magazine in my pistol with a fresh one, leaving me just one extra. The empty mag clattered off the wood floor as it dropped out, the pistol's slide gliding forward with a metallic click as it shoved a fresh round into the chamber. Dave pushed the ammo I gave him into the loading port of the shotty, pumping it with a new shell.

With explosive force, the weakened door gave way crashing inward. The old iron hinges snapped like peanut brittle as the creature on the porch slammed its angry fists against it. The door came slapping down onto the cabin floor in front of us kicking up a whirlwind of dust, blocking our vision. Behind us, my wife shook the flashlight in panic one last time, yelling,

"Come on, you piece of shit!"

It was as if the inanimate light would somehow obey her frantic command.

As the dust settled, the light came on. Its beam centered on the face of the demon of the flesh that stood towering in the middle of the doorway, lighting up the creature's green eyes making them appear almost fluorescent. His dark greasy hair hung limp. The sunken hollow cheeks of the demon looked even deeper in the shadows. The frothy slime that leaked from between its lips was black like ink.

The ghoulish terror stood in the doorway swaying back and forth. Dressed in black slacks and a pale yellow sweater, his clothing was still damp and sagging from the rain. Black liquid oozed out of the multiple bullet holes that riddled the undead monster's chest.

Standing in the light, the ghoul let out a bellow as its mouth dropped open. Reddish-brown saliva like liquid spilled out onto the porch floor. Raising its arms, it stepped forward, towards us.

Without raising the shotgun, Dave squeezed the trigger. Hitting the beast in the left hip, the shot almost tore off its leg. He pumped the action back, firing again. Meat and bone filled the air as the next slug smashed into the side of the monster's ribcage sending it spinning to the ground.

The ghoul struggled on the porch to get up. Rushing over, Dave pumped the action once more and fired into its chest to where the heart was, knocking the undead man back down. Dave stood over the creature staring down into the cavity that was once its ribcage. The demon of the flesh began to sit up. Raising the shotgun over his head, Dave brought the butt of it down repeatedly, bashing open the undead horror's head. The cracking of skull filling the night air several times as the monster's brains spilled out onto the porch floor. The creature now lay motionless as Dave straddled over top of it breathing heavy with fear, the adrenaline still coursing through his veins.

Out of the silence of the night came the same earsplitting growl that we had heard earlier. We all shook as the howl sent shivers running up our back. Dave looked over to his right from where the spine tingling roar came. Rushing to the doorway, I looked past Dave.

A monstrous Black bear stood straight up on its hind legs sniffing the air, its cub sitting behind. In front of the bear, four walkers advanced on it. As the monsters neared, the furry beast dropped to all fours. The bear began to woof and swipe at the dirt in front as if to draw a line, daring the walkers to cross.

The undead continued their course. The bear, now visible angry and distraught, pointed its ears back and charged. Its mighty paws smashed one of the creatures backwards to the ground as the furry beast let out another huff. The bear rushed the second walker. The ghoul grabbed hold of the bear's front leg, trying to sink its teeth into it. The Black bear pulled the demon into its grasp, hugging it. Rolling to the ground the furry giant clamped its teeth onto the monster's head, tearing the flesh from the ghoul's scalp.

The remaining two undead creatures turned their attention towards the baby bear as the cub sat chewing on a twig, oblivious to the dangers at hand. As the walkers closed in, the cub got up and ran around the ghouls.

The small cub ran in circles, playing with the pair of undead, taunting them to catch him. The demons of the flesh staggered around after the baby, slowly swiping at it, trying in vain to catch the speedy little fur ball.

Seeing this, the mother bear let go of the tackled walker and rushed to her cub's aid, knowing all too well that this was not a game. She barreled into both of the creatures, knocking them to the ground violently like a linebacker cheaply blindsiding a quarterback.

Pushing her cub through the forest with her nose, the two bears made their escape. The small bear whined and continually looked back for its playmates as they went.

The first attacking creature did not get back up. The back of its head oozed brain matter from the open gash caused by the large boulder it crashed into. The bear hugged walker stood up facing us, its scalp peeled open, hanging from its skull. Out of the two tackled ghouls, only one got up. The other's legs had been badly broken. It was obvious by the manner in which the demon lay, contorted in the mud, struggling to get up.

The two standing corpses stumbled towards the shack, the fallen branches from the trees crunching under their heavy footfalls. The fallen walker slowly dragged itself through the mud, the wet leaves now covering its body. The soft muck squished through its fingers as it pulled itself along the floor of the woods.

Turning towards the cabin, I yelled in at my wife,

"Time to go..."

Looking back to the oncoming demons of the flesh as they slowly crept closer, I finished my sentence, the urgency darting through the air into her ears,

"...NOW!"

I could see that she was thinking way ahead of me and was already packing up our gear. Stuffing the bread back into the knapsack, my wife met Dave and me at the door of the cabin. I grabbed the pack from her and threw it on.

The three of us walked quickly away from the shack. The emanating moans of a larger more threatening group of walkers began floating towards us through the woods. In what little daylight remained, we could see the glowing orbs of the small hordes' eyes dancing in and out between the trees as they approached. Dave apologized,

"Sorry, they must have followed me
here."

My wife stated,

"They would have found us
anyways. They always find us."

Our pace quickened as the moans from the forest encircled us, coming from all directions.

The three of us hurried in and out through the trees of the forest sometimes breaking into a jog. The beam from the flashlight my wife held danced through the branches that reached towards us like icy fingers of doom.

We were all tired and wanted to rest but we knew that that was not an option, not here, not now. It would surely mean certain death for us all.

As we continued through the woods, the sounds of the undead

followed in our ears. They taunted us to sit down and rest, daring us to close our eyes and sleep. How long had we been running? How deep were these woods? Were we heading into them deeper? All these questions but not one answer. That theme seemed to repeat itself lately.

I had no idea what time it was when we reached the shack but it was nearing midnight so I figured we had been on the run now for at least three hours. It was a long, terrifying three hours with the moans of the undead seeping out of every darkened crack in the trees—but we had yet to encounter one.

The light on the handheld torch flickered the odd time in our journey through the woods. The beam began to dim permanently. It was clear that we would soon be without any light at all. Fifteen minutes later the batteries were dead.

My wife stopped, jiggling the flashlight once again as she had done previously in the cabin. Maybe it would work once more. As me and Dave continued our quick pace, I looked back into the darkness towards her. I was just five feet away and she was just barely visible to me. If it had not been for the rattling of the batteries, I might not have found her at all. Knowing that if any of us stopped even for a second without the others being aware, they would be lost in the inky blackness of night—and at the mercy of the creatures that prowled around us. I ordered my wife to,

"Keep moving."

Tossing the used up flashlight to the ground, my wife ran to catch up.

Without the small beam of light from the torch, it was impossible to tell who was walking beside me. For all I knew we were walking amidst the animated corpses. We would not even know it until they grabbed hold of us.

It became desperately clear that the three of us wanted out of this forest of fear. We rushed to find a way out, the undergrowth tugging on our pant legs. The three of us truly believed it was the undead clawing at us from the ground as we danced our way through the trees.

In the far off distance, we heard a man's scream for help. Another survivor had made their way down into the woods to look for a reprieve from the carnage that was taking place everywhere. Unfortunately, seemingly no place was without the horrors of the undead as the demons of the flesh roamed the lands freely, searching for their next feeding.

The screams for rescue rang through the darkness. The three of us kept right on going, stumbling our way past fallen branches and over the thick foliage, ignoring the stranger's pleas for help. There was no way in hell we would find that person, not without a light.

Even if we had a light, there was no way of knowing how many of those—"things" were out there hanging around for the feed. None of us were about to take that chance. Maybe if we had heard gunfire or possibly saw some muzzle flashes, something that gave us some sort of sign that the guy might still be alive when we got there. Then we might take a chance at helping. But just screams in the dark—fuck that and forget it! For all we knew the undead monsters already had the pour soul down and were about to dig in.

The man's wails confirmed our thoughts as they turned from screams of rescue to shrieks of agony. As the man's blood pumped up into his windpipe, it gurgled out through the howls of his painful death. Then all was silent.

The fiendish moans of the walkers went silent as they hungrily feasted upon the man in the woods. The only thing we heard was the crunching of the fallen branches and twigs under our feet sounding like the devouring of bones. We made our way through the low hanging arms of the trees, their fingers angrily clawing at our faces with the occasional,

"Ugh!"

and

"Ah!"

coming through our panting breath.

Crunching through the woods, the three of us stopped at the bottom of a small hill. Over the top of the hill some light cut through the trees. It looked like the illumination from a fire. Its orangey glow silhouetting the trees as it broke through the darkness.

Seeing the light reach through the trees at us, I could not help but wonder if this is what death is like. If we could get to that circle of light maybe all would be better. Salvation lay beyond that orange glow—or death.

It was obvious that we all thought the same thing. We quickly scurried up the hill, stumbling to the top as if playing a game of "last one up is a rotten egg." I was the "rotten egg." The backpack weighed me down like a boulder on my shoulders. The multiple battles with the undead demons slowly took its toll on my body, wearing me down.

That is how the walkers beat you. Not with a lightning fast blitzkrieg but with a lethargic almost unperceivable pounding that continues draining you slowly until when you do finally realize that you cannot continue—it is too late.

As we crested the hilltop, the three of us squirted out of the black grip of the woods and out onto the street. My wife fell to her knees as tears of joy rolled down her cheeks. She giggled and cried at the same time. I bent over to catch my breath placing my hands on my thighs to prevent myself from keeling over. My legs shook with exhaustion. Dave and I looked at each other and we both smiled, grinning from ear to ear. We made it! We had escaped the consuming darkened canopy of the trees that had only offered us fear. We were safe—for now. However—for how long—we did not know.

CONVENIENCE

Standing on the road, the three of us stared at the small town that lay deserted before us. The fire that lit up the night sky came from what used to be of the local paint supply store. Located at the end of the town's main drag, the various flammable goods that the store once offered for sale burned out of control. No firefighters would show on that night to extinguish the inferno.

Walking up the sidewalk of the main street of the town all appeared quiet, the fire raging off in the distance. The glow from the blaze lit up the small town in an orangey hue. The roads were vacant of the abandoned automobiles. Just the odd newspaper lay scattered here and there.

Picking up a page from the newspaper, I turned the paper to catch some of the glow from the fire. It was just local news about an upcoming Cactus Festival. What the—a Cactus Festival? There were no cacti around here. From what I could read there was nothing about the violence or the outbreak. Although, the uprising of the army of the dead happened so fast and so widespread it would be hard for anyone to do anything but try and survive.

The weirdest thing about this small town was there was no sign of any people. Where had all the people gone? The streets were void of the bodies and gore that we had witnessed in all the other places on our journey. Not a single sole, body, or corpse—alive or dead, was to be found. Not even a speck of blood. It was a modern day ghost town. The windows of the shops were now nothing more than mere shards of broken glass on the sidewalk, the remnants of the windows crunching under the soles of our shoes as we made our way by the rows of stores.

Instead of cooling things down, the earlier violent rainstorm made it an unusually hot and humid night. It made the stifling air feel heavy and difficult to breathe. Our damp clothes clung to our skin. The cracking and crunching of the glass beneath our feet broke the silence, sounding twice as loud in the still night air.

Looking in at the empty shops, their turned over shelves were left bare from looters. Our shadows danced across the walls inside the stores ghoulishly, the light of the fire silhouetting us as we walked. Yet, one question still remained—where had everyone gone? Had they all gotten away? On the other hand, did they all die and just wander off?

The lack of blood and bodies made me want to believe that the people managed to escape the carnage. It was a small town so maybe someone got word to them of the impending apocalypse. Maybe they pooled together and were holed up in a survival camp or something.

Nearing the end of the town's main drag, we spotted a convenience store at the corner. The windows, like the rest of the shops, had been smashed out in the looting but this tiny shop had an added feature. Iron security bars blocked the variety store's empty window frames. Even the door had the black bars in it providing further protection. This would make a perfect place to stay the night. The fire across the street lit up the inside of the store well, and the iron bars would barricade us from the threat of any monsters that might arrive.

I looked at Dave and inquired,

"What do you think?"

I could tell by the glint in Dave's eyes that he liked the way this place was fortified. His long drawn out two-word answer came with the sound of assurance,

"Awww Yeeeah!"

As Dave and I turned back to the storefront, it was obvious that my wife had already made up her mind. She pushed open the steel framed door, the door sweeping away a pile of debris left by chocolate bars and broken open bags of potato chips.

Propping the door open with her foot my wife bent down and began to munch out of a heap of what looked like Sour Cream and Onion potato chips. She reached down with her other hand and threw a couple of chocolate bars at Dave and me. Looking down at my wife in her feeding frenzy, Dave said whimsically,

"I think you broke the five second rule."

That just pissed her off as my wife let out a stern but muffled,

"Shut-up."

As my wife sat on the floor gorging in munchies, Dave and I checked out the store. The rows of metal shelves, some over turned onto the floor, were bare of anything of value. There was still a wide assortment of DVDs for rent in the back of the store but I was sure there would not be any renters anytime soon. Next to the section of movies stood a bookrack still full of cheap preteen romance novels, the kind that teenaged girl fantasies are made from.

Behind the cash register, all the goodies that I desperately wanted were gone—no cigarettes, no cigars—not even a lighter. The cash drawer was still full of money. If this was the case then the people had to know what was happening. If not then why leave the cash?

Refrigerators lined the one wall. Now dark with the lack of power the row of fridges were dry of beverages and foodstuffs. Several open tubs of sour cream lay on the floor in front, their white creamy contents oozing out of their cracked open containers.

Dave walked towards the movie section at the rear of the store, passing by the overturned Slushy machine. The ice all melted, the Slushy mix was a purple puddle on the floor. As Dave strolled through the gooey mess, it made the bottom of his boots tacky. Sticking to the linoleum floor as he walked, Dave's feet sent out tiny clicking noises. Dave stopped in front of the shelves of movies and began browsing through the new releases as if he would get one to watch later.

As the other two kept themselves occupied, I dropped my backpack on the cash counter and headed through a doorway to my right. It led to the back storeroom. Stepping on a dog's toy squeak bone, I scared the shit out of myself. Its loud "EEP!" making my sphincter tighten as I stiffened.

The dim lighting in the backroom made it difficult to see at first. It did not catch much of the glow from the fire outside as the front of the store did. As I waited for my eyes to adjust, I made my way to a pair of loading doors just barely visible in the dark. Two heavy steel doors with the locks still intact blocked any entrance from the outside. The security bars that protected the front of the store complimented the one tiny window in the back also.

My eyes, finally getting used to the dim lighting, searched the room. Empty milk crates sat on the floor stacked underneath the tiny window. Bags of garbage and folded up cardboard filled a corner. Crushed items littered the floor, swept off the shelves in the looting as in the front. Once again, all the useful items were gone—or were they? Sitting on one of the shelves were several combination bike locks, complete with plastic encased wire. These would be perfect for securing the front door for the night.

Scooping up three of the locks, I headed back out front. As I emerged from the back storeroom, I found my wife still seated on the floor but now with her back leaning against the cash counter. Her mouth hung open as she clutched at her belly, moaning,

"Ugh, I think I ate too much."

Dave was still at the back of the store holding the shotgun by his side in one hand. In the other, he held a DVD high in the air to catch the dim light of the fire outside and whispered to himself,

"Huh, I haven't seen this one yet."

Spinning the DVD case around Dave squinted to read the back cover as if getting ready to pop it into a player and watch it.

Walking over to the front door, I pushed it open and gave one last look up and down the quiet street. Good, it was still clear of any undead. The only sound that filled the air was the crackling of the blazing inferno down the street. Ducking back inside the store, I began the task of securing the front door.

Wrapping the wire of the locks around the bars in the door to the frame of the windows, I locked the front door closed. Giving a tug on the door, I checked my handiwork. The door barely budged. I stood back admiring my handiwork as I said,

"There, that should keep those
bastards out."

Turning, I walked behind the cash counter to take another look.

Suddenly, my wife pounced up from her moaning state on the ground, blurting,

"Idiot!"

"You left the combination stickers on the locks."

She hurried to the door and began peeling the stickers off the back of the locks. Laughing, I replied,

"Somehow, I don't think they can read."

Dumbfounded, Dave glanced over at us, hearing another of our absurd conversations. My wife, her head now bowed down, knew how silly her actions were and squeaked sheepishly,

"Better safe than sorry, right?"

Shaking my head, I bent down behind the counter, muttering under my breath,

"That's what I get for marrying a blonde."

Sifting through a stack of papers at the bottom of the counter, I found a pack of scratch tickets hidden under some inventory sheets. Holding the tickets up in the air, I said,

"Hey, look what I found."

Seeing what I held in my hand, my wife hopped up and bounced over to me excitedly, saying,

"Oooh, I want some!"

Dave dropped the DVD on the floor and walked up to the counter. Seeing the handful of tickets, he cried,

"Sweet!"

Doling out the wad of lotto tickets between the three of us, it gave us each four chances to win a million. My wife quickly scratched hers and not to my surprise, all her tickets were losers. The scratch tickets in my hand were also losers. Dave, his first three tickets losers also, began to scratch away the silvery coating on the last. The first square revealed fifty thousand dollars. The second also revealed fifty thousand dollars. He slowly began to scratch the last square on the card—fifty thousand dollars! Dave's eyes opened wide as he exhaled an excited,

"Holy shit!"

My wife also screamed with delight at the site of Dave's winnings. I gave a half-hearted,

"Right on!"

I knew there was no way he was ever going to cash that thing. I only did it to take our minds off of the chaos that still surrounded us outside.

As I finished my feeble attempt at being excited for our friend, a moan came from near the bars in the window. The three of us immediately looked over to where the groan emitted. Outside the bars stood a walker, its form blackened to a silhouette by the glow of the fire behind. The ghoul's arms reached up, grabbing the security bars of the window. The light of the fire behind illuminated the top of its arms and hands, revealing its tattered flesh and exposed bone.

The demon of the flesh teetered back and forth beyond the safety of the barred window. Moaning and groaning to get it, a second walker joined him—then a third—and a fourth. As they congregated outside, the stench of their death wafted over to our noses. Within minutes, there were about a dozen demons at the windows and door. They pushed on the bars attempting to get inside the small convenience store. It was a good thing that the dead only pushed on things and not pulled. If they were intelligent, they might have figured out how to pull on the door and tear it from the hinges.

Seeing that the door and windows appeared secure and there was no way that the monsters could possibly break in, my wife began to look around the tiny store once more. Routing through a bunch of stuffed animals, she found an overturned box of hair elastics on one of the still standing shelves. Grabbing one of the elastics, she pulled her hair back into a ponytail. I always loved the way ponytails looked on a woman.

Dave sauntered over to the security bars and held his ticket up to one of the ghoul's face. It reached through the bars, struggling to grab him.

"Yeah, check it out shithead!"

"Fifty thousand dollars!"

Dave went on, teasing the monster,

"Bet you wish you won this, don't ya?"

"Instead of being all fucked up and dead."

He dangled the ticket in front of the creature's outstretched hands, taunting him, jerking it back as the undead creep pawed for it. He played this game with the walker for a few minutes.

Dave then ran along the length of the bars high-fiving the demonic beings that struggled to break in. As if, he was a football player coming out of the tunnel at Super Bowl time. As Dave ran back and forth, he imitated the roaring of the crowd while cheering himself on,

"Woohoo!"

My wife jumped up. She ran up and down the isles cheering along with him.

Dave stopped, standing in front of the demons of the flesh, breathing hard. My wife continued to jog around cheering. Stuffing his fifty thousand dollar ticket into his pocket, Dave lifted up his balled fist and stuck out his middle finger,

"Fuck you!"

"Fuck you all!"

Dave then turned, plopping down on the floor in front of the cash counter. Picking up a chocolate bar from the floor, he tore open the package and bit of a hunk. The gooey warm caramel filling of the candy bar dripped down in strings over Dave's dry cracked lips. With a mouthful of chocolate and caramel he mumbled,

"Assholes."

I sat down beside Dave leaning back against the counter. My wife walked over and squeezed in between us, giving her the illusion of increased safety. If those things got in, no place in here was safe.

The three of sat on the floor together. Hidden from the glow of the fire outside by the shadows of the darkness of the night, we listened to the monsters rattling at the bars. The security of the store made us relax. As the dizziness of exhaustion filled my head, I quietly said,

"Let's try and get some sleep."

"We'll figure out what to do in the morning."

With that, our heads filled with black as we quickly drifted asleep.

I am not sure if the others dreamed that night but I had the same reoccurring dream about the dead coming to me. Their glowing eyes piercing through the darkness towards me. A muffled bang from a distant explosion awoke me that night.

I awoke in a cold sweat as usual, the noise sending my eyes

darting to the convenience store front, my sight still blurred with sleep. It was probably just an aerosol can blowing up in the paint store fire. I could barely make out the dead, still outside the bars, reaching to get in. Their moans sounded like howls from dying animals. As the haze of sleep washed over me again, my vision turned to black.

The next morning my wife had to shake me awake. I was still exhausted. My body ached and my muscles were now stiff from my encounter with the walker in the forest. If only I hadn't forgot the pain pills at the Diner. I could really use some now. My shirt smelled disgusting from the juices of the monster's internal organs that stained it a brownish black.

Standing up, I stretched my spine, the cracking of my bones sounding as if they broke. I did not even have to look over towards the front of the store to see if the dead were still there—I could hear them. I wanted to make sure this was not a dream so I looked anyways.

Moaning and groaning like a pack of dying mules with their rotting flesh hanging off, the demons of the flesh continued to paw at the inside of the tiny store. That is when I noticed something strange and yet at the same time amazing. Underneath the patches of their torn off flesh, new flesh had grown back. The bodies of the dead were actually regenerating. Could the DRED-not be doing this?

Was it possible for the DRED-not to be keeping the demons animate and growing new tissue to replace the decayed? If so, as creepy as it was, it was an astonishing feat of biological engineering. The new flesh still seemed to decay but more grew back in its place. That meant the bodies of the dead would be walking around for a long time.

How could we defeat something like this? There was no way in hell that we had enough ammo to kill every one of them. Sure, they were slow and lumbering but there would be millions, if not billions, of these unholy undead walkers. We tired—they did not. We did not even know if there were any other survivors left.

I decided to keep my revelation to myself hoping that the others had not noticed. It was time for other things—time to figure out how the heck to get out of here now. Looking to the others, I said,

"Let's get the hell out of here before

more show up."

My wife replied in bewilderment,

"And how are we supposed to do that?"

The only thing I could think of to try popped into my head as I came back with,

"We'll just walk out the back door."

My wife fired back,

"Are you crazy?"

It sounded like a ridiculous idea but the only evidence of the following pack of undead came from the front of the store. Maybe they all congregated out front because they could actually see us. Maybe we could just walk out the back door. Why not? It was worth a look at least.

I grabbed the backpack off the cash counter and the three of us made our way towards the back room of the store. Stopping my wife at the entryway to the back, I said,

"Stay here and make sure they can see you."

"Flash 'em your tits or something"

I continued,

"We'll check outside to see if it's clear."

Smacking me on the arm, my wife remained in the doorway, waving to the monsters outside.

I squinted out the tiny window as the morning sunlight's glare blinded me. I was now able to see what awaited us outside in the light of day. A dirt alleyway ran behind the store. Across the alley, tall weeds ran back into the forest. All looked clear outside.

Dave stood to the side of the doorway aiming the shotgun towards the opening as I unlocked the door and pulled it open. The alley was quiet. The two of us stepped out into the alley and I called back to my wife,

"O.k. Let's go!"

The three of us ran up the hardened dirt alley, the heavy thud of our shoes echoing off the buildings. The morning air was cool and felt refreshing. The dew on the weeds glistened in the early sunlight. The forest, now lit by the daylight, did not seem as foreboding as it did the night before. The branches of the trees reaching out to us seemed to tempt us back into its grasp. As if to read my mind, Dave looked to the trees and said,

"I don't think so."

We continued up the alley at a slow jog until we spotted an older model Cadillac crashed nose first into the wall at the end, its trunk popped open hiding the inside of the vehicle from our view. Above the Caddy, a giant billboard hung sloped to one side, the crash loosening all but one of the bolts that held it in place.

A large picture of a smiling mustached man wearing glasses filled one side of the billboard. The hair on his head was quite obviously a toupee and his smile looked as phony as his hair. Underneath the picture of the man, small white lettering identified the man in the picture as "Mayor 'Buddy' Hawthorn." The other half of the billboard read "Re-elect 'Buddy' Bill Hawthorn" printed in large white letters. On the right of the Cadillac, a laneway ran out from between the two buildings back to the main street of the town. To the left, a main road parted the tall weeds.

As we neared the car, we slowed to a walk. A slow banging, like the beat of an off-key kettledrum, echoed from the front of the Cadillac. Walking up the side of the big car, the cause of the noise became visible. The impact into the brick wall slightly buckled the old car's hood. Pinned between the wall and the front of the Caddy, the Mayor laid across the front of the car slowly thrashing his bloody hands off the hood, the congealing blood stringing from the bottom of his palms.

We peered into the car's windows as we made our way closer to Buddy. It was empty and the passenger door left ajar. The keys were still in the ignition and the car was still in drive but the gas tank was empty.

The Mayor stopped pounding as we approached. He stretched his arms towards us, his glazed lifeless eyes staring through us. Buddy's toupee hung near the back of his head by its tape, flung off by the force of the collision. His jaw, broken from smashing off the hood, hung open. Buddy's nose lay flat across his face, smushed sideways.

Black tar like drool slid out onto the crumpled hood of the Caddy as the Mayor repeatedly huffed through his crushed face. It was as if he was trying to catch his breath. Every now and then, Buddy stopped huffing and let out a loud bubbling gurgle from his throat.

On hearing the first gurgle, my wife threw her hands up to her mouth. She turned away and dry heaved. The sound was indeed sickening to hear as it turned all our stomachs.

Dave stepped forward and pointed the shotgun towards the Mayor's sunken decomposing face. Dave's actions almost seemed to anger the Mayor. Buddy's top lip raised in a snarl, imitating the fake smile on the billboard above. The shotgun blast was deafening in the quiet morning air causing my wife to let out a small hop.

As the slug exited the barrel and slammed into the Mayor's head, his toupee blew up into the air, landing in some tall weeds about five feet away. Buddy slumped down onto the hood of the car revealing the blood spattered brick behind him.

We did not have time for this. The walkers from the front of the store would be coming around the corner any minute. It was time to go. I walked away with my wife in tow, saying,

"Come on. Let's go."

Dave turned to follow then stopped and pumped another round into the chamber of the shotgun. He turned back towards the Mayor's slumped over corpse and fired into the top of his head. Startled by the second blast from the shotty, my wife and I spun around thinking that maybe the rest of the party had arrived. However, there were no walkers, just Dave standing there with the shotgun, the smoke still rising from its barrel.

We looked on as Dave turned back towards us. With a loud snap, the billboard let go from its last bolt and spun down onto the top of the Cadillac. Crashing off the roof, the giant metal poster hurtled into Dave's spine. My wife shrieked in horror as the huge sign smashed into Dave. I ran as fast as my legs would go to Dave's side.

The blow from the billboard had sliced Dave's back wide open. Dark blood flowed from under his shirt, slathering the dirt path. He gasped for air as pink froth bubbled from his lips. Squatting down beside him, I lifted Dave's shirt and knew this was the end of the line for him. A large gash in the middle of his back revealed his spine was broken in several places as the bones poked through his flesh.

At first, I thought we might carry him back to the safety of the store. But Dave was as big as both my wife and I put together. There was no way the two of us were going to move him anywhere.

As I squat down beside him not knowing what to do, I repeated softly,

"Oh shit, oh shit, oh shit."

The panic in Dave's eyes confirmed that he knew his situation was grave. As I knelt beside him, the moans and groans of the dead made me aware that time was not on our side.

Coming from the main street, the pack of walkers from the front of the store rounded the corner into the alley. I was not sure if it was the dire situation that Dave was in or if it was that the oncoming monsters were hungry but they seemed to move down the alley incredibly fast.

As the demons of the flesh closed in, I picked up the shotty. Standing up, I aimed the gun down at the top of Dave's head. I could at least spare him from the horrific death that the oncoming entourage of evil brought with them. I pumped the chamber and fired. Nothing came out. The gun was empty. I did not have time to dig into my pocket to reload more shells into the shotty. The dead were quickly lurching down the alley and would be on us in not time. My pistol was almost out of ammo and having two weapons was a top priority.

Looking down at Dave, I could see his eyes rolling backwards into his skull, his lips pulling back as death slowly crept in on him. He would not feel a thing. Watching the gathering undead move in towards the Caddy, I knew there was no time for sentiments as I quickly spit out,

"Sorry bud."

Turning, I ran towards my wife. She was already ahead of me, running through the tall weeds towards the main road. I looked back over my shoulder as we ran away. The demons of the flesh tore into Dave's upper torso, ripping it from his crippled legs. They fought over his innards like kittens playing with a ball of yarn, his intestines trailing behind as the ghouls lifted them in the air like a trophy. The walkers had claimed their fifty thousand dollar prize. I wanted to think he was already dead when this happened but there was no way to be sure.

My wife stumbled down a small embankment into a ditch that ran along the side of the road. Clambering up the other side and onto the two lane highway she paused in the middle to regain her breathe as she waited for me. Catching up to my wife, we stood in the middle of the road looking back and forth, trying to decide which way to go in. In one direction, nothing but road flanked on either side by trees, the other led back into the city. As we pondered our dilemma, I said what I knew she wanted to here,

"There was nothing we could do."

"He was already dead."

SURVIVORS?

When travelling, we liked to stay in open places and always in daylight. It made it easier to spot the walkers. Although, if you went through tall grass it was not the walkers you had to watch out for—it was the creepers.

The creepers were the ones who had their limbs torn from their bodies when killed. The ones eaten beyond recognition but still managed somehow to survive or the crippled and incapacitated. They were the ones who crawled around on the ground through the mud and debris, silently searching out their next meal. They were not fast or much of a threat but if you got careless and missed one...

We made the choice to head back into the city in hopes of finding others. The only thing we found away from the city was more walkers so at that time it seemed like our best option. There had to be others out there that survived the initial carnage as we did. Maybe we would have luck if we stayed away from the core of the city and stuck to the outskirts.

Approaching the last house that rest outside the city, we paused out front. It was a large white farmhouse with wooden plank siding. A set of five stairs led up to a wrap around porch that circled the entire house. The white wooden shutters that once flanked the outside of the windows left their images in the faded paint. The large brown wooden door, cracked and hanging from the bottom hinge, leaned inward.

I looked at my wife and asked,

"Well, you want to check it out?"

She nodded with a,

"Sure, why not."

Walking up the gravel driveway, I reloaded the shotgun. Handing the shotty to my wife, I drew my pistol. Examining the dried mud on our weapons, I could not help but think of the misfortune of a jam. They needed a good cleaning and as soon as possible. I stopped and replaced my pistol to its sheath on my side. My wife stopped, wondering,

"What's wrong?"

I replied, grabbing the shotgun from her hands,

"Nothing."

I unloaded the shells from the shotgun and stuck them in my pocket. Wiping the shotty as clean as I could with my t-shirt, I reloaded it and handed it back to my wife. Taking my pistol back out, I unloaded it and also gave it a quick wipe. With both weapons now somewhat clean and reloaded, I had a bit more reassurance that they would not malfunction if we needed them.

"O.k. Let's go."

The two of us once more started up the gravel driveway towards the house.

Cutting across the front lawn of the farmhouse, the more we neared, the slower our approach became. Standing in front of the stairs that ascended to the porch and led to the front door, we paused. We stood staring at the multiple reddish brown handprints and smears that blanketed the outside of the white house. The two windows that bordered the door were smashed inwards and devoid of glass. The remaining shards lodged in the window frames caught the chunks of flesh from the monsters as they crept in.

Going up the steps, the smell of rot and decay slapped at our noses. Navigating through the dried blood left by the creatures' relentless attack, we went to the door and peered in. Rays of light stabbed through the broken windows, lighting up the tiny dust particles that floated about, filling the air with an eerie white glow. The shutters, once used to bar entry, lay on the floor now streaked in blood and gore. Splintered wood and shards of glass cracked beneath our feet as we stepped into the living room of the farmhouse.

The two doorways leading into the living room remained blocked and secure. One with a large wooden antique dining room table and the other with a small rectangular kitchen table also made of wood. A heavy old wooden coffee table tightly nailed to the one window in the rear barred entry from the back. The old, ripped, yellow floral patterned couch was now filthy with mud and blood from the multiple footprints of the undead. The matching chair lay in the corner on its side. The feet of many smashed the cheap glass end tables, crushing their glass and thin metal frames.

The security of the sealed doorways inevitably sealed the fate of the occupants inside. Once the front windows and door failed, there was no way for them to escape the rush of the oncoming demons of the flesh. They had trapped themselves inside. Their hunks of flesh strewn across the floor, what little remained of the victims was now claimed by the swarms of flies and wriggling maggots. We had seen enough. It was doubtful that we were going to find anyone here except maybe a straggling walker. Quietly backtracking, we headed back for the driveway.

Once back on the gravel driveway, we paused to take a few deep breathes. It was hard to escape the stench of death. It was everywhere and on everything. As we cleared our nostrils with a few deep breathes, I asked my wife,

"Are you o.k.?"

She replied with a sigh,

"Yeah, I'm o.k. I just don't like the stink."

I answered back,

"Somehow, I think it's going to be around for a long time."

We continued to the road and began our trek back into the city. Off in the distance, we could see the damage that the walkers had brought. Steady streams of dark smoke rose up from the fires of the night before. Towering in the sky, they escaped through the grasp of grey fog that now blanketed most of the city. The majority of the fires had burned themselves out and now just smoldered with hotspots.

As we walked along the road, the rains came once more. It was only a light drizzle but enough to make you miserable, as if we were not already miserable enough. The rain did not last long. Just long enough to make our clothes wet and clammy again. The bonus was that it did help wash some of the stink of death that had clung to us all night.

The glass towers and tall buildings of the city, now just skeletons of scorched steel and concrete, stretched high into the sky and as we approached the outskirts. The horrible death of Dave was still fresh. Our minds replayed the image of his body torn in two by the demons of the flesh. The hungry grunts and groans of the dead as they wrestled over Dave's shredded corpse, the slurping and smacking of their mouths as they gnawed off his still warm flesh.

The city streets were barren of life. Lined with abandoned, burned out and wrecked autos that all pointed out of the city, it did not appear that many made it out alive. Our situation appeared more disheartening the farther we went. The deeper into the city we travelled, the more debris from fallen structures clogged the streets. The discarded belongings of those that had attempted to flee now crushed and trampled by the legions of undead. The thick clouds of smoke choked at our lungs as we ventured further into the city. Down one of the side streets, two dogs fought over what appeared to be either an arm or a leg bone. They tugged back and forth, as they snarled and growled at each other.

Clearing the thick blanket of smoke and haze, I searched my pocket for my cigarettes. Damn, they were crushed and wet. As we slowly walked past the rows upon rows of derelict autos, I glanced inside each one in hopes of finding some smokes. It eventually paid off.

I walked over to a car with the door open. The remains of a victim lay sprawled across the front bench seat. The nubs that had once been full legs hung out of the open door. As I neared, the knobs of flesh began to wiggle. Drawing my pistol, I stepped closer. With no arms and only stumps for legs, the ghoul on the front seat was nothing more than a hunk of rotting meat.

Following the chewed nubs up and across his blood soaked shirt, I spied the pack of cigarettes tucked inside the breast pocket. Replacing my gun to its holster, I reached in, plucking the smokes from his shirt. The monster's torso wriggled at me as its mouth opened and closed, burping foul air. I opened up the cigarette pack.

Sweet! The pack was almost full. Grinning, I leaned over the demon's face and whispered to him,

"Don't you know these things will
kill ya?"

Having not brushed my teeth in over a day, I was sure that my breath must have been almost as bad as his was.

Giving the ghoul a quick wink, I backed out of the auto. Pulling a smoke from the pack, I lit it and offered my wife one. She snatched it out of my hand, remarking,

"For a while there I thought I would
be forced to quit."

We leaned up against a wrecked automobile and enjoyed our cigarettes. We did not speak until we were done. Finished, I asked,

"Ready?"

My wife answered with a nod and we continued our journey into the city.

The weather had continued to be miserable, drizzling rain on and off. We were wet but not cold. It was another one of those hot, humid days where your clothes cling to your skin. The fact that we had not showered in a while just compounded the stickiness.

After all that we had been through, I still managed to take a long hard look at my wife's breasts. Her wet, spandex top pressed tightly against her ample bosoms as they fought back against the tension of the material. They swayed back and forth and bounced up and down as she stepped unsteadily through the rubble that had once been a grand city. My wife's erect nipples pointed straight out as if guiding us in which direction to go. Ah, I was still sane.

Out of the corner of her eye, she caught me ogling at her protruding nipples. Cupping her mammoth jugs, she squeezed them together, and stuck her tongue out at me. Smiling, thinking about how I would love to be stuffing my face into her big tits right now, we heard the pop, pop, pop of a standard military issue M-4 assault rifle. Its 5.56mm bullets making an unmistakable sound that I immediately recalled from my past as an Infantryman. The shots tore my attention away from my wife's bouncing breasts and quickly brought me back to reality.

Instinctively, I crouched down running for cover, ordering my wife to do the same. We darted across the street and knelt down in front of the burned out hulk of a car, its paint colour now soot black. The car's windows were smashed out, the plastic trim of the interior melted by the heat. The driver, now also blackened, was still inside, frozen in time in a grotesque pose. The body, burned badly beyond recognition, held its arms up high as if someone had said,

"Stick 'em up!"

Hands up and with the palms facing forward, the curled over fingers looked like scorched twigs. The corpse's back arched in the seat with the chest sticking outward, the black leathery flesh stretched across the ribs. Its head leaned towards the rear of the car over the blob that was once the headrest. The tight charred skin of the face pulled the mouth open into a large black oval, the white teeth eclipsing the outside.

We scanned the horizon for the spot from which the shots rang out. The gunfire was coming from a field of dried up waist high grass that, from a distance, looked more like straw. It was only about a small city block away so we decided to investigate.

The multiple rows of scrap cars that lined the street would allow for ease of movement to our destination. We skulked along the street weaving in and out of the abandoned wrecked autos. We made our way slowly towards the field of tall grass and the origin of the shots.

Wading into the tall light brown coloured grass, we hunched over to sneak in for a closer look. The two of us paused in front of a wheelchair hidden amongst the tall hay like grass. The wheelchair lay tipped over on its side, the occupant missing.

Fighting the heat, my wife reached out and grabbed hold of the arm of the wheelchair to steady herself. She quickly drew her hand back. Strings of gore streamed off her fingers as she yanked it away. With the grimace of disgust on her face, my wife wiped the blood and meat onto her pant leg leaving a dark smear. At least she didn't dry heave this time. We peeked through the blades of tall grass over in the direction to where the shots rang out.

There they were—the demons of the flesh. There were only about a half dozen or so, moving slowly towards an abandoned Dodge Charger. It was the new model that I thought looked sharp. At one time, I had thought about buying one. It was the first new car that I actually liked the way it looked.

Kneeling on top of the Charger was a soldier, an American

soldier! We were in Canada! With the rifle sling wrapped around his left arm to help steady his shot, the soldier was carefully taking aim and dropping the monsters one at a time. The 5.56mm rounds punched tiny crimson blossoms into the ghouls' foreheads. The spray of blood and brains was visible as the gore exited from the back of their skulls, the puffs of red mist filling the air.

The trooper did not get one shot, one kill but he came damn close. Keep your cool, do not panic and take your time and you may just have a chance. This guy knew what he was doing and was doing it well.

Once the last creature crumpled to the earth, we called out to him. We wanted to make sure he knew we were survivors and not just some more wandering walkers coming for lunch.

The soldier waved us over to his perch in the grass. As we neared, I could see by his AA shoulder flashes that he was a paratrooper with the 82nd airborne. He was a Staff Sergeant, about 35 years old.

When we finally got to him, he was still all business. Reloading his magazines and checking his remaining ammo and kit, he asked,

"Which way did you come from?"

I coldly replied,

"It doesn't matter because its not there anymore."

I continued,

"We are here now."

The trooper stated,

"Fair enough."

I did not mean to be rude but it was hard not to be with all that had happened to us.

We joined him on top of the car and introduced ourselves, as did he. Sergeant Coulter he said his name was. It was obvious that he had not seen any living humans in quite some time. The more the soldier talked, the giddier, like a little school girl, he became. He had a story and it was easy to see that he wanted to tell it. So, I let him.

Sergeant Coulter said he was on route flying in a C-130 Hercules preparing to be dropped along with other troopers. They were on their way to reinforce some congressman from butt fuck no where's escape route. About an hour into the trip one of the paratroopers succumbed to the sickness.

The inside of the plane was dark, the only illumination coming from the glow of the red jump light. The soldiers kept busy checking their gear one last time before their deployment. No one took any notice as the dead soldier sat there limp, his head drooped down. He may have just been resting before the jump like so many others sometimes did.

When the motionless trooper did re-animate, the guy next to him was as good as dead. He got it in less than a second, one bite that went almost halfway through the right side of his neck. The newly risen ghoul's teeth slid through the skin and muscle as if it were a piece of sweet vanilla cake. The soldier's blood streamed out of the gaping wound in his neck. The warm gooey liquid squirted across the plane's interior showering the paratroopers, blinding one. Now there were two.

Pandemonium unleashed as the others noticed the fate of their comrades. The living soldiers retaliated, pulling their daggers from their sheaths. Due to the amount of extra weight and gear that they carried, the trooper's parachutes and full battle kit restricted their movements. For the walkers, the burden meant nothing.

The soldiers stumbled, falling over one another. They struggled in the dark with their gear, stabbing at anything that appeared threatening. The undead attack was relentless. With a knife buried up to the hilt into its cheek, one demon still managed to bite off the hand that plunged it at the wrist. Leaving both knife and hand dangling from its face, it continued its unforgiving attack. Even over the deafening roar of the engines and through their helmets, the pilots could hear the screams. The shrieks of terror came from the live, but soon to be dead, cargo in the back.

There were only two survivors, Sergeant Coulter and a Corporal Singleton. Singleton was 26. They were the lucky ones near the door and the farthest away from the bloodshed.

Not thinking twice once the carnage had ensued, the two men hooked up their lines and jumped, not knowing where it led. Singleton's parachute wrapped around itself, sending him hurtling towards the ground below. He tried desperately to untangle it. The treetops screamed in at him as he fell faster and faster. Until the billowing of the chute's canopy finally yanked him upwards.

The paratroopers floated down, away from the chaos above.

They hung helplessly, watching the cargo plane bank steeply to the right and dematerialize into the forest. The cargo plane disintegrated in a burst of flames leaving nothing more than a plume of thick black smoke.

As the two soldiers floated down to the earth below, they slowly drifted away from each other. The two remaining troopers landed about a half a mile apart. Coulter landed just like all his other jumps—textbook perfect.

The Corporal on the other hand, was not so lucky. He landed hard. Singleton crashed into a tree, the blow knocking him unconscious. He tumbled through the limbs like a rag doll, the arms of the tree pushing his heels skyward as he fell. A branch broke his fall—and his spine. The Corporal's chute lines tangled in the massive wooden fingers above. Singleton dropped to the ground, the lines eventually catching him. It left him hanging there, crippled and unconscious, his boots suspended approximately three feet from the ground.

The Corporal awoke a short time later to find the three walkers that had begun to feed on him from the waist down. Singleton tried desperately to kick them off his legs but it was futile. The Corporal's legs no longer worked.

There was no pain for him, just the shock of dangling there, watching it all take place, and not being able to do one damn thing about it. Eventually, Singleton did die. Either the shock or loss of blood would have done the job equally.

Upon landing, Coulter immediately set out in search of his comrade. He headed in the direction that he had last seen Singleton's chute. Sergeant Coulter found the Corporal about half an hour later. The demons of the flesh must have had their fill or could not reach anymore, for they had abandoned their feast.

Just the top half of Singleton remained, hanging from the tree, mimicking a broken marionette. The few remaining parts of the corporal that worked twitched at the sight of the Sarge, hoping for him to come closer so he could have a taste.

Coulter drew his pistol from its sheath at his side. Cocking the hammer back, he took aim at the monster that was once his friend. The Sarge lined the sights of his pistol up with the top of the Corporal's head. Coulter was not a religious man. No god could ever allow this to happen to anyone. There would be no prayer.

The Sarge told us that he had prepared a barricaded shelter in a nearby apartment building, pointing over in its direction. Coulter continued to tell us about his bunker,

"You have to climb up to it but it
works."

We could see his jerry-rigged rope ladder from where we sat.

Sitting atop the car, the three of us shared a little food and water while we made a bit of "normal" chitchat. Like a nightmarish picnic, the bodies of the deceased lay only a few yards from us, stinking up the stagnant warm air as we sat atop the car. Coulter looked up to the sky saying,

"It will be dark in a few hours so it's
best to get indoors."

We agreed. Packing up our meager supplies, we prepared to head out. The trooper was the first to jump off the top of the auto. I handed him his M-4 and climbed down after him. Coulter waded off into the tall grass towards his shelter.

As I turned to help my wife down, we heard the Sarge yell out,

"Fuck me!"

I spun to see Coulter stumble to his left then let loose at the ground with a full auto burst from his rifle, unleashing hot death to whatever lurked at the soldier's feet.

Empty shell casings arced out, blood and flesh showered into the sky above the grass. I could see his mouth open, yelling a long, drawn out,

"Cocksucker!"

The gunfire muffled his voice as the Sarge emptied the entire magazine earthward. Coulter's chest heaved as he shook, clearly distraught with the events that had just taken place. The Paratrooper seemed to stand there for an eternity looking down, the smoke drifting off the barrel of his assault rifle. Then with his chest out and shoulders back, the trooper turned, hobbling back towards us.

Bending down, Coulter rolled up his pant leg. We could all see the bite. The Sarge let out an angry,

"Fuck me!"

It was not a large bite and it was not deep. Nonetheless, it was a bite. We all knew if the Sergeant was infected, he had but three days at most to live.

Coulter stripped himself of his weapon and combat equipment placing them on the hood of the Dodge. He had no need for them where he was going. He did keep his pistol. Tiny droplets of water formed in the corners of the trooper's eyes. As the Sergeant felt the moisture releasing from his now glossy orbs, he tried to stem the flow. He was trying to be strong but the tears came regardless of how tough he wanted to be.

His eyes welling with tears, Sergeant Coulter turned to limp away. My wife yelled after him,

"Maybe you're not infected."

Coulter kept walking knowing well that he was infected. He knew he was doomed to become one of the things that he had despised so much for taking his friend earlier.

My wife called to him once more, asking,

"Where will you go?"

The Sarge paused, looking back. His tears were gone now. Nothing but pure hatred seared from the soldier's eyes.

"To Hell!"

It was too late—we were already there.

SALVATION

Picking up Coulter's weapon and gear, my wife and I headed for his shelter. The bunker that the Sarge had constructed was located on the second floor of a burned out building. A pick-up truck sat on the sidewalk across the street from Coulter's makeshift shelter. The truck's bed was overflowing with corpses, each body with a bullet hole or two in the head. Pools of dried blood dotted the street below the balcony of the bunker above.

The building was a small three-story walk-up. Destroyed by the fire, the apartment's main stairs had collapsed. The only way up was the makeshift rope ladder that Coulter had tied to the balcony. Climbing up, we entered the Sarge's sanctuary.

The inside of the shelter was a plain bachelor type pad with an old sofa bed, mismatched chair, and a milk crate doubling as a coffee table. A small fridge sat against the back wall. Beside it, a hotplate sat on the counter next to the single sink. The orangey brown, 70's era wallpaper that hung in the room was peeling, the glue having dried up over the years. Popped from its hinges, the door to the entrance of the tiny one room apartment was missing. Possibly someone had removed it to barricade another apartment. Around the entrance of the doorway, the walls were black from the soot of smoke damage. The smell of burnt wood filled the room giving it that wintertime fireplace scent. Across from the main entryway, another doorway led into the bathroom. A map was pinned to the wall beside the bathroom with a large red circle scribbled not far from our current position. Obviously, there was something of value there. Maybe the red circle marked a location of some supplies or perhaps survivors.

Walking over to the open doorway, I stuck my head out into the hallway. It opened up into a large foyer. A U-shaped balcony with a white wooden railing ran the length of the opening with the main stairwell running up the middle towards the back. The fire blackened the corridor. The railing that ran the length of either side of the hall to the main stairs had several sections missing. Tumbling to the floor below, they joined the remnants of the staircase in a heap of smouldering burnt timber. A discharged fire extinguisher lay on its side on the hall floor. Its wide powdery contents sprayed across sections of the floor and walls.

Across the hall, the wall of the opposing apartment had also burned away in the fire. It revealed the charred insides and the previous occupants. Two bodies lay stretched out on the burnt couch. With their arms tightly wrapped around each other, the fire fused them into one crispy mass. A charred gas can lay tipped over on floor beside the blackened sofa. Seeing the outbreak of the dead they must have thought it best to die together. Lighting themselves ablaze, they held each other in their arms. What courage it must take to knowingly light oneself on fire and wait to die. In one way, I admired the couple for their bravery. And yet, I despised them for their cowardice of not standing up for themselves and fighting. I turned back into the small one room apartment.

I dropped my pack beside the small sofa bed and rest the M-4 up against the arm. My wife stood over by the map still holding the shotgun. She cradled it in her arms as if it were her child. I walked over and took stock of the supplies that Coulter had managed to pilfer.

A 20 litre bottle of water, two cases of baked beans minus a few cans, a half dozen boxes of soup crackers and a variety of single cans of soups sat stacked against the wall next to the bathroom. Beside the pile of foodstuffs, five rifle magazines filled with 5.56mm ammo rest atop an open cardboard box teaming with loose rounds. Next to the box of ammo, I saw something that in a strange way excited me. The hideaway, stocked with plenty of ammo and food, even had toilet paper!

Knowing that neither my wife nor I had gone to the washroom lately, I went to check the toilet. A half used roll of toilet paper sat on top of the back of the tank. I placed the roll on the side of the tub and lifted off the lid to the toilet tank. Sure enough, there was water in the toilet.

As I stood there staring down at the filled tank I could feel my bowels sensing the relief and begin to loosen. I called for my wife, who was still busy studying the small map. Being a gentleman, I let her go first. It felt like an eternity. I danced back and forth outside the closed door waiting for my turn.

When I did get in, I could barely get my pants down fast enough, not caring if the odour of a fresh shit floated in the air around me. It felt terrific to have a good crap. I really needed that. I am sure we both did.

Flushing the commode, to my amazement, it refilled. That meant there was still running water! I turned on the shower taps. Water began to flow. I stuck my hand under it. The water was warm. I yelled to my wife,

"There's warm water!"

"Hurry up and have a shower."

My wife stripped off her clothes as if they were on fire. I smacked her playfully on her tight heart shaped ass as she ran past me to the tub. She giggled as she stepped in.

I was certain the water was not going to be warm for long and I was right. Halfway through my shower the water began to turn cold. I did not care. It just felt good to be clean. Now the simple things in life that we had once taken for granted seemed to elate us. You never think of the little things such as going to the bathroom in a safe comfortable environment. It was now a luxury. After our showers, we both gave our clothes a good scrubbing and hung them over the shower rod to dry.

After enjoying our quick clean up, I built a small fire in the sink to cook our meal. The tiny sink would keep the glow of the fire to a minimum and be somewhat safe. We sat naked, having some baked beans and crackers as our dinner. The hot meal bringing back colour to our faces as our harrowing journey had begun to give us the resemblance of our undead foes.

Still chewing on my last mouthful of beans, I walked over and studied the map. It appeared that it was a street map of the local area. Coulter had highlighted some sort of building. It was only about five clicks away but with the massive destruction in the streets outside it might be tough going.

There was not enough daylight left for a return trip to the spot marked on the map. Seeing as how the shelter seemed secure and well stocked with plenty of supplies, we decided that we would rest for the remainder of the day. We would hunker down for the night and hope to get a good night sleep for once. In the morning, we would make the trek to the location on the map.

If it were a wasted journey then there would at least be enough time for us to return in the safety of daylight. In addition, seeing as how Coulter worked so hard to organize and stock his bunker, we were not going to let it go to waste.

Our sleep was not as pleasant as we had hoped. I still had my nightmares and the moans from the few wandering dead echoed in the still night air outside. Without the normal drone of civilization, the groans from the demons of the flesh travelled a long way off. It did not sound like there were many out there—but they were there. My wife and I did manage to have a bit of intimacy for the first time since all of this madness had begun.

The two of us awoke in the morning to the pop, pop, pop of more gunfire. Grabbing our still slightly damp clothes, we hurriedly dressed and ran to the balcony. Scanning the area below, we saw them. Up the street they came. It was a military squad of six men. A seventh man pulling up the rear followed them. They advanced, walking in a firing line, eliminating all the undead that roamed the land.

After taking down a walker, the seventh man would go up to the fallen corpse and search the liquidated ghoul. Were they looking for money, jewellery, what?

The squad was heading right for our position. I was not sure whether to fear for my life or to yell out to them with excitement. My emotions spun back and forth, toying with my mind. One second scared, the next joyous. Were these another pack of hunters? Maybe the Sarge had gotten the word out where he was and they were searching for him.

Ducking back inside our hideout, my wife and I sat quietly,

covering the balcony with our weapons. Out of the silence came our names. How did they know who we were?

I looked at my wife, whispering to her,

"Stay here."

I slowly crept to the balcony and peeked down to the ground. Outside, I saw that the six soldiers had now formed a circular perimeter. They stood at the ready underneath in front of the balcony while the seventh man still searched the disposed walkers. A message squawked from one of their radios,

"Wills? Did you acquire the subjects?"

Tipping his head down to the handset on his shoulder, Wills replied,

"Unknown at this time. Wait one."

Once again, the trooper called our names and asked if that is who we were. I replied,

"Yes, how do you know who we are?"

The lead trooper, Wills, got back on his radio and spoke into it,

"Subjects acquired."

He continued,

"On route—ETA approximately one hour fifteen."

Looking up at us, Wills ordered,

"Hurry up and pack up your shit."

He went on,

"—'cause you're coming with us."

Who the fuck were these guys—and why the hell were we subjects? It made us sound like some kind of goddamned experiment. If this was some kind of an experiment, it was most definitely fucked up. Most of the planet is destroyed and dead people are walking around eating what little remained of the living. You can't get any more fucked up than that.

Looking down at the men on the ground, I noticed that they were a mixture of Canadian and American soldiers. Half of the trooper's wore some type of night vision goggles—but it was daytime. Their faces were well shaven and their uniforms were clean, so wherever they came from it had to be pretty good—and secure.

The seventh man walked up to the lead trooper. He did not wear a uniform like the rest and did not carry any sort of weapon. He carried a number of small cloth bags. The seventh man handed

Wills one of the bags. Wills then handed it off to another soldier who put the cloth bag into the butt pack that was attached to his load bearing equipment.

The seventh man wore grey coveralls covered in dirt and stains. Wearing gore soaked rubber gloves, the man reached into his pocket and put whatever it was he grabbed, into his mouth. It was obvious that the man had no teeth. His jaw wiggled up and down and from side to side in an attempt to gum the item in his mouth. The sinking of his face from the lack of teeth gave him the look of a walker. The man's hair was not cropped short like the soldiers'. It was shoulder length and greasy. Black with grey streaks, his hair snaked out from beneath the dirty ball cap that he wore. The seventh man was also much older, looking to be about sixty. Scribbled in black marker over one of the pockets on his coveralls was "Ponds."

I looked back to my wife then back to the ground and said,

"Give us a few minutes."

A yell came back as I ducked back inside the tiny apartment,

"That's all you have—a few minutes
and no more."

My wife said with concern,

"We don't even know who they are."

As I packed more supplies into my pack, I discussed our situation with my wife.

"We will be a lot safer with them
than staying alone."

She agreed and picking up our weapons, we returned to the balcony.

Climbing down from our small safe haven, we moved out as a group, heading back towards the field where we last saw Sergeant Coulter. Ponds tagged along behind. I pulled out my pack of smokes and handed one to my wife. I offered one to the rest of the soldiers as we walked. They all declined. Ponds hurried up to me and asked,

"Can I get a smoke off you?"

Taking a cigarette from the pack, I extended it towards him,

"Sure."

Wills grabbed Ponds by the back of the coveralls tugging him to a stop, saying to me,

"Don't give him anything."

Wills shoved Ponds to the back and yelled at him.

"Smoke your own, asshole."

With a cartoon like cackle, Ponds reached into his pocket and dug out his own cigarettes. He took out a bent half-burned smoke, lighting it.

As we walked, Wills talked,

"Sorry about having to walk but our chopper is out of gas."

It was their helicopter!

They were the ones buzzing over us since we had begun our trip into hell. Another soldier added,

"We got lucky at the gas station."

He went on,

"We were on our way back to base, flying on fumes, when we spotted you."

"We..."

Another trooper cut in,

"We wanted to pick you up but we lost you in the trees."

Wills took over again,

"We figured you would run from us after what happened at the diner."

He continued,

"We already weren't sure if we were going to make it back on the gas we had so we couldn't keep chasing you around."

I replied,

"It's ok...we made it."

I began to tell them about Sergeant Coulter when I was interrupted. Wills explained that the Sarge did know he was looking for us. He went on to say,

"Coulter was an advance scout. His job was to keep a look out for the two of you."

"He was to keep you at his shelter until reinforcements came."

I was stunned,

"So, Coulter lied to us about how he came here."

Wills corrected me,

"The story about the plane is true."

Adding that,

"Singleton—along with the others— is dead."

The troopers were to drop into our neighbourhood to recover us but the plane never made it. Coulter was searching for us each day. It's funny how we found him instead. Without us knowing, the Sarge had dropped a locator beacon at the car as we sat and had lunch the day before. He was trying to delay us for the team's arrival. The one thing the Sarge did not count on was becoming a demon of the flesh. Puzzled, my wife asked,

"Why are we so important?"

Wills answered,

"Don't worry you'll find out soon enough."

Were we travelling to our own deaths? I thought not. By the way that they treated and seemed to protect us, we felt more like a king and queen travelling with their bodyguards.

Our trek took just little over an hour with the dead posing little threat. As the soldiers made their way to us, they had previously cleared the area of all of the undead horrors. There was the odd new walker that had wandered in to fill the void but the troopers put them down before they even got close.

Upon seeing the dropped walker, Ponds ran over to its corpse. He searched through the fallen cadavers of the walkers, every so often sticking something shiny into the pocket of his coveralls. Giggling to himself, Ponds laughed aloud with his cartoon character chuckle. Wills yelled at him,

"Never mind stealing shit, just do your fucking job!"

Then finished it off with a quiet,

"Fucking retard."

At that warning, Ponds pulled a small tube out of one of the little bags that he carried. Taking a small knife, he cut off a hunk of brain from the undead ghoul. Wills yelled at Ponds again,

"Cut away from your body!"
"You cut yourself again and I'm
leaving you here for the monsters."

A mist floated up and out of the small tube when Ponds opened it. Wills, still watching Ponds, said to my wife and me,

"It's liquid nitrogen."

As the rest of the soldiers formed a defensive circle, Wills continued,

"We take the samples back to the
lab to be analyzed in hopes of
finding a way to stop this."

Ponds took the tiny sample and dropped it into the tube. Replacing the cap, he put the tube back into the small bag and ran back. Once more, he handed the small bag to Wills who handed it off yet again.

Our journey was coming near to a close when we arrived at a place in which the soldiers referred to it as:

"Beelzebub's bottleneck or the
Gauntlet."

Upon hearing that name, I knew it could not be good. You do not give something a nickname like that unless it is bad.

The bottleneck was a long stretch of street that consisted of large tall buildings running along either side for about two blocks. Glass littered the ground on both sides from the buildings' windows falling to the pavement below. The towering concrete structures blocked out the sun, casting most of the street in eerie shadows. Rubble blocked off any entrance or exit to the side streets. The only way through was straight down this street. At the end of the neck, the road opened up into a field. Off in the distance, near the end of the street, a small concrete wall was visible. It looked like a detour or construction barrier of some sort.

Farther past the small wall, in the middle of the field, sat a larger concrete structure flanked by two towers. The group began to slow as we approached. This cannot be good, I thought to myself. Glancing over to my wife, I shot her a quick smile, hoping in some way that she had regained a small piece of confidence back.

The soldiers stopped and began to check their weapons. Wills stood in front of them and barked,

"Mags full, safeties off."

Then turned to us and said,

"Make sure your weapons are full,
check your fire, and stay close."
"We call this running the gauntlet."

Reloading his own rifle with a fresh magazine, he told us to get ready to run and,

"No matter what happens, do not
stop."

Looking at us, Wills asked if we were ready. Who the hell would ever be ready for this? We all nodded. With the order of,

"Go!"

we took off, racing down the street. What was the big deal? We were running down an empty street. A few bodies lined the street scattered here and there but nothing out of the "new" ordinary. The "new" ordinary that consisted of destroyed burned out buildings and vacant streets devoid of any signs of life.

Nearing the first corpse, it began to sink in why we were running. The dead on the ground were both undead and soldiers. Ponds did not stop here to take samples. He ran as fast as he could like everyone else. As my eyes rose from the decaying remains on the ground to where our destination lay, time slowed to a near stop. Our goal seeming to whip away from us the more we ran towards it. That is when the moans started.

Just a few groans at first, then increasing the more we travelled. It seemed the farther we went, the more excited and agitated the dead became. Like a demonic race, the demons of the flesh were on the sidelines, cheering for the winner—eating the losers.

We had nearly reached our goal of the open street. Then the bad feeling I had earlier came to a reality. Hundreds of hungry ghouls came streaming out of the ground floors of the buildings to both sides of us. They swarmed in, trying to block our exit in front. Out of the open doorways and pouring over the glassless windowsills, the dead flooded into the street.

The undead creatures slowly gathered, closing in around us. My wife, with a scream, was the first to fire. The blast from her shotty tore into one of the oncoming demon's torso. Splitting its stomach like a gory piñata, the ghoul's entrails spilled out onto the ground like candy for the damned. The rest of us began to open up with our M-4s, riddling the oncoming monsters with bullets. The stray rounds thumped harmlessly off their chests as the demons of the flesh continued to creep forward. My legs began to feel shaky and weak. It had felt so long since I had had a good night's sleep. Over the monster's loud moans came the repetitious yell of Wills',

"Run! Run! Run!"

The lead trooper screamed at us as we rushed through the gauntlet.

The dead began closing in on us like the slamming of a book. Pushing my way through, I felt the undead trying to rip the rifle from my hands. Letting it go, I drew my sidearm and attempted to fire at the oncoming horde.

The walkers were at such close range that their ghastly hands pawed at the pistol as I fired, most of the rounds ineffectively blasting off their gnarled fingers. Grabbing at me like a bunch of crazed groupies at a rock concert, I struggled through the crowd.

The ghouls ripped at my pack, pulling me off balance. Shedding my backpack, I shoved my way through the growing horde. I saw a small opening between the mass of monsters and made a run for it. Catching up to my wife, I pushed her forward from behind. Struggling through the legions of undead, I felt a sting and the sharpness of a demon's teeth drag across my left forearm. My hot sweaty skin tore open, jetting my blood skyward. Shit! I had been bitten. The soldiers ran to our aid, pushing the monsters away and pulling us through the swarms of hungry walkers. Clearing the last of the undead creatures, I looked back to see if everyone had made it.

Behind us, the advancing waves of the undead washed over the last soldier who was guarding our rear as the pour soul's weapon ran dry. He managed to take out at least three of the ghouls with just a knife and his bare hands before the monsters could pull him to the ground. We could no longer see the soldier's body as we cleared the gauntlet, just a massive frenzy of clawing undead. The dying soldier's shrieks were barely audible over the grunts and groans of the hungry horde as they began their feast of the flesh.

Pointing to the small concrete wall, Wills screamed,

"Take cover!"

Our small group ducked in front of the barricade and waited for our next order. The demons of the flesh slowly turned and began making their way towards us. The air filled with the echo of a 30mm cannon. The crack, crack, crack of the huge rounds blasted at our ears as they left the barrel, passing within inches of our heads. Leaning up against the wall, I sat and watched. The high-powered projectiles slammed into the crowd of creeping carnage, disintegrating the victims they found, sentencing them to eternal damnation. The air above grew hot as the bullets streaked across, travelling down range.

I had always been taught forgiveness by my parents, who, I was sure were long since dead. But how can you forgive something like these—things? There was no forgiveness, no pity—only hatred. Not one shred of amnesty was in my voice when I muttered under my breath,

"Die you fuckers."

Only about twenty shots came out of the cannon before Wills yelled again,

"Let's go!"

Following closely behind Wills, I could see the two steel towers with 30mm cannons mounted in them. A soldier stood, manning only one of the two towers. The second tower sat empty. A long concrete shaft ran from the top of the towers into the ground. The remnants of the chain link fences that once surrounded the towers were now crumpled on the ground, the armies of the undead having long since destroyed them. Panels of reddish-brown steel lay twisted haphazardly around the outside of the concrete structure. Was it dried blood or rust?

In my mind, I wanted to believe that the reddish-brown coating was rust and tried to convince myself that that was in fact true but knowing the current state of despair the world was in, that was more than likely not the case.

A concrete structure filled the void in between the two towers. The building was not very high. It was only about fifteen feet tall, just high enough for the demons of the flesh to be unable to scale its smooth sides. The remains of disposed walkers smoldered in a heap. The pile of burning creatures reached the height of a three-story apartment dwelling.

Running towards the structure a soldier rose on top. Casting down a rope ladder, the soldier said,

"This way—up here."

My wife was the first to go up, then myself. The remaining soldiers followed, with Wills being the last.

THE COMPLEX

Our little group stood atop the short concrete building. The structure stretched out across the ground spanning about the size of a football field. Solar panels lined the rooftop, many of them cracked and broken. A hatch that was similar to one that you might find on a submarine sealed the world out. The helicopter that we had seen several times buzzing around during the last few days now sat idle at the rear of the concrete building. We turned, looking back to the Gauntlet through which we just came. The demons of the flesh still advanced slowly. More of them poured out into the narrow street behind those that still came to us.

The soldier with the rope ladder began to pull it up.
Wills, helping the trooper pull the ladder, said to him,

"We lost Peterson, Stokes, and
Noble."

The soldier's reply came,

"Shit! That's ten this week."
"A few more weeks like this and
there won't be anyone left but the
docs."

Wills seemed confident, adding,

"I think things are about to change

for the better."

The soldier fired back with uncertainty,

"Yeah, I hope so."

The small horde of undead stood below just mere feet from us. They pawed up at our boots, stretching, reaching for our warm flesh. My wife and I stared down into the mass of monsters. The trooper with the rope ladder looked at us and said,

"Don't worry. They'll leave—
eventually."

The group of soldiers walked us over to the hatch. Wills lifted it open. A metal ladder descended deep into the opening. One by one, the troopers began climbing down the metal ladder and into the complex that lie far below. Wills grabbed my wife by the hand, helping her into the opening. I stood there looking down into the deep hole that descended into the earth. Pointing down inside the hatch to the metal ladder, Wills looked to me, ordering,

"Let's go."

As he turned towards the open hatch, I grabbed Wills by the shoulder, stopping him,

"I can't."

I rolled my arm over, revealing the fresh teeth marks in my flesh and continued,

"I got bit."

Rolling his eyes at me as if to say,

"Who gives a shit?"

Wills said,

"Don't worry about it."

"Just get your ass down the hole,
buttercup."

What the fuck? First pretty boy and now buttercup. I answered back to Wills,

"O.k.—I hope you know what you're
doing."

Reluctantly, I grabbed the rungs of the ladder and started my climb down, muttering under my breath,

"Yeah, I'll show you buttercup."

"If I die, I'm eating you first."

I didn't think Wills heard my mumbling but the small chuckle he let out said otherwise.

The rungs of the ladder felt cold to my grip, the sweat from my hands making them slippery. The cool air of the complex below whisked past me, blowing away the hot humid air above. Tiny lights lined the inside walls of the shaft giving off a dim glow. The climb down seemed to take an eternity as the clanging of our boots against the rungs echoed off the round walls of the tiny descending tunnel. It must have been at least forty feet below to the ground.

Reaching the bottom, the descent took us into a vast underground complex. An entrance to a long round hallway was our way in. A set of thick double glass doors sat at the end of the hallway. Behind the glass doors, a large sterile looking room opened up. Two armed guards stood with their weapons at the ready. They wore hard composite body armor from head to toe.

The armor covered the soldiers completely, looking more like a high tech spacesuit. By the ease in which the troopers moved, the armor must have been lightweight and comfortable. The body armor even covered the guards' joints. The guards also wore what appeared to be some type of night vision goggles. Just like the same ones a few of the soldiers in Wills' group had worn but these ones were built into the face shields of the hard composite helmets that the guards wore.

A third guard sat beside them off to the right at a metal control panel. He sat watching a monitor, his hand poised ready to push a red alarm button on the console. The third guard was not armed or armored like the other two. He looked more like some sort of lab technician with the long white smock that he wore.

Stepping into the long corridor, a heavy steel door slid closed behind us. My wife and I turned at the grating sound as the door slammed shut behind us. The steel door had several dents and dings in it from multiple bullet strikes. Wills also turned. Not from the sound of the door closing, but instead to make sure the entrance was sealed shut. He took no notice of the damage that the door had sustained. Tiny holes, spaced about four feet apart, dotted the length of the round hallway. A computerized voice spoke from speakers in the ceiling,

"Scanning"

The artificial voice emitted from the roof as our group slowly walked. Upon reaching the heavy glass doors, we stood there until the voice above granted us access with,

"Area Secure"

The glass doors slid open as Wills described how the hallway was a way to monitor all incomers for the DRED-not and D.R.E.D. virus combo. It was what made the dead walk. Mounted in the walls were cameras that would scan the subjects as they walked through.

The security system was similar to that of an x-ray machine. If a person came in with the DRED-not combo in his or her body, the scanner would show the infected host up on the guard's monitor. The guard would then send out a general alarm that there had been a breach of the complex.

When reinforcements arrived, the troopers would eliminate the threat. If need be, the doors could be opened via remote from other control hubs spaced throughout the facility. They have had several breaches in which returning soldiers had received a bite while out in the field and had tried to sneak back in without telling anyone. Guess they thought that they might not be infected and not become one of the undead. It resulted in swift termination.

The goggles the security detail wore also showed the DRED-not combo but they were still in the Alpha testing phase. Wills said that so far the goggles worked. But why had it the security system not detected the DRED-not and D.R.E.D. virus in me? I had been bitten. Technically, I should be infected.

Stepping through the doors, the cool clean air of the artificial climate blew against my face. Standing in a large square room that consisted of sterile white walls and three corridors, I heard the "shoop" of the heavy glass doors closing behind. Looking over to my wife, I could see that she was now happy. The ear-to-ear grin on her face said that she once again felt safe.

The armored troops confiscated our weapons. No firearms were allowed freely inside the facility unless used for security purposes or weapons research. Upon entering, all weapons were to be taken to the armory and locked up. I guess it made sense. It would limit the drunken mishaps and the suicide attempts.

Glancing down, I looked to my wife's breasts knowing what lay in store. The air conditioning made her nipples stand fully erect once again. I would never get tired of seeing those. Looking back towards the two guards in their funny goggles, I could tell that they were staring also. Realizing that every male eyeball in the entire room ogled her boobs, my wife hunched over. She blushed as she attempted to hide her bosoms.

They had everything down here. I could see the signs on the walls pointing down the various halls to the directions of a lab, cafeteria, lounge, games room, barracks, armory, even weapons testing, and a firing range. I don't think they missed anything down here.

Two more troopers that wore the composite armor showed up pushing a wheeled cart. The soldier in our group with the samples took out the bags and handed them off to Wills. The group of soldiers then placed their weapons on the cart and headed off in the direction of the barracks to clean up. The trooper that confiscated our guns handed them over as well and they joined the other weapons on the cart. The two troopers wheeled the cart away towards the armory. Wills held his hand out towards the lab, showing us the way.

As we walked down sterile hallway after sterile hallway, Wills went on to tell us that the bunker at one time had been surrounded by a high fence and hidden from view by an old steel building. It did not take long for the demons of the flesh to destroy those. The construction of the bunker was in case a global pandemic took place. It was not a military stronghold built to ward off hundreds of thousands of walking dead.

There also, in the beginning, used to be four towers. Two of the towers no longer existed. Now destroyed, they sealed the entrances with concrete at the surface. The remaining two defensive structures still stood but with resources dwindling fast, there was only enough ammo and manpower left to run one at a time. The complex maintained a twenty-four hour guard in the towers.

Wills went on to say that,

"The facility is a self-sustaining
environment, with back-up
generators and solar charged
batteries. It even has a small
nuclear powered generator."

The roof of the structure opened to reveal the solar panels. Many of the panels, damaged from fallen debris during the destruction of the outside were beyond repair. There was still plenty of power and,

"If we had to, we could stay down
here for about a year."

Providing all of the resources held out. Manpower was becoming a key issue. Well, lack of it.

"If it was not under control by then,
we had lost."

Following Wills, we passed through the complex heading to the lab, pausing by the lounge. Rows of chairs cheaply upholstered in an orange fabric filled the small room. A large central television sat fixed to the wall, high above the chairs. Several off duty soldiers sat and laughed as they smoked cigarettes while watching, of all things, a low-budget zombie movie.

On the television, a group of people ran from the invading zombies. They fired their guns into the hordes of monsters as they ran. The demons of the flesh in the movie were different from the ones that we fought. The ones on the television ran quickly, attacking fiercely. I was glad that we were not up against these ghouls. I preferred the slow gait of the monsters that now inhabited the earth. Once running out of ammo the people in the movie became victims themselves. The creatures savagely tore them apart in the same manner that we had recently witnessed.

How could the soldiers be watching something like this when they had to live with it everyday? Were they trying to desensitize themselves to what was going on outside? I found my eyes fixating on the television screen and actually enjoying what the soldiers watched. Maybe it was human nature not to care. After all, the walkers were dead.

The speakers of the surround sound system that filled the room pumped out scream after scream from the woman in the movie. Her image flashed across the big screen as the zombies began tearing into her. Wills' touched me on the arm. Looking over to him, I saw his jaw move as he mouthed some words but I could not make out what it was he was trying to say. The noise from the lounge was overbearing.

Wills stuck his head into the lounge and screamed louder than I have ever heard anyone yell. The anger and authority in his voice were evident.

"Turn it down!"

One of the soldiers hopped quickly to his feet and complied,

"Sorry sir!"

He tried to explain to Wills,

"We were just..."

Wills stopped him,

"I don't want to hear it."

He continued, giving the men a lecture,

"Have some respect—you guys
aren't the only ones down here."

This time, all the soldiers piped up an apology.

Wills looked to my wife and me again, pointing down a side corridor,

"As I was saying, the lab is this
way."

Continuing on our walk, I caught a whiff of the aroma of the cafeteria food coming from another branch in the corridor. Oh, that smelled good. It was steak. I could go for one of those right now. A nice hot juicy medium rare steak topped with fried onions and mushrooms. My mouth watered as the smell filled my nostrils with joy.

Making our way along our short tour of the facility, we came across a series of rooms with large plate glass windows. Between the windows sat a set of large double doors. The door handles had a white powdery finish to them and appeared to be made of zinc. The sign on one of the doors read,

"Weapons Research"

Wills said that there had been other facilities around the world such as this one. The practice was to capture and bring in a few live walkers as test subjects for weapons research.

"That practice changed this
morning."

"All the facilities have been
destroyed one by one due to internal
infection."

"We lost contact with the last one a
few hours before we set out to find
you."

Now the facilities were underground bunkers filled with the roaming demons of the flesh. Eventually, those too will have to be cleaned out of the dead.

Well, there were still two complexes in China but they were as good as dead. When China launched the several nukes within their own borders, the leaders failed to take into account as to where these facilities lie. The two remaining bunkers now sat in the middle of the irradiated zones buried under mounds of rubble. The people trapped inside would be in there until the outside world dug them out—and help was not on its way anytime soon.

Upon losing contact with the last facility, all of the remaining animated monsters inside the complex were shot and disposed of. The new practice was to bring in only dispatched walkers. The scientists worked around the clock, studying the corpses as best they could in hopes of finding a way to battle the bodies filled with the DRED-not.

Walking by the Weapons Research rooms, I stopped and took a quick glimpse of what was taking place in there. Rows upon rows of metal gurneys lined the room, each one topped with a freshly deceased walker. The monsters' heads poked out from beneath the crisp white sheets that covered them. The creatures were all shapes and sizes consisting of both male and female. Even a few child ghouls lay there. It was easy to spot them by the size of their small forms hiding beneath the white sheets. The inanimate demons of the flesh stared up at the ceiling waiting patiently for their chance to become the next test subject.

At an autopsy table, two male scientists or possibly doctors dressed in their white lab coats worked over the current test subject. They had the insides of the walker pulled open and pinned back revealing its internal organs. A dark green liquid oozed from the corpse onto the metal table. The liquid seemed to flow through the entire creature. Maybe the fluid was the DRED-not. Maybe it's what kept the bastards walking.

A female scientist sorted through slides of the walker's internals in another part of the room. Several microscopes lined the desk that she worked at. Placing one of the slides under one of the microscopes, she hunched down and began studying it.

Over to the far right side of the room, through thick glass doors was a single firing range. On the shooter's end sat several different plastic boxes holding various types of bullets. It looked as if they were manufacturing a new type of hollow point ammunition, each type of ammo tipped with a different colour. A soldier cradling his M-4 stood at the front of the range. Several magazines, each containing one type of round, sat on the table in front of him along with three sets of hearing protectors.

At the far end of the firing range, the wall was stacked with sandbags. Several holes dotted the bags from the multiple bullet strikes. Sand leaked out of the tiny holes forming little mounds on the floor. A gurney sat pushed off to the side. Two more guys in white lab coats worked. The two men hung a naked deceased female walker in a harness. Attached to the ceiling, the harness made her stand upright. The creature did not have the telltale signs of death such as the blackish pooling of blood. Her muscles and skin still seemed pliable. She did not have the tightly drawn back lips or the sunken hollow cheeks of death. For the most part, she looked like she might still be alive.

The two men finished hanging the female ghoul into the harness. They then hurried back to the soldier who stood patiently waiting at the other end of the range. The three men picked up their hearing protection from on the table. They pulled the earmuffs down over their ears to get ready.

Selecting one of the magazines off of the table in front, the trooper loaded his M-4 assault rifle and chambered a round. He took aim and fired at the hanging demon of the flesh. The bullets thudded into the front of the female walker sending puffs of green mist into the air. The trooper continued to fire until the weapon was dry. Having expended the magazine's ammo into the corpse, the soldier checked his rifle saying,

"Clear."

Reaching over a button on the wall, he pushed it. That activated a massive exhaust fan, sucking out all of the bloody mist from the air.

The two men in lab coats quickly hurried down to the female walker. Removing her from the harness, the lab workers dumped the demon of the flesh onto the gurney and hurriedly wheeled her back into the main room. Immediately, the other doctors gave up on their current test subject and began working on the new one.

I stood at the windows engrossed at what went on in the room. I watched, observing the effort that was going into destroying these monsters. Leaning back away from the glass, I failed to notice that my wife and Wills had continued to walk away, leaving me behind. With no sign of Wills or my wife, I hurried down the hall following the signs that pointed to the lab. I wandered through the vast complex taking passage after passage feeling as if I was going in circles. From down one of the corridors I could make out some loud conversation followed occasionally by laughter. I headed towards the noise. Maybe they could tell me a quicker way to get to the lab.

Approaching the room, I heard a group of soldiers talking. I poked my head in. Six soldiers sat in pairs at small tables, eating. Ponds sat in the room at a table by himself, nibbling out of a dirty bowl filled with pasta. He was still dressed in his gore-covered coveralls, his blood soaked rubber gloves hanging from his back pocket. The soldiers, engrossed in conversation, never took notice to my presence at the doorway. One soldier asked Ponds,

"Your name isn't Ponds so why do
they call you that?"

Ponds just sat there ignoring the question, gumming his pasta and moaning. A second soldier replied,

"You don't know how Ponds got his
name?"

The first trooper shook his head,

"No."

The second soldier smiled and began the story of how Ponds received his name.

In the first few hours after all the chaos began, it was common practice to send out teams to capture a few of the walkers for study. The team would go topside and taser a monster or two. The problem with the taser was that you could never be completely sure if it worked. Sometimes the demon of the flesh would fall but it wasn't out cold. A few guys got it that way.

Once incapacitated, the walkers were fitted with gags and hogtied. The captured creatures were then brought down into the facility for scientific and weapons tests.

"At first, we lowered the walkers
down on ropes."

"After the first few, we just said fuck
it and dumped them down the
shaft."

Another soldier cut in, laughing as he said,

"You should've seen those fuckers
tumble the forty feet to the bottom
below."

As they watched the falling undead, the soldiers would laugh or yell mock screams as the demons of the flesh tumbled down. A soldier screamed aloud,

"Ah, I've fallen and I can't get up!"

They did put football helmets on the ghouls so that they didn't crack their skulls open in the fall. The soldier that inquired about Ponds' name cut in,

"Yeah, I remember, I took part..."

The explaining trooper held up his hand to cut him off in mid sentence and continued.

They were out looking for some of the undead bastards when the team saw a few of the creatures wandering around a street side department store. The team went in to round up a couple of them. Once they bagged a few of the walkers, they put the rest down. The soldiers could hear a faint moaning and groaning coming from over near the make-up isles. The team had thought that they had cleared the department store. They approached the area silently and cautiously. With their weapons at the ready, the soldiers prepared to take out any monsters that they might encounter. Rounding the corner of the sales counter, they saw Ponds.

Ponds sat on his knees. Beside him, the body of a twenty-something year old girl lay face down. Her blonde hair flowed from beneath the cash register that crushed her head. She was dressed in her white lab coat and a short black skirt. Chewed off at the shoulder, the girl's right arm was missing. Ponds knelt between the black hose clad legs of the girl. In his hands, he held the girl's right arm. Ponds moaned and groaned like one of the dead, stroking himself with the dead girl's hand, her palm slathered in Ponds Cold Cream. It oozed out from between her icy dead fingers as she unwillingly gripped him. Littering the floor beside Ponds was the empty jars that he used for lubrication.

The story-telling soldier looked over to the soldier he told his tale to. The listening trooper sat in shock with a grimaced look on his face then slowly turned to look at Ponds. Ponds sat there making groaning noises, still gumming away at his dirty bowl of pasta. The storyteller finished with,

"I gave him a kick and he followed us back."

"He's been known as Ponds ever since."

Another soldier cut in,

"You should have seen him trying to get the hand off his dick with the rigor mortise."

Ponds let out his cartoon cackle,

"And it was free too!"

Ponds continued to cackle as the rest of the soldiers laughed at him—not with him.

After the laughter settled down, I spoke out,

"Can you guys tell me how to get to the lab?"

Without looking up, a smartass soldier shot back,

"Just follow the signs."

Well, no shit. I already figured that one out. Knowing these guys were not going to be much help, I gave them a sarcastic,

"Thanks."

I left the doorway once more following the signs to the Lab. As I walked away, I could hear the wisecracking soldier say,

"Dumbass."

The other troopers once again burst out into laughter.

A group of four soldiers passed me in the hall. Stopping, they whispered back and forth all the while staring at me. They watched me walk, staring at me as if I had done something wrong. I decided it was in my best interest to take a corridor that approached up on my right. Hurrying down the side passage I looking back to see if the soldiers had followed. They did not.

As I continued quickly down the bare hallways, I came to another set of double doors with the same zinc handles. Once again, large thick windows flanked the doors casting my reflection back at me in the glass. They did not seem to hide anything that they were doing down here. It was all wide open and for all to see. Possibly, to show them the reality of what it exactly was that they were dealing with. Pausing once more, I put my hands up to the glass and peeked in.

The room, simply labeled "Manufacturing" was quite vast in size and well lit with fluorescent lighting. Music played from a small stereo that sat on one of the several workbenches that filled the room. Several workers clad in coveralls toiled feverishly making various items for war.

On one side of the room, a tall metal rack held numerous sizes of the hard composite armor that the security detail wore. In front of the rack, four workers continued making more of the ballistic suits. They poured some kind of liquid plastics material into the different types of molds. They placed the filled forms into a kiln and heated them. I guess that made the armor harden.

Across the massive room, contained in a clean room, workers dressed from head to toe in white cloth coveralls made the strange goggles that many of the soldiers wore. They also made riflescopes. The finished products rested on a shelf mounted behind the workers.

Watching the workers with my nose pressed into the glass, I couldn't help but think that with all this work going on down here that we might actually have a chance at winning the battle for topside. Standing there deep in thought, a bang on the glass beside my head startled me. I jumped back, the oily imprint of my nose clearly visible on the glass as I pulled away. Beside me, Wills stood staring at me, his eyebrows raised out of impatience, his hand still mashed against the window. At the end of the hall, my wife stood with her arms crossed, sending me a stern look. Wills said plainly,

"Let's go."

He continued,

"I am not going to chase you all over this place."

"You'll have plenty of time to sightsee later."

This time Wills followed me to make sure I did not straggle off again. Approaching my wife, she gave me her usual smack on the arm, saying,

"What the hell's wrong with you?"

Shrugging my shoulders, I knew that the two of them would reject any response I gave. The three of us continued down the repetitious stark white hallways towards the Lab with Wills pointing the way.

Mankind was now in an entirely new age of warfare. The hundreds of years, the human race had invested in finding and perfecting better and more efficient ways to kill each other had now gone to waste. Not all the bullets, tanks, or bombs that we had could win the battle that we now faced. It would take a completely new arsenal to deal with our new enemies, who were in fact still human. Down in the belly of this vast complex the people made every effort to find new ways of destroying the ghastly foes that roamed freely above.

Conflict was what made many countries thrive. Arms sales were big business and big bucks. Strife was a good thing for economies. The benefit of global atrocities used to be that somewhere, someone needed guns and there was always someone else to prosper from selling them what they needed.

Now, there were no economies left to gain from this current conflict of man versus monster. Now, it was a battle for the very existence of mankind itself. Mankind as a whole acted as a monster but we could still create life and show compassion. We can nurture and care for things, whether it be plant, pet, or person. The walkers were something completely different. The demons of the flesh were a new modified breed of humans that wandered the planet. Their goal was to do one thing. They were here to exterminate the living. With no pity or remorse, it came easy for them. If we were to survive, mankind would have to become just as evil and malevolent as our new foes. The problem was is that our time was slowly running out.

THE LAB

Arriving at the Lab, it was just a single door set into the wall. The Lab did not have the large windows on the sides of the door like most of the other rooms had. A small thick reflective window provided a view to the hallway from inside. They kept this room in secrecy and away from the prying eyes of others. Whatever went on in here they did not want the others to see. The handle had the same white powdery finish as the others throughout the complex. An intercom adorned with a security card swipe and keypad jutted out from the wall beside the door.

I glanced over to my wife and saw that she had the same sinking feeling that I now felt. If this room was off limits to most of the others, what in the hell were they going to do to us in there? Wills, noticing the look of despair in our faces, gave us a reassuring smile and said,

"Don't worry, you'll be fine."

Digging inside his uniform tunic, Wills pulled out his keycard and swiped it. The door unlocked with a beep and he yanked it open.

The room looked as sterile as the rest of the building with its plain white hospital walls. Three pictures hung on the walls. The largest contained in a mahogany frame, showed a foggy dirt road flanked by trees. Along the right side of the road ran a white picket fence. A wire horse fence with wooden posts ran along the left. The fences faded off into the fog—into the unknown. Was it to symbolize the long unknown journey that sat before us? The painting was as dreary as how the world sat in its current state, echoing my own feelings of despair.

The other two pictures were smaller and surrounded by white pine frames. Both of animals, one was a lone wolf. The other was a lone dear. Both animals stood in a winter forest. Perhaps the two paintings signified mankind and the battle at hand—one the hunter and the other the prey. I pondered which animal I had become. Was I the wolf or the dear? Was I the hunter or the hunted?

White metal tables sat against the walls, their tops filled with test tubes and beakers. Two chairs, the kind you might see in a dentist's office sat in the middle of the room. Placed beside each chair was a small table. On top of the tables sat trays with needles and empty blood sample tubes. Off to the left of the room was a door with large glass windows on either side.

The room to the left was a clean room. Four scientists, all wearing rubber biohazard safe suits, worked on experiments of whatever it was they were doing here. Lab cultures filled the tiny room as the scientists ran test after test. Microscopes filled the long metal table in front of them. Tanks of liquid nitrogen filled one corner. The biohazard team worked diligently. Taking out new slides, they injected them with something and began to observe them under their microscopes. The liquids that they injected into the samples looked in similar colour to the tips of the various bullets in Weapons Research.

Examining the stark white walls of the Lab, I had no idea why they would shroud this place in such secrecy. Everyone in the facility knew what was going on up top. Nothing in the room cried out,

"Hide me."

Maybe they just did not want the distraction of others.

Straight across the room from where we stood was a heavy reinforced-steel man door with an electronic card reader beside the handle. To the right of the door sat a plastic chair. A pair of the rubber gloves that you can put your arms in to work on the inside of the room but remain sterile on the outside hung down above the chair. Below the gloves was a slot fixed into the wall. Above the gloves was a long glass window with blue opaque curtains.

Upon entering the Lab, a woman stepped forward to greet us. Wills nodded to the woman and handed her the small bags,

"Doc."

She introduced herself as Dr. Reiniger.

Dr. Reiniger was a blonde German woman in her mid-thirties. A tightly pulled ponytail held the doctor's hair back. Her green seductive eyes captured everyone who entered the room with their beauty, including my wife. She wore the traditional doctor/scientist white smock left open revealing her fit figure hiding underneath. She did not wear scrubs like the rest of the doctors or scientists that we saw in the complex. Beneath her smock, Dr. Reiniger wore a tight white blouse. With the top buttons opened to reveal plenty of cleavage, she tucked into a dark grey skirt that rose just above the knee. Black pantyhose and black high heel shoes complimented her outfit. The doctor knew she was sexy and enjoyed showing it. The keycard to the heavy steel door across the room hung around her neck, sharing the same chain as her dog tags. Dr. Reiniger's perfume wafted over to my nose giving off the faint aroma of a floral bouquet. I closed my eyes drinking in the fresh scent of the doc's perfume, the sweet smell cleansing my nose of the past couple of day's stench of death.

Taking a deep breathe, I opened my eyes and glanced at my wife. She was busy checking out the doctor. The look on my wife's face was one that said,

"I am the hot bitch here—not you."

Was she jealous? Looking back to the doctor, I found that she too had the same look. Neither of them seemed to like the competition that the other offered.

I extended my hand to her and she quickly stepped back, saying,

"We don't want to risk the chance of
any further contamination."

"There will be plenty of time to get to
know each other later."

Dr. Reiniger walked over and placed the small bags of samples on one of the tables near the clean room. I followed the doctor's slender legs, listening to the sound of her heels clicking off the tile flooring as she went. The doctor turned to come back. Feeling the daggers from my wife's eyes stabbing at me, I stopped looking and tried to stare inconspicuously at the walls. I thought I should be whistling and rocking on my heels with my hands in my pockets. Like nothing happened. Smiling, Wills shot me a look as if to say,

"Give it up, you know you got caught."

The doctor continued,

"First, we must quarantine you two for three days to make sure there is no infection."

"We don't want you turning on us and trying to eat us now would we?"

She went on,

"It is only a formality."

"You understand, don't you?"

Finally, she added,

"We can't be too careful."

Nodding our heads, we knew it was for the best and we followed her to the heavy steel door. She unlocked the door with the keycard.

As we stepped inside the small room, Wills stood at the doorway saying,

"I'll see you two after."

"If you can endure this minor setback, I have a feeling that you two are going to change the outcome of the battle."

Minor setback? At the time, I had no idea how exactly we were going to change the outcome of the raging war against the undead. What did he know that we didn't? Wills turned and saying his goodbyes to the doctor, left the Lab.

The door locked behind us with a click and I stood looking around the room. I thought I was in paradise. This room was not painted white like the rest of the complex. The walls in here were a nice shade of light blue, except for one wall. Painted to resemble a lakefront, the wall looked similar to where we used to keep our boat.

The room also had nice plush wall-to-wall carpeting. A warm looking comfortable bed rest pushed up to one wall. Its neutral coloured, diamond patterned duvet was pulled back as if it were inviting me to crawl in. Fresh clothing for the both of us, consisting of combat fatigues lay folded on the bed. In the mural on the wall, a hidden door led to a sanitized washroom complete with a shower and hot running water. Across from the bed, a flat panel widescreen TV sat inside a cherry wall unit with a surround sound stereo and a DVD player.

A soft couch and wooden coffee table rest in front of the cherry wall unit. Matching cherry shelves lined the walls with numerous videos. Video game systems sat over on a desk in one corner with every game imaginable. Compared to the last couple of days, this was heaven. We were safe, secure and had everything we needed to entertain ourselves. Underneath the rubber gloves, hanging from the wall near the door was a chair and a small table topped with needles and blood sample tubes.

From outside the room Dr. Reiniger walked over to where the rubber gloves hung. Drawing back the curtains, she sat down. Sticking her arms into the safe gloves, she said,

"Let's take a look at that arm."

I had completely forgotten about the small bite on my arm. A trail of blood dotted my route around the facility. Looking down at the red spotted floor and carpet, I said,

"Sorry, I seem to have made a mess."

The doctor replied,

"It will be cleaned up as it was to be expected."

Picking up her folded stack of fresh clean clothing from the end of the bed, my wife made no hesitation as she headed into the bathroom for a shower. Disappearing into the wall mural, she said,

"I'll see you in half an hour."

Dr. Reiniger finished bandaging my arm and began to clean up. The door to the Lab opened and a person entered. I could not tell if it were a man or woman since they wore one of the thick biohazard suits. The person pushed a large cart full of cleaning supplies. Kind of like a Molly Maid from outer space. I am not sure what looked creepier, the cleaner, or the undead ghouls roaming above outside. The "maid" followed my trail of blood specks and promptly cleaned them off the floor, first spraying the area with a disinfectant and then mopping it up.

Dr. Reiniger unlocked the door to our tiny prison allowing the cleaner access to finish the job. As the vacuum seal from the door broke, I could feel the rush of incoming air from the Lab. I caught another whiff of the doctor's sweet fragrance as it floated towards me in the gentle breeze. Once again, it was a nice change to smell something other than the death and decay that had filled my nostrils over the past few days. In the background, the hairdryer supplied for my wife gave off its drone making everything seem normal once again.

The cleaning technician entered. I could see by the eyes that it was a woman. A loud muffled voice came from her thick suit as she competed with the sound of my wife drying her hair,

"Can you please step back against
the wall?"

The doctor followed in behind the maid. Dr. Reiniger grabbed the bottle of disinfectant and the scrub brush that girl had switched the mop for to clean the carpet. She then gave the cleaner an order,

"Wait outside."
"I'll take care of this."

Dr. Reiniger began to scrub the carpet to clean up my mess. Without looking up, she said,

"Almost everyone down here is
afraid of you."

Staring down at the doctor as she worked, I asked,

"Why, is it because I have been
bitten?"

She came back with,

"Oh, no, it's nothing like that."
"If you became one of them, the
security team would just come down
here and put a bullet in your head."

Dr. Reiniger went on,

"And besides, you are immune to
the bites of the undead."

With a puzzled look on my face, I inquired,

"How the hell can I be immune?"

Looking at me as if I should already know this information, the doctor said,

"You are patient zero."

I replied, almost yelling,

"What the hell do you mean—I am

patient zero?"

As Dr. Reiniger answered me, the colour in my face drained. The room began to spin and the drone of the hairdryer ceased. The blood rushed to my head pounding through my ears like a heartbeat. I thought I was going to faint as the doctor's voice continued fading off into the background,

"You are the person that started this
hellish nightmare."

The "click" from the opening of the bathroom door sent my eyes over to its direction. The door opened and the steam from my wife's hot shower filled the doorway, rolling out onto the floor like the deadly fog that seemed to precede the undead. The mist cascaded out, blanketing the waterfront mural on the wall as if to shroud it in doom. My wife stepped through the mist with a brush in her hand, streaking it through her long golden hair. She looked like an angel sent down from the heavens arriving to ease my pain and suffering.

Pausing in mid stroke, my wife looked over to me. The way my eyes fluttered towards the back of my skull and the pale look on my face, she knew something was wrong and asked,

"Are you ok?"

The room stopped spinning as the doctor's words slowly began to sink in. I no longer felt sick or faint. Now, every cell of my body overflowed with anger. Hatred from what I had just learned streamed from my voice as I yelled my wife,

"No, I am not ok!"

I had never raised my voice in anger to my wife before but at that moment, no matter how hard I tried, I could not bring myself to remain calm.

"I just killed—what—a billion
people?"

I actually had no idea how many people had died or how many had survived the atrocities that were running rampant in the outside world but a billion seemed like a fitting number. Staring at my wife, my anger now turned to sadness as I said,

"I am patient zero."

"I caused all of this fucking mess."

Walking over to me, my wife wrapped her arms around me, tears welling up in her eyes. She did not ask how this could be. She did not care. All that she knew was that she still loved me. I had brought her this far and together we would make it the rest of the way. My wife continued to hug me as we plopped down on the side of the bed.

Sitting on the edge of the bed, I continued to listen as Dr. Reiniger went on,

"That is why everyone is afraid of you."
"You see, everyone here knows that you are patient zero."
"They know that you and you alone are responsible for this whole monstrosity."
"Most people in here want to kill you but are too afraid to come close for fear that you might infect them with the virus."

I jumped in,

"But I don't have the DRED-not in me."

The doctor answered,

"They are afraid of the virus itself."
"Some of us know that you are not contagious but the others..."

She went on,

"They are just naive and scared."
"They would rather have you alive and for us to find a way of stopping this insane madness than to destroy the very hope of eliminating the ongoing massacre outside."

The last statement the doctor made left me wondering if I was to make it out of this alive as she put forth the reality of my situation,

"After we find a cure, who knows, your guess is as good as mine."

To most of these people, I was no better than the monsters that ravaged the planet above. But, I was the key, which is why they had fought in vain to find me. I was now the biggest mass murderer on the face of the planet. In any other instant, there would be no hesitation to shoot me dead where I stand. Nevertheless, they needed me to find a cure. If I was gone, there was no way to eliminate the undead horrors that now took control of the earth.

Handing the scrub brush and disinfectant back to the maid, Doctor Reiniger sat down at the small table near the door. She began explaining the D.R.E.D. virus to us as best she could.

The virus that my wife and I carried was in itself harmless. The mutated virus however was incredibly deadly. It attacked the body similar to Pulmonary Anthrax. Anthrax in itself was not contagious. Somewhere during its mutation, the disease crossed with smallpox giving the virus its contagious properties. During its change, the sickness encapsulated itself making it all that much stronger. The D.R.E.D. virus now lasted outside the host for an extended period of time. Sometimes up to weeks. The longer it floated around the globe, the tougher the virus became. The scientists have even witnessed the virus mutate in the Lab right before their eyes. As they exposed the D.R.E.D. virus to extreme cold, it built up a resistance to it forming a new strain. How many strains were out there? They did not know. I cut in asking,

"So up north is infected also."

Dr. Reiniger replied,

"We are not sure exactly how far it
has spread."

She did know that, once mixed with the DRED-not, the virus survived in almost everything.

Once the DRED-not combined with the virus, it made the bodies of the dead re-animate. The DRED-not joined with the virus on a cellular level keeping the muscles and tissue of the deceased pliable so they could still move. It fed off the bacteria of decomposition and generated new cells in their place. As the new skin cells replaced the old, the bacteria would eat them, decomposing them once more. It was almost like a perpetual motion machine of the cycle of life and death. There were no living virus victims to test out the DRED-not on. The scientists did the best they could with what little they knew about D.R.E.D. The DRED-not did work—just not as planned.

My wife cut in this time,

"So they are still alive?"

The doctor replied once more,

"Technically speaking—no."
"They are in fact dead."

Dr. Reiniger continued to explain,

"The cycle of decomposition leaves their brains with a sensation that they are hungry and need to feed."

"The dead have no thought process or will."

"It is the DRED-not that controls them and their actions."

Destroying the brain of a walker did put it down but the DRED-not and virus cycle remained active in its body. Even in death, they were still dangerous. If you crossed blood with a dispatched demon of the flesh, there was still a chance that you would become one.

Knowing that the DRED-not itself, bonded with the D.R.E.D. virus, the new task was to set out in finding a way to destroy the DRED-not and the virus together. They had plenty of samples of DRED-not and could eliminate that one its own. But they needed a sample of the origins of the D.R.E.D. virus to complete their goals.

The new goal was to be able to target any part of a walker's body to eliminate it, actually destroying the cycle that is taking place in their bodies. We needed new weapons to fight a new foe. That's what was taking place deep within the walls of the complex. The facility was just one huge underground weapons plant.

Lying back on the bed, I stared up at the ceiling. Folding my hands behind my head, I said,

"Well then, let's get to it."

"Let's find a cure."

Dr. Reiniger pulled over the box of needles on the small table and said,

"I'll need you to roll up your sleeve."

She requested blood samples from the two of us. I was happy to oblige, as long as I got one of those steaks.

THE HUNT

The first day in our so-called captivity passed quickly. My wife and I mostly slept. Over the second day, Wills came to visit us several times. Usually, we just shared general conversation like how he spent three tours in Iraq. How he was glad that he was not there anymore when the D.R.E.D. virus spread. Wills enjoyed the short time he had been at the facility. It was an easy gig for him. He did what he wanted and when he wanted. He didn't have to endure any of the crap he put up with in the regular Armed Forces. Down in the complex, it was much more laid back. Sure, there were still rules to follow but you could pretty much do what you wanted as long as you got the job done.

Wills wasn't the top brass at the facility but everyone trusted him and listened to what he had to say. Wills was not only an excellent soldier at fighting the living; he was an expert at dispatching the dead. That's why everyone trusted him. In the few days since the demons of the flesh had risen, Wills became an expert in what they now called Walker Warfare. If you went out with Wills, chances are, you came back.

Every time he went out in the field, Wills could look at the terrain before him and predict with uncanny accuracy as to where and when the undead would arrive. And usually, he knew how many. It was as if he himself became one of the undead legions, sensing their movements and feeling their hunger. The other soldiers all knew the walkers could not think or reason. So how could Wills predict where and what they would do? Did he have some kind of heightened smell for the dead? They did not know. All the soldiers knew was that they trusted him like no other.

Sometimes Wills would tell us more about the complex. How approximately ten years ago, various governments from around the world built these facilities in the event that a worldwide pandemic occurred, although, no one ever counted on the dead coming back to life.

Wills went on to tell us that the facility had once housed over two thousand personnel but that their numbers had since dwindled considerably from battling the infestation of the undead. Friendly fire killed some. Others, falling victim to the masses of undead never returned. The rest were shot trying to sneak back in to the facility while infected. The outbreak was unlike anything anyone had ever dealt with before, so it was still a new learning curve.

During another conversation, Wills asked us if we remembered Ponds. How he searched the bodies of the deceased walkers. Wills told us how,

"When we kill a walker, if at all
possible, Ponds will search the
corpse for ID."
"We catalogue the deceased when
we get back."

They knew Ponds liked to touch the dead bodies. They knew he fondled them, both male and female. As creepy as it was, he was the best choice for the job. No one else wanted it. You did have to watch him constantly to make sure that he did not steal any of the belongings from the dead. Wills did allow Ponds to take the occasional trinket just to keep him happy.

They cross-referenced the deceased with the records kept from when they handed out the DRED-not injections. This way they could get a rough estimate as to how many of the undead remained and to how many they still had to dispose of. They could also keep track of the masses of walker's movements by comparing the origins of where the disposed demons of the flesh had come from. Since the DRED-not stopped the rate of decay, the dead would be roaming virtually forever.

Dr. Reiniger indulged us with the fact that they figured out from tracing the various hospital records, that I was patient zero. They had come to our house to search for us but we had already fled and the corpses were rising too fast to conduct a mass search. If they had taken a blood sample at the hospital that day, they would have been ahead of the game. But they did not. So, they needed one from me personally. I said,

"I guess that's good for me isn't it?"

They sent the helicopter to either rescue us or to help us along on our journey and keep us safe. The problem was, is that we proved to be just as elusive to the soldiers as we were to the undead. Now we were here and hopefully, we had enough time to figure out a way to overcome these monsters and claim the planet as our own once again.

On the third day, I was almost saddened when I heard the click of the door unlocking. Dr. Reiniger stood in front of my wife and me with a big shit-eating grin on her face. She spoke four words,

"We found a cure."

My wife jumped into my arms at the sound of the doctor's good news.

Dr. Reiniger explained how, since the DRED-not reacted with the virus, and because I was patient zero, I was immune to both the virus and the DRED-not. That is why it did not show on their scanners. That is how they had managed to synthesize a cure from my blood. It was the bite that had helped. The DRED-not simply floated around in my body giving them what they needed to find a cure. Since I was too pig-headed to stand in line, without the bite there would be no DRED-not in my system and thus no cure. Dr. Reiniger went on,

"Well, it actually isn't a cure."

My wife's smile disappeared as her grip on me loosened. The doctor clarified herself,

"It is a weapon."

I smiled even wider as I grabbed my wife tightly again,

"Good enough for me."

The Weapons and Research Lab had capped the antidote to the DRED-not into the tip of a new type of hollow-point bullet. When fired, the new round could hit any part of the undead giving almost instant results.

I could not see how this was possible since the demons did not have a beating heart to send the cure coursing through their veins. Dr. Reiniger explained,

"If the DRED-not had just entered
the blood stream then bleeding out
a ghoul would have solved the
problem. But..."

She went on,

"We know the DRED-not targets the
cells in the body so we went after
that."

The new round would target the DRED-not directly in the cells of the monsters. Therefore, there would be no need to target the brain.

Shooting a walker with one of the new bullets, it would take approximately ten seconds for the antidote to work. Yes, in the heat of a battle that is a long time. Those ten seconds could be the difference between life and becoming one of the dead. They were working on a quicker acting round but that is what they had for now.

Once hit with one of the new rounds, the undead will slow. If that is possible since they were rather slow to begin with. The shot walker would then move erratically as their brain slowly begins to shut down. The DRED-not will be repelled from the ghoul's system, finally dropping them dead for good. They still had a long way to go but they were making progress. They had their first weapon in this new age of warfare.

The goggles that the soldiers wore to distinguish the dead from the living had finally been perfected. Hunting the demons of the flesh could now be done day or night. The modifications made included an up to ten times zoom. The scientists had named them Viravision goggles. The soldiers called them gore glasses.

Wearing the goggles prevented the troops from having to see the gory decaying of the undead as they hunted and disposed of them. It also made it easier in the event that the soldiers ran into someone, a loved one, or a friend perhaps, that they had known before all of the carnage had begun.

All of the undead became merely targets. Through the goggles, the demons of the flesh appeared as dark human shapes with thick red veins in their bodies. Live humans showed up in the goggles as having blue veins. The goggles also helped in the event that the Search & Destroy Squads came across any more survivors. Instead of shooting them at far range as suspected walkers, which had happened so many times before, the teams could now retrieve the survivors.

The riflescopes worked but not nearly as well as the goggles. The scopes were still first generation and unreliable. The soldiers pressured the scientists to make better scopes so they would no longer have to wear the goggles in the day. For many of the soldiers there was nothing better than the gore glasses. The undead couldn't hide from them.

All day and all night Search and Destroy Squads travelled out of the complex in shifts to destroy the walking dead. Only one team at a time left the base due to the dwindling numbers of manpower affecting the facility and in an attempt to limit the friendly fire incidents. There was also the problem with the lack of ammunition. Yes, there was new ammo but we had to scrounge for the supplies to make it. Ammunition itself was still in short supply.

The S & D Squads started as close to the complex as possible. For the first few weeks, the teams never left the roof of the building. The walking dead always seem to refill the previously cleared areas. Being on the roof was the easiest and the safest. If you ran out of ammo, you just went inside.

As the Search and Destroy Squads gradually moved out and away from the complex, the walkers stopped re-populating the cleared areas, creating small safe zones. These zones were not actually completely safe. You still had to be on alert and keep a close watch since the odd undead straggler always wandered through. The areas populated with walkers were referred to as the dead zones. If you went into these zones by yourself, you became dead.

I had heard that while out on a night hunt, Ponds was killed. Two soldiers, having just finished a battle with about sixty walkers, stood relaxing. Pausing to have a smoke, their gore goggles dangled loosely around their necks. From behind, they could hear the moaning and groaning as it slowly approached. The soldiers stood frozen, one saying to the other,

"You smell that?"

With that they both spun, swinging their rifles up. The sunken-cheeked face of the monster stared back at them mouthing some kind of indistinguishable garble. The demon's arms stuck outstretched towards them and the smell—the smell was horrible. The two troopers gagged on the foul odour as they fired their weapons that night. The muzzle flashes from their rifles lit up the darkness and their target as the rounds punched into it.

The two soldiers stepped over to their freshly disposed of victim. Looking down at the unmoving body on the ground, they realized what they had just done. Staring back at them from the hard cold concrete was Ponds. His mouth full of crackers, pink froth and a thick doughy paste bubbled out onto the side of Ponds' sunken cheek. In his hands, he held the tiny bags filled with IDs. He was trying to hand them over to the two soldiers. The two troopers stood there, watching Ponds' eyes slowly turn empty and die. Their only response was,

"Oh, shit."

"How do we explain this?"

Then one asked,

"Well, what the hell was that smell?"

The other replied,

"It was him—the fucker never washed!"

"Wills said not to take our eyes off him."

The two soldiers returned and told Wills their tale. The two troopers were not reprimanded in any way. Ponds did stink beyond what any walker ever smelled like so it was an understandable mistake. We also could not afford to waste manpower keeping soldiers locked up for what was clearly an accident.

After time, my wife helped in the complex in any way she could. Usually, she worked in the lab making more of the anti-toxin or in the weapons research department perfecting the next generation Viravision scopes for the rifles. And I—well—I was to join in the hunt.

My first hunt was a night shoot. They say it is actually easier to stalk the walkers at night because the undead show up more clearly in the Viravision goggles.

Sure, it was harder to walk around in the dark without tripping on all the rubble left by the destruction. You still had to watch out for the creepers as well. But only seasoned veterans of the goggles could use them during the daytime.

In the daylight, the images in the goggles were not as clear and visible as they were at night. In the daytime, the living and the dead were hard to differentiate. Sometimes the sunlight gave both a purple hue. So that was when most of the friendly fire incidents took place. There were also a substantial number of undead soldiers wandering about. From afar, it was easy to mix up the living with the dead.

That first night, as soon as I stepped outside of the bunker I immediately noticed a difference. The wails of the demons of the flesh had become quiet, virtually non-existence. The multiple piles of the burning corpses from the dispatched walkers lit up the night sky, the disposal crews also working night and day.

The stench of death was slowly disappearing. The air smelled fresh as it filled my nostrils. Now free of all the pollution from the factories and car exhaust that ceased to exist.

Taking a cigarette from my pack and lighting it, I looked down the street once called "The Gauntlet." It was now clear of the debris and bodies that had blocked it before. The glow of the new rows of streetlights shone down brightly lighting the road. A full moon hung high in the sky giving off additional light.

Adjusting the brightness in my goggles, I stepped down the retractable steel ladder that replaced the rope ladder on the side of the bunker. It had been a month or so since I had actually set foot on something other than tile, carpet, or concrete.

I smiled as I felt the soft earth squish under my boots. It had rained. My nostrils filled with the sent of the oncoming dew of the night. Inhaling a drag from my cigarette, I looked down to the damp ground. I thought about the earthworms. I wondered to myself how the worms had faired with all that has happened. I stood there breathing in the cool night air and realized what a stupid thought that was. But that was all I could think about—the worms.

I wished it were daylight so that I could see the sun once again. It had been so long since I had felt the warmth of its rays against my face. All of our faces had become a pasty white from hiding out in the underground bunker. We had become an army full of mimes.

The rest of the squad stepped down onto the dirt beside me and we lined up to check our equipment. One soldier spoke out,

"I heard that we are going out with Wills."

It was his first time under Wills' command. The soldier continued,

"I heard once that Wills fought off an army of undead with nothing more than his hands."

I put forth,

"I'd believe that."

I played with the guy, adding,

"I heard he fought his way all the way back from Iraq."

The soldier looked at me in awe,

"Really—wow!"

I knew what I had just told him was utter bullshit but for some reason I couldn't help myself.

Wills came down the ladder and stood in front of us. He had become a good friend to me and he was to lead this hunt.

Standing before our small squad, Wills spoke,

"Listen up!"

"I'm only going to tell you once and once only."

"Do what I say and you might just get to fight another night."

"Don't and maybe tomorrow—we hunt you."

Wills started his orders,

"Check your gear and your weapons."

"Exterminate with extreme prejudice!"

Wills continued,

"This...!"

Wills said, sweeping his hand across the horizon.

"...is where we belong."

"...On top."

"Not hiding from the walkers in some underground bunker."

"This is our little section of land and
we are going to keep it."

He added,

"In a hundred years when all of this
is over and your grandkids'
grandkids have finished rebuilding,
they'll look back and remember all
the heroes that have ever fought in
any war."
"And they will remember you men
most of all."
"You not only fought for your
existence—you fought for everyone's
existence."
"Be it white, black, yellow or
brown…"
"You are the ones that fought for the
very existence of humans as a
species."
"Without you there would be no
tomorrow."

Wills finished with,

"Now—let's go kill us some stink
bag, rotting, zombie fuckers!"

The squad replied with a war cry of,

"Oorah!"

As our team headed out, I dropped my smoke to the ground, twisting it into the earth with my boot.

With six men in our squad, we worked as three, two-man teams. Spread out in a line, the squad advanced forward through "The Gauntlet" and down the street. Each man carried sixty extra rounds of ammunition. With one magazine in the rifle, it gave us a total of ninety bullets with which to exercise our extreme prejudice against the walkers.

We were a good two hours into our hunt before spotting one of the demons of the flesh. Lifting up my goggles, I watched the walker stagger into the light of the moon. An old woman about the age of eighty came wandering into our path. Her cheeks hollow from the lack of teeth in her mouth. I giggled to myself at the image of her joining a pack of attacking monsters as she tried to gum her victims to death.

I heard the "pop" from my partner's rifle then his voice in my headset,

"Johnnie down."

The soldiers had started calling the walkers "John" or "Johnnie" after the Scotch Whiskey named Johnnie Walker, which for some time, was the only alcohol available in the complex. The name came from a drunken joke that went around before my arrival to the bunker about a soldier who had drank too much and was as mindless as one of those things outside.

Pulling my gore glasses back down over my eyes, I zoomed in on the old woman. I followed the image of grandma in my goggles as she staggered back and forth, finally falling over face first onto the concrete. When she hit the ground, she spit something out onto the pavement. Walking over to her now still corpse, my partner bent down to search the old woman for some identification. I stood guard. My partner startled me when he blurted out,

"Holy shit! She could have eaten someone!"

Looking down, I saw the single tooth that had tumbled out as she hit the pavement.

It might have taken a year or two to finish a hand but I guess she could have done it.

Failing to find any form of identification, we left the fallen granny and regrouped with the others. A small pack of a dozen or so "Johnnies" tumbled out of a broken storefront window. As they closed in around us, Wills yelled out,

"Waste those fucks!"

The walkers did seem to move much faster when they had not feasted in some time. They were still slow and still staggered but their gait had quickened as if they could anticipate the taste of their next meal. For this dozen—there would be no next meal.

The muzzle flashes lit up the night as our rifles peppered the oncoming group. Their red images danced in our gore glasses as the ammo took effect. In about ten seconds, it was all over. The creatures lie crumpled in a mound of corpses on the ground, now motionless—as the dead should be.

Gathering what info we could from the fallen "Johnnies", we

checked and reloaded our weapons. We then continued our hunt for the demons of the flesh.

Gradually, things were getting back to normal. The dead were still visible as their image roamed back and forth in my goggles. But now, one bullet hitting them anywhere would rid us of these hideous creatures.

The new weapons that we had made for our war against the walkers proved to be the catalyst for our return above ground. We eradicated the undead and bit by bit, our borders expanded. The progress was there but the battle was far from being over. For the demons of the flesh, their quest was nearly complete—the total annihilation of mankind. For us, the battle had just begun.

Cresting over a mound of loose rubble, I sighted the image of an undead horror in my gore goggles and aimed my rifle. I watched the little figure wander aimlessly in the night. Still clutching its teddy bear tightly in its hand, I could not help but think. Who were the real monsters—them or us? I squeezed the trigger of my rifle and whispered into my throat mic,

"Johnnie down..."

The End—or is it just the beginning?

www.ingramcontent.com/pod-product-compliance
Ingram Content Group UK Ltd.
Pitfield, Milton Keynes, MK11 3LW, UK
UKHW020132250726
13967UKWH00002B/600